RESTLESS

"It's no use, Charley. I've tried to stay away from you, but I can't."

His mouth rocked over her lips, persuading and cajoling, sensually nipping her lower lip until she was reeling. Restless male hands wandered over her back, caressing her. She was helpless against this loving attack.

"Do we have to deny ourselves?" Shad muttered. "I don't see any reason to pretend I don't want you. Do you know what I mean?"

"Yes." The aching admission was torn from her throat, the ability to think lost. "I want you too . . . just as much."

It was the answer he had been waiting for as he swept her off her feet and into his arms.

from "The Traveling Kind"

BOOK YOUR PLACE ON OUR WEBSITE AND MAKE THE READING CONNECTION!

We've created a customized website just for our very special readers, where you can get the inside scoop on everything that's going on with Zebra, Pinnacle and Kensington books.

When you come online, you'll have the exciting opportunity to:

- View covers of upcoming books
- Read sample chapters
- Learn about our future publishing schedule (listed by publication month *and author*)
- Find out when your favorite authors will be visiting a city near you
- Search for and order backlist books from our online catalog
- Check out author bios and background information
- Send e-mail to your favorite authors
- Meet the Kensington staff online
- Join us in weekly chats with authors, readers and other guests
- Get writing guidelines
- AND MUCH MORE!

**Visit our website at
http://www.kensingtonbooks.com**

JANET DAILEY

Ranch Dressing

ZEBRA BOOKS
KENSINGTON PUBLISHING CORP.
http://www.kensingtonbooks.com

CONTENTS

THE TRAVELING KIND

Chapter One

The sun-warmed air blowing in through the open windows of the pickup truck was fragrant with the resiny scent of pines, but Charley Collins was too preoccupied to notice it in more than a passing way. Her mouth was set, lips pressed together in a concentrating line. A tiny crease in her forehead marred her smooth features, and there was a thoughtful look in her hazel green eyes.

Her attention was fixed on the highway she traveled, her gaze rarely lifting from the road to the Idaho mountains. She drove the truck with a competence born of long experience, an experience that came from learning to drive almost before her legs were long enough to reach the floor pedals. It had been the same with horses, learning to ride before her feet reached the stirrups.

The winding stretch of forest-flanked road was broken by the appearance of a building that housed a combination gas station–café–general store with living quarters in the rear. Charley slowed the truck as she approached her destination. Swinging off the highway, the pickup rolled past the gas pumps to stop in front of the wooden building.

With the gear shifted to park, Charley switched off the ignition and opened the door. The riding heel of her western boot dug into the gravel as she stepped from the cab. The faded blue denim of her snug-fitting Levi's had been worn soft, a comfortable second skin stretched over her slim hips and long legs. The long sleeves of her plaid blouse were rolled up, revealing tanned forearms, and the pearl snaps of the Western blouse were unfastened at the throat to hint at more suntanned skin.

There was a supple grace in the looseness of her stride as she walked to the entrance door. A tortoiseshell clasp held her thick, sandy hair together at the back of her neck, its heavy length swaying as she walked.

The bell above the door jingled as she went in. She was greeted by the tantalizing aroma of homemade doughnuts and freshly brewed coffee from the café section, set off by a horseshoe-shaped counter. Charley paused to close the door and glanced at the outfit propped against the wall: a rolled duffel bag, an A-fork saddle that was well made and showed use, and a wool saddle pad and blanket, along with an assortment of other gear that bore the earmarks of quality. The tools of his trade said a lot about a cowboy. Normally Charley's curiosity would have prompted her to study his outfit a little longer, but she had other things on her mind.

Her searching look briefly noted the cowboy

slouching at the counter on a high stool. Since he was the only customer, he was also the likely owner of the outfit by the door. A noise from the kitchen drew her attention and a smile widened her mouth when a stocky man in a bibbed white apron appeared.

"Hello, Frank." Her long, graceful strides ate up the short distance to the counter. "How've you been?"

"As I live and breathe! Charley Collins!" He came forward to gladhand her, his lined face wreathing into a smile, a salting of gray in his brown hair. "I haven't seen hide nor hair of you since spring."

"I've been busy." Which was an understatement.

His expression immediately became regretful. "How's Gary? We were all sorry to hear about the accident." Then he motioned toward the stool she was standing beside. "Sit down. I'll pour you a cup of coffee on the house."

"No, thank you, but—" She tried to protest but he'd already set a cup on the counter and was filling it from the glass pot. She sat one hip on the stool, keeping a foot on the floor while the other rested on the foot rail around the counter. "Okay. If you insist." She took a sip from the cup to be polite. "Gary is doing much better, although he's fit to be tied."

"I can imagine." Frank Doyle laughed, the laughter fading into a compassionate smile. "With him not able to get around, you must be doing most of the heavy work."

"Yeah. Actually, that's why I'm here." Charley took the opening she'd been given. "Gary is going to be in that cast for another six weeks. I was hoping I could hire Lonnie to help me out on the ranch for the rest of the summer." Lonnie Doyle was Frank's teenage son. He'd worked part-time for them before when they'd needed an extra hand. Charley knew he was a good worker and dependable.

"Sorry. Lonnie has a full-time job as a laborer on a road crew this summer. I know he'd help you out on the weekends if it would help."

Charley blew out a tired sigh and managed a wry smile. "We need someone every day. Between taking care of Gary and the ranch work, I have my hands full. It's more than I can handle alone," she admitted. "But I may have to settle for someone part-time. So far, everyone I've asked already has a job."

"What about Andy Hollister?" Frank suggested.

"He's drinking again. I can't depend on him." She dismissed that possibility with a decisive shake of her head.

As she started to lift the steaming mug of black coffee to her mouth for a second sip, a third voice intruded on the conversation with a soft, interested drawl.

"Excuse me, but did I hear you say you're looking for someone to do ranch work?"

Charley set down the cup and turned to face the cowboy seated at the top of the horseshoe counter. A sweat-stained brown Stetson was pushed to the back of his head, revealing heavy black hair. Long hours in the sun had weathered the skin that stretched across the angular planes of his face. Its teak color combined with crow-black hair to contrast with the glittering blue eyes that returned her gaze. He was sitting loosely, all muscles relaxed. His large-knuckled hands were folded around the coffee cup, nursing it, his browned fingers showing the roughness of calluses.

His expression had an air of knowingness and there was a faint, ironic gleam in his eyes that said he wasn't easily fooled. Probably in his midthirties—okay, in his prime, Charley thought uneasily hc was handsome in the craggy way of a man of the West.

With him sitting down, it wasn't easy to judge his height, but she could guess at the corded muscles beneath the faded blue and gold plaid of his shirt. There was another quality about him that Charley recognized: the restless streak of a drifter. She felt a twinge of regret that it should be a trait of his . . . and then snapped out of her momentary reverie to answer his question. "Yeah, I am. I need an experienced hand."

He shot her an amused look that made her wish she hadn't used the word experienced. Clearly he was that and then some. "I could use the job," he stated in that same lazy drawl. His slow indifference was deceptive. His gaze was alive to her, sweeping over her in an assessing way.

Charley felt the earthy sensuality in his look, but there was nothing offensive in it. Just honest male admiration for a member of the opposite sex. But it made her feel vulnerable all the same.

Her glance darted to the outfit propped against the wall near the door, aware that it spoke for his competence. So far, this stranger was the first—and only—applicant for the job. Although she would have preferred hiring someone local, the situation was getting close to desperate. She couldn't afford to be too choosy.

But common sense insisted that she ask about his background. And get references. "Where have you worked before?"

"I worked for Cord Harris on the Circle H in Texas, Kincaid's spread in Oklahoma. Most recently for the Triple C in Montana." He picked up a pen that a waitress had left on the counter, and a paper napkin, then jotted down a few phone numbers and one name—she guessed it was his—handing it to her without further comment.

"Oh. Well, we have a small, two-man operation, nothing close to the size of the ranches you've mentioned," Charley explained, impressed by the list. "There's a lot of work that has to be done on foot." She'd learned the hard way that some hardline cowboys turned up their nose at any task that couldn't be done on horseback.

He glanced down at his large, work-roughened hands, then lifted his gaze, sharply blue and glinting. "I've done physical labor before . . . and survived."

"We can't pay much," Charley warned. "You'd get a salary, plus room and board." Without thinking, she named a sum she and Gary had agreed upon. Only then did it occur to her that she should have called first and checked on this guy. Charley felt like kicking herself.

"Sounds fair to me." He shrugged his acceptance and uncurled his hands from around the coffee cup, flattening them on the counter. He used them to push off the stool, dismounting almost as if it was a horse. Reaching into his pocket he pulled out some change and laid it on the counter to pay for his coffee, then moved around the corner to Charley, extending a hand. "The name is Shad Russell."

"Right." She set down the napkin and acknowledged the introduction as her hand was engulfed in the hugeness of his. He was taller than she had expected, easily six foot. Charley slid off the stool to offset some of the difference in their height. "Okay, Mr. Russell," she began, watching with reluctant fascination as lines broke from the corners of his eyes over his cheekbones when he grinned at her. It was quite clear that he was a man with a big appetite for many things—excitement, life, women and adventure.

"Make that Shad. I'm not much for formality," he said.

"All right." Her mouth curved into a smile that was deliberately casual. Charley realized with a flash of chagrin that she wasn't indifferent to his particular brand of potent charm. "Guess that's your gear over there, huh?" With a what-do-I-do-now look, she turned to Frank Doyle, who had been silently observing the exchange.

He came to her rescue. "Charley, I was talking to Shad for a while before you came in. Turns out we know a lot of the same people," he said.

"Oh." She smiled very slightly at the waiting cowboy. "Guess that's as good a recommendation as any."

"Well, I can't recommend him," Frank amended.

"But I can vouch for him." He slapped the other man on the shoulder. "Do everything her way and do it fast. Charley doesn't fool around."

"Thanks, Frank," she said, feeling a little miffed but also grateful for his protectiveness.

"No problem. Don't go so long between visits," he said and added as Charley started to move away from the counter, "Give my regards to Gary."

"Will do," she promised and tried not to notice how effortlessly Shad Russell swung the heavy saddle onto the back of his shoulder with one hand. His free hand reached down to pick up his duffel bag. "My truck is parked outside," she said. "Do you want to follow me or are you on foot?" She didn't recall seeing any other vehicles parked out front.

"On foot. I was riding my thumb," he stated and waited for her to walk out the door ahead of him.

A hitchhiking stranger. Charley hesitated on the threshold for a fraction of a second. Then she caught Frank's reassuring wink. She knew without him saying so that she was safe, and exited with Shad.

Once outside, Charley waved a hand in the general direction of the truck's rear bed. "You can put your gear in back," she instructed him and walked around the cab to the driver's side while he swung his belongings over the side of the truck's bed. When he had sprawled his lanky frame in the passenger seat beside her, she started the motor.

As she turned the truck onto the highway her glance flickered to him. The weathered Stetson hat was pulled low on his forehead, half-shielding his features. "How come you left your last job?" she asked.

His arm was draped along the back of the seat, not far from her shoulder. "I got tired of the flatlands and decided I wanted to see some mountains for a change." It sounded like a flip answer, but Charley didn't doubt his reason could be as flimsy. Drifters often needed no more motivation than that.

"Where were you headed?"

"Bitterroot country." Then he asked a question. "How did your husband get hurt?"

She glanced his way, startled for a second, then gave him an amused look before refocusing on the highway. "Gary is my older brother, not my husband. The horse he was riding lost its footing on some mud, fell and rolled on him before Gary could kick free. He ended up with a compound fracture of the upper leg bone. He's in a cast up to his hip . . . and will be for another six weeks."

"That's rough."

An understatement, Charley thought, and Shad Russell was soon to find out why. "You don't know the half of it. He hates the cast, totally hates it. He lumbers around the house like a bear with its paw in a trap, growling and snapping at everything, so be prepared. He acts more like a rebellious teenager than a thirty-year-old."

"How old are you?"

She turned to find him studying her through heavy-lidded eyes, so blue and sharp with male interest. She fought down the sudden acceleration of her pulse. "Twenty-six. Why?" She managed to keep her tone even. Answering a question with a question was an easy way to distract most people.

"Divorced?"

Evidently that strategy didn't work with Shad Russell. She wanted to tell him flat out not to get too personal, but on second thought she decided against it. A measure of openness seemed to be in order to establish a friendly relationship. Might help keep him around for the rest of the summer . . . if Shad stayed that long.

"Never been married," she said casually.

"No fiancé in the wings, either?" His sidelong glance moved over her body and the cleanness of her profile.

"None." Her reply was cheerful, if a little defiant.

"For a woman of twenty-six, that usually means she was jilted somewhere down the line and hasn't recovered from a broken heart," Shad observed. "Especially a pretty woman like you."

The last comment was designed to have an effect on her and it did, but Charley didn't let it show, except to laugh it off. "Sorry. There's nothing so melodramatic in my past."

"Then how've you managed to stay single?" His curiosity was aroused. She could hear it in the inflection of his voice.

"Actually, it was easy." She cast him a bland glance. "Around here, if you don't marry your high school boyfriend or find someone in college, there just isn't much husband material. The men are either already married or too young or too old—or like you."

"Like me?" Her remark caused him to lift a dark eyebrow and give her a look that she couldn't quite interpret.

"Yup. You're the traveling kind—just passing

through on your way to some other place, never content to stay anywhere too long." She had recognized his type right from the beginning, which didn't lessen his attractiveness. Men like Shad Russell were magnets for women who weren't exactly raring to settle down either. Charley counted herself among them.

"Is that a bad way to live?" Shad Russell sounded amused . . . almost mocking.

"Not for you, maybe," Charley conceded. "But it could be bad for a girl who's foolish enough to think she can change you."

"Well, that wouldn't be you. You're nobody's fool." It came out soft, a borderline challenge.

"No, I'm not." She smiled without humor and continued to look at the road ahead. She was nearing the turnoff to the ranch and slowed the truck to edge off the pavement onto the dirt lane. "This is Seven Bar land. The ranch house sits a couple of miles back from the highway."

Although he didn't change his relaxed position, Charley was conscious that he became more alert to his surroundings, the sharpness of his gaze taking mental notes on the abundance of graze, the condition of the cattle and fences—things a cowboy needed to know to do his job. She didn't question his ability, trusting her own instincts on that. Given that she'd known him for less than an hour, the major flaw in his character was that broad streak of wanderlust. Something told her that it would never do to rely on him too much. The thought saddened her, but she didn't examine too closely the reason why.

The mountain lane wound along the slope and

opened into a meadow where the ranch headquarters was situated with a panoramic vista of the surrounding peaks. Besides the two-story white wood house, there was a log barn and shed and corrals fenced with rough-cut timber. It was a small operation by modern standards but its clean, well-kept appearance was a source of pride for Charley. A half-used stack of last summer's hay stood near the barn, with the summer crop yet to be cut. The horses in the corral whickered a greeting and rushed to the front rail as she slowed the pickup to a stop in front of the house.

"You probably noticed that there's no bunkhouse," she said. "But there's a spare bedroom you can use."

A herding dog trotted out from the shade of the house to greet her. The sight of the stranger climbing out of the cab of the truck changed the dog's pace to a stiff-legged walk.

The dog sniffed suspiciously at his legs but a low word from Shad started its tail wagging and a panting grin opened its mouth. Charley observed the dog's acceptance of the new hired hand without comment and waited at the porch steps for him to join her.

Leaving the saddle in the back of the truck for the time being, Shad lifted out his duffel bag and started toward the house. There was no hurry in his long stride as he made a slow study of the ranch and its buildings. When his eyes stopped on her they held a glint of approval. The curve of her mouth softened under its light.

"It looks like you and your brother have a sound, well-run operation here," he observed.

False modesty didn't come naturally to her. "We like to think so." She turned to climb the steps. "Come in and meet my brother and I'll show you where to put your things."

He followed her up the steps and across the porch floor, his footsteps an echo of her own. She pulled open the screen door and entered the front room with Shad behind her. The loud thumping of crutches sounded from the downstairs bedroom.

"Is that you, Charley?" Her brother's voice called impatiently as the steady thud of the crutches moved closer to the front room. She opened her mouth to answer but he spoke again before she had a chance. "Damn it! Where have you been all this time? You said you'd only be gone a couple of hours!"

"It took longer than I thought," Charley replied and would have said more but her brother appeared in the archway of the hall leading off the front room. When she saw him she didn't know whether to be embarrassed or laugh at his predicament. A bulky plaster cast encased the whole of his right leg. His chambray shirt was half-buttoned, the tails hanging free but not concealing the jockey shorts he was wearing. A pair of jeans was trapped between his left hand and the crutch on that side. Her brother stopped short at the sight of the stranger beside Charley, a dull red creeping up his neck.

"Meet our new hired hand, Gary." She just barely managed to contain the smile playing at the corners of her mouth. "This is Shad Russell. And the half-naked man with the broken leg is my brother, Gary Collins." As she turned toward Shad she caught a glint of amusement that he quickly suppressed.

There wasn't any way for her brother to gracefully get out of his embarrassing situation so he chose to ignore it. "Russell," he repeated the name in a searching way. "You from around here?" He frowned at his inability to place the name.

"No," Shad replied and volunteered no more information than that.

"Frank vouched for him," Charley said simply. She knew her brother would give her the third degree later. Why don't you follow me, Shad?" she suggested, moving toward the staircase. "I'll show you where you'll be bunking."

"Good idea." His lazy blue gaze slid from her brother to her, aware that she was rescuing her brother from an awkward situation.

The door to the stairwell stood open. Charley preceded him up the steps and paused in the hallway of the second floor. When he stood beside her, there didn't seem to be as much room as she remembered. It took her a second to realize that she was feeling the effect of his nearness, the breadth of his shoulders and his towering height. She opened the door across from the staircase.

"This is the bathroom." She pointed to the door below the washbasin. "The towels and washcloths are kept in there." She saw his gaze light on the makeup, lotions, and other girl stuff on the surrounding counter and didn't bother to mention that they would be sharing the facility. "You'll have the bedroom to the right of the stairs." He backed out of the bathroom doorway and let her take the lead.

When Charley entered his assigned room, she found herself avoiding the area where the double bed stood. She walked instead to the closet. "There are extra blankets on the top shelf if you need them. And wire hangers in the closet for your clothes. Let me know if you need more."

When she turned, she realized he hadn't been paying much attention to her. His gaze was skimming the contents of the room, skipping the furniture to inspect the pictures on the wall and the assorted knickknacks on the bedside table and dresser. None were special or out of the ordinary. Charley was confused by his attention to them. He was silent until his gaze shifted back to her and his mouth twisted in a self-mocking smile.

"It's been years since I've slept in an actual bedroom," he explained. "I'd forgotten some of the little things that make it different."

Her glance ran around the homey room, suddenly seeing it through the eyes of someone who had spent most of his time in bunkhouses. The personal touches did stand out. She began considering the loneliness of his existence, then told herself not to be so sentimental. He'd chosen to live that way. He had the ability to change—if that was what he wanted to do, which it obviously wasn't.

"I'll leave you to unpack and settle in," she said briskly, moving toward the door. "Come down whenever you're finished."

Without waiting for a reply she left the room and ran lightly down the steps in search of her brother. She found him, still half-dressed, rummaging through her sewing basket, balanced unsteadily on his crutches.

"Gary, what on earth are you looking for?" she asked with a hint of exasperation. He'd become almost childlike.

"I'm trying to find the damned scissors," he grumbled.

"Scissors?"

"Yes, scissors," he snapped irritably. "So I can cut the pant leg off these jeans. I can't get them over the cast and I'm tired of running around in a bathrobe. I want some clothes on for a change."

"If you asked me nicely, I might do it for you," Charley suggested.

He glowered at her over his shoulder. She stood with her arms crossed in front of her in silent challenge. His hair was a darker shade of brown than her own light color but he had the same hazel eyes. His build was heavier and carried more muscle than her slender frame, but a stranger would instantly guess they were brother and sister. Their resemblance was strong in other ways, too. Both possessed the same proud, stubborn streak that often produced a contest of wills, as now. This time it was Gary who surrendered.

He sighed tiredly. "Would you cut my pants for me, please?"

"Of course." Her smile was wide and filled with warmth as she reached out to take the jeans from him. "The scissors are in the bureau drawer, not the basket."

Gary leaned on his crutches and watched her snipping at the leg of his jeans. "How come you hired him? I thought we agreed to get one of the local boys." It was a statement, not an opening for an argument.

"They're all working. When I stopped in at Frank's to see if his son was available, this Shad Russell was there and asked for the job," she said, aware that it wasn't much of an explanation.

He frowned. "Where is he from?"

"Here and there. I didn't ask specifically," Charley admitted. "But Frank said they knew the same people."

"Uh-huh. Frank knows everyone for hundreds of miles around, but he isn't a rancher. What kind of experience does Shad Russell have?"

"Oh, a couple of previous employers right out of Who's Who in the cattle business," she replied dryly as the scissors sliced through the last bit of cloth. "Sit down in that chair and we'll see if we can get your pants on."

Gary maneuvered awkwardly to sit on the edge of a straight chair, resting his crutches against the side. With the cast holding his leg stiff, it was a struggle working the jeans to where he could get both feet through the pant legs. When he could finally stand up again, Charley pulled the Levi's the rest of the way up.

"What you're saying is this guy is a drifter." Gary succeeded in balancing himself on the crutches long enough to fasten his pants.

"That's right." She returned the scissors to their place in the bureau drawer. "I didn't think it mattered since we wouldn't want him to stay past summer anyway."

"No, it doesn't, I guess," he agreed. "What are you going to fix for lunch?"

Charley glanced at the clock. It was an hour before noon. "All you think about anymore is your stomach," she chided him. "As much as you've been eating lately, you're going to gain twenty pounds before you get that cast off."

"You try dragging this deadweight around on your leg"—he gestured toward the cast—"you'll work up an appetite, too."

"During these next six weeks that you're convalescing, why don't you learn to cook?" Charley suggested. "Starting with breakfast. That will be one less chore for me to do."

"You mean I have to master eggs over easy and things like that? Hey, I don't have the hand-eye coordination to manage crutches and a spatula, Char—"

The good-natured spat was interrupted by footsteps on the stairs. Charley turned as Shad Russell emerged from the stairwell. His blue glance rested briefly on her, then shifted to her brother. Yet, in that second, all her senses were brought to full awareness.

"I thought I'd take my saddle and tack to the barn, then have a look around," Shad said.

"I'll come with you and give you a rundown on our operation," Gary volunteered, adjusting the crutches under his arms to hobble over to the man. "Charley can get lunch ready while we're gone."

A few minutes past noon, they sat down at the kitchen table to eat the lunch Charley had fixed. During the meal the conversation centered on the ranch, ranging from repairs that needed doing to the cattle market and futures. Charley could tell her brother was impressed by Shad Russell's in-depth knowledge. His experience in the business was wide and far-reaching, yet it was revealed in a manner that could only be described as offhand.

She liked the thoughtful way he dismissed ranching methods that didn't suit their operation and discussed others that could be incorporated to improve their present system. Shad never made a critical comment and he didn't attempt to force his suggestions on them. Ideas were mentioned, explored and judged on their own merits, to be either considered or rejected.

Shad Russell was becoming more and more of an enigma to Charley. He had traits she admired in a man—his intelligence, his tact and his quiet authority—but she didn't permit herself to forget her first impression that he was a drifter. Today he was here, but he might be gone by sunset.

Dessert was a fudge cake that Charley had baked the day before, and strong black coffee. When it was consumed, Shad leaned back in his chair, stretching with the contentment of a man whose stomach is full. His dancing blue gaze swung to Charley and she watched again as a smile broke from the corners of his eyes, slashing lines in his lean bronze cheeks.

"It's been so long since I've sat down to a home-cooked meal, I had forgotten how good it can taste."

It was a sincere compliment with no attempt at flattery. He'd spoken directly and warmly to her, and it felt . . . like a caress.

But it wasn't. She told herself silently that she'd been lonely for too long if just making and sharing a meal could feel so good and so right. And she was surprised that a man like Shad appreciated it so much. As surprised as if a wolf had come over and put its head in her lap. Shaken by the thought, for she knew it wasn't possible to permanently tame a wild thing—it would always revert to its old ways—she warned herself again not to become involved with a man who was only passing through her life.

So she took his compliment and responded to it with a casual reply. "My mother was an excellent cook. I was taught by the best." She rose to clear the table. "More coffee?"

"No, thanks," Shad refused with the same lazy smile in place. "I thought I'd spend the afternoon riding around to familiarize myself with the layout of the ranch. Is it all right if I take my pick of the horses?"

"Ride whatever one you want." Gary waved a hand in the general direction of the stables.

When his departing footsteps became echoes in her mind, Charley paused in her stacking of the dirty dishes to glance at her silent brother. He was staring thoughtfully into space. A shooting twinge of pain broke his reverie and he grimaced, his hand reaching down to grip the hard cast encasing his thigh.

"Have you taken any of those pain pills the doctor prescribed for you?" Charley eyed him, already guessing the answer.

"No," he admitted defensively. "I don't want to start depending on pills."

"You want to be the big, strong hero gritting his teeth in the face of pain," she chided him.

Gary ignored that comment and changed the subject. "Hey, I think you were right in hiring Shad. He's a walking encyclopedia about ranching. I feel as if I've just spent an hour in school. That guy is sharp."

"Yes." Charley turned back to her dishes, feeling uncomfortable even if her brother had said she was right about something for once.

"Too bad he isn't going to stick around," he remarked. "But I can't help feeling we were lucky that you stumbled onto him. The man knows his business, I have no doubt about that. What do you suppose makes a man with so much going for him drift from one job to the next?"

"I really don't know." But she wished she did.

Her gaze lifted to the window above the sink with its view of the barns and adjoining corrals. She saw Shad riding away and recognized the horse instantly. Dollar was a solid bay gelding without any markings except for a circle of white on his forehead the size of a silver dollar. He was the best all-around horse in the string, which showed that Shad Russell was a good judge of horseflesh. Just one more thing in his favor.

Chapter Two

The alarm clock went off precisely at five o'-clock the next morning. Charley rolled over with a groan while her hand fumbled over the nightstand to find the button that shut it off. The urge was strong to go back to sleep and ignore the strident summons but her conscience wouldn't let her. She tried to rub the sleepiness from her face without success and lethargically swung her legs from beneath the bedcovers onto the floor.

Her eyes were heavy, not even half-open as she stumbled to the chair where her cotton bathrobe was lying. She slipped into it out of habit rather than conscious direction and made for the door. Outside her room, the second floor was quiet—nothing and no one stirring. Not fully awake, yet not sleepwalking, either, Charley drifted down the stairs in a hazy consciousness that fell somewhere between the two extremes.

By instinct she went to the kitchen. Her mind had memorized how to make coffee until she could literally do it with her eyes closed. When the coffeemaker was switched on, she leaned back against the counter and let her head rest against the upper cupboard. Propped in a standing position, she let herself sink into a half sleep until the aroma of freshly brewed coffee would stir her. But it was a man's voice that roused her first.

"Good morning."

Her lashes flickered long enough to give her a glimpse of the tall, lean man with crow-black hair and clear blue eyes as he came into the kitchen. She was too sleepy to be disturbed from her relaxed position.

"Is it? I haven't been able to wake up long enough to find out if it's a good morning or not," Charley murmured with her eyes closed.

There was a pulse beat of silence before the low, drawling voice came back. "You need to be kissed awake."

For some reason the comment struck Charley as being pleasantly amusing and her lips slanted into a faint smile. Then a pair of hands clasped her waist, pulling her away from the support of the kitchen cupboards. Startled by the unexpected contact, her eyes flashed open to see the roguish glint in Shad's blue ones. Her hands came up to ward him off but when they came in contact with his muscled chest, they lost their purpose. Surprise made her tip her head back, bringing it into line with the one bending toward her. His mouth was just above hers, his gaze hypnotizing her with its steady regard.

When he claimed her lips, she felt a heady rush of sensation. Her pliant body allowed itself to be enfolded by the circling pair of arms and yielded to his dominating, hard maleness. The delicious fire of his kiss warmed her through and through, and ignited a response that had her kissing him back. She was more than content in his embrace, filled with a sense of rightness that had no basis in reality.

A coolness swept over her lips when he ended the kiss and stood up straight. A little dazed, she blinked her round hazel eyes at him. Uh-oh. She had been kissed by a stranger—a hired hand at that—and liked it. A lot. Her early morning wooziness wasn't enough of an excuse. She wondered why on earth she'd allowed it to happen and why he had done it.

He turned away from her, reaching for a coffee cup to fill it from the freshly brewed pot. "You're awake now," he observed.

"Yes." Awake to the needs of her body and awake to him—the sharply cut profile, the sure touch of his hands and the masculine scent of his aftershave. But most of all she had been awakened by the sheer pleasure of his kiss.

"Would you like me to pour you a cup?" His sidelong glance was knowing. He was well aware of his effect on her.

"Yes," she repeated, finally stirring from her position at the counter and frowning at him. "Why did you kiss me just now?"

"Seemed like the thing to do." He turned to offer her the cup in his hand and held her gaze, much more in command of himself and the situation than she was. "There you were, half asleep, with your hair all messed up, looking very kissable. So I kissed you."

"I see." She didn't.

"There was just something so domestic about it. You know, the little woman waiting for her man to come downstairs for that first cup of coffee. In her robe."

His glance skimmed her from head to toe in a way that prompted Charley to pull the cotton robe more tightly closed in front and comb her fingers through the heavy tangle of her hair. It didn't help much. The mocking glint of laughter in his look brought a trace of pink to her cheeks. Charley wasn't sure whether the rush of heat came from anger or embarrassment—or the intimacy implied in his use of the words "little woman" and "her man."

"Like I said, a morning kiss seemed to be in order," Shad finished his explanation and moved with a gliding stride to the table. Pulling out a chair, he sat down and let his gaze return to her. "I've never been one to observe the rules of proper conduct. I'd be lying if I apologized for my behavior. I can't imagine being sorry for kissing a beautiful woman, even if she happens to be the boss's sister."

Something—his blunt words, his calling her beautiful—made her tremble. But she had found too much pleasure in his kiss to want him to regret it had taken place. What was she supposed to do, play the outraged female? She had totally responded to him and he knew it. But she felt obliged to make sure it wouldn't happen again.

"Mr. Russell—" she began in a crisp, authoritative tone.

But he interrupted. "Shad," he corrected with a mischievous glint in his eye.

"Okay, Shad." She conceded that formality at

this point was a little ludicrous. "I think we should make a few things clear. In a couple of months or less, you're going to be moving on—to another job, maybe to another state. Men like you always think there's greener grass somewhere else."

"Maybe. Maybe not."

"Um, I'm not the grass."

"I'm not real sure what you mean by that, Charley."

"I mean you're a good-looking man but—"

"Your eyes were closed," he pointed out.

"Just shut up, okay?" She had to smile a little. "And listen to me. While you're here, you can practice your charms on someone else."

He sipped his coffee and studied her over the rim of the cup. "I don't need practice."

Charley put her hands on her hips and glared at him. "Oh, please."

"Okay, maybe I do. Did you enjoy the kiss?" he asked absently, as if he really didn't care about the answer.

"Don't distract me. I don't want to become involved with you, Shad. I don't do meaningless relationships. We can be friends but that's all. You'll have to find someone else to provide your female entertainment."

Her statement had turned out to be more of a speech. When she finished, his expression had become sober and withdrawn, his gaze never leaving her. He lifted his cup in a toasting acknowledgment, his mouth twisting into a rueful line.

"Got the message. Received and understood," he said, letting his gaze fall to the black depths of the liquid in his cup. "I don't think you could make it any plainer, Charley." Then a reckless smile edged the corners of his mouth. "Maybe that's the key. If I keep calling you Charley long enough, I'll start forgetting about the body that goes with the name." He looked up in time to see the flush of heat warm her face. His glance lingered for a stimulating second on the jutting swell of her breasts beneath the thin cotton robe. "Sorry if it embarrasses you, Charley, but you don't have a brick out of place."

"It doesn't embarrass me," she insisted, but his observation was unnerving. She wasn't sure that she wanted him to find her physically attractive. But she was asking for trouble by staying in the same room with him when she was wearing only a nightgown and robe. She set her untouched cup of coffee on the counter. "Excuse me. It's time I was dressed."

"I couldn't agree with you more," Shad murmured against the rim of his coffee cup, thus hiding the smile Charley suspected was lurking.

Twenty minutes later she came downstairs dressed in her work clothes for the day: worn Levi's and a rust-colored blouse with its long tails knotted at the front. The aroma of bacon permeated the air and Charley faltered in midstride, then continued toward the kitchen where the smell was stronger.

Shad was standing at the stove when she walked in. He glanced at her over his shoulder. "How do you like your eggs? Scrambled? Over easy?"

"Over easy," she responded without thinking, the

frown of surprised disbelief not leaving her face. "You didn't have to fix your own breakfast. I was coming down to do it," she said sarcastically.

"Some women take longer than others to dress. I wasn't sure which category you belonged in." Shad spoke with the certainty of experience. "I wanted to get an early start today so I decided against waiting for you. Do you object to someone else cooking in your kitchen?" he asked as an afterthought.

"No," she replied with a shake of her tawny hair, watching him deftly flip an egg in the hot skillet without damaging the yolk. It was obvious he was no stranger to a kitchen.

"Is something wrong?"

"No. I guess I'm just amazed that you know how to cook. You don't look like the type. A lot of men don't bother to learn—my brother, for instance. Why did you?" There seemed to be any number of things about Shad that separated him from the crowd.

"It was a case of necessity," he replied with an indifferent lift of his shoulder as he scooped up the fried egg and slid it onto the plate warming on the stove. "And frying an egg is no big deal." Using a pair of tongs, he added a few strips of bacon and handed the plate to Charley. "The way I live, I have to be self-reliant. There's toast on the table."

The table had been set for two and Charley sat down in front of one of the place settings to eat . . . a breakfast prepared by someone else. It was a novel experience, a definitely pleasant change of pace. She was spreading dewberry jam on her toast when Shad joined her at the table, plunking down a plate of food for himself.

She finished her first piece of toast while her glance ran over him, noticing the strength and raw vitality in his face and the smiling knowledge of life in his eyes. Not to mention a knowledge of eggs. She poked a fork into hers. Perfect.

"Can I ask you a personal question or is it too early?"

"Go right ahead," he said.

"Where are you from originally, Shad?" She wondered about his background and what had prompted his restless life—never staying anywhere too long, always passing through to some other place.

"I was raised mostly in Colorado." He began to eat, giving her the chance to formulate another question.

"Do you still have family there?" Charley tried to picture his parents and guess at their concern for their footloose son.

Shad paused for the briefest of seconds, then shook his head. "No." He looked up from his plate to her. "How long have you and your brother been running this place alone?"

"Since we lost Dad two years ago to a massive heart attack." The passing of time had allowed her to speak of her father's death with only a minor twinge of grief. "Our mother died five years before that, from pneumonia. Dad was never quite the same after she was gone."

"So now it's just you and Gary."

"Yes." She snapped a strip of crisp bacon in two and began munching on the smaller half.

"And neither of you have plans to enlarge the family circle." His chiseled mouth crooked in a doubting line. "Hard to believe you don't have a man in your life. It doesn't seem natural."

Charley shrugged, aware of the flurry of her pulse as the conversation began to focus on her love life. "That's none of your business. Anyway, I'm not seriously interested in anyone."

"Ah." It was a smooth, knowing sound and his eyes danced with it. "That's the key to the puzzle, huh? Maybe you're not 'seriously interested' in any man, but I bet there's someone who's interested in you."

She considered denying it, but didn't.

"All right, yes," she admitted with a vaguely challenging look. "So far I haven't been able to convince him that I only care about him as a good friend and neighbor. He thinks I don't know what I want yet. As long as he's patient and persistent, he figures that sooner or later I'll come to my senses."

"He's your neighbor?"

She nodded. "Yes, Chuck Weatherby. He owns the adjoining ranch."

In her mind's eye she pictured her would-be suitor. Close to forty, he was of average height, with a stocky build and a developing paunch. Unlike Shad, hours in the sun had not given Chuck Weatherby a dark tan; rather, the fair complexion that went with his auburn hair had given him a perpetual sunburn. He was a good, solid guy with unwavering loyalty and unquestionable devotion. He had a lot of qualities that Charley could admire, but he didn't spark any romantic interest. His kiss didn't stir her senses the way Shad's had a little while ago.

"Chuck Weatherby," Shad repeated the name and followed it with a chuckle. "Chuck and Charley?"

An amused smile lightened her expression. "It does sound kinda ridiculous."

"I think a person could safely say it's unusual," he agreed with a wink. "What is your given name? Charlotte or Charlene?"

"Charlotte, but no one ever calls me that. It's always Charley." She gave a little shrug that showed she had no objections to it and took a sip of her coffee.

"That's because it suits you." His gaze traveled over her in a way that seemed to take some of her breath. "A masculine-sounding name always makes a woman seem more feminine. The reverse isn't true, however. It would never work if your brother, Gary, was called Mary."

"That joke is lamer than he is," she said dryly.

"Sorry." Shad changed the subject with a grin. "I'm surprised your brother isn't married by now. A young, good-looking rancher should be a likely candidate for the single girls in the area."

"I suppose he is," Charley conceded. "A year ago he was almost out of circulation but the engagement was broken. Since then he's sworn off women."

"That's a noble vow, but it won't last." He seemed to speak from experience as he pushed his empty plate back and set his coffee cup in front of him. "What went wrong? Do you know?"

She shook her head, the mass of caramel-colored hair brushing her shoulders. "Gary doesn't like to talk about it." She wasn't sure if she should have even told Shad about it. He was virtually a stranger and here she was spilling the family secrets. Of course, Gary's broken engagement wasn't exactly a secret. It was the discovery that she was talking more freely to Shad than she did with most people that she found disconcerting. Charley switched the subject. "How about you? Have you ever been close to walking down the aisle?"

Shad smiled at the question and took a swig of his coffee. "No, I haven't even been close enough to catch the scent of orange blossoms."

Charley realized she had been wondering whether a woman had started him out on his wandering path. It had seemed logical to assume he was running from something, but apparently that wasn't the case.

Silence stretched for a span of several seconds, broken by the scrape of a chair leg on the tiled kitchen floor as Shad came to his feet with lithe ease. Her upraised glance encountered the smiling light in his blue eyes.

"It's time I started earning my keep."

"Thanks for fixing breakfast. It was good."

"So was the company. Food always tastes better when you don't have to eat alone. I know," he said with a wry twist of his mouth.

That last comment caused Charley to fall silent. As he turned away from the table she studied his muscular body, admiring the width of the shoulders that tapered to a lean waist and hips. He moved with the loose-limbed ease of a horseman. He paused at the back door to take his brown

Stetson from the brass hook and push it onto the midnight black of his hair.

As he walked out the door without looking back she tried to imagine what the life of a drifter was like—traveling down so many roads, and meeting a lot of people but never staying long enough to call any of them friend.

Depressing, she thought. And lonely. But maybe it worked for him. Shad always had a trace of humor in his expression. He seemed to be embracing life and living it to the fullest.

Still, even considering that she hadn't known him long at all, Charley sensed he was searching for something. Perhaps it was a place to call home. The thought brought a vague stirring of hope, which she quickly squashed. It wasn't wise to dream of such things. That led to a fast road to heartbreak with the drifting kind like Shad Russell.

While she nibbled on the last slice of toast, she cleared the table and stacked the dishes in the sink. The uneven thump of a pair of crutches heralded her brother's approach to the kitchen. Charley glanced over her shoulder as he entered the room.

"You're up early this morning," she said. Since he'd come home from the hospital, he'd been in the habit of sleeping until nearly eight.

"My leg was bothering me," he explained, and she could see the whiteness of discomfort in his tanned face. He paused inside the room, leaning his weight on the crutches. "I thought I smelled bacon. What did you do—eat without me?" His gaze centered on the dirty dishes in the sink where Charley was standing.

"Uh-huh. Shad fixed breakfast this morning. For a change I got to eat somebody else's cooking." She moved away from the sink as Gary hobbled toward the table.

"Shad fixed breakfast?" he repeated with questioning surprise. While Charley held the chair steady, Gary lowered himself into it.

"Yes. You should take a lesson from him," she chided and scooted a second chair closer so he could prop his broken leg on it.

"Maybe he's discovered that's the way to a woman's heart," Gary suggested, giving her a curious look that Charley couldn't quite meet.

"I doubt it." She laughed away the suggestion. "He was fixing his own breakfast so he could get an early start. When I came down he just threw another egg in the skillet for me."

"Maybe it wasn't such a good idea to hire him," Gary murmured thoughtfully.

"What makes you say that?" She started for the refrigerator to get his bacon and eggs.

"He's a good-looking guy. In case you haven't noticed."

I noticed. Charley took her time to pick an egg from the identical half dozen that were left. Her brother kept right on talking.

"Hey, you haven't had what could be described as an overabundance of male company lately. The two of you are going to be working together and living in the same house. You're pretty cute, Charley. Sooner or later he's going to make a move. And I'll lay you odds that he's the kind that loves 'em and leaves 'em."

She didn't dismiss her brother's words of caution. All she had to do was remember the sensations that had flowed through her when Shad had kissed her early this morning. The sexual chemistry between them was intense and volatile—definitely something she had to be on guard against. She decided not to mention the incident to Gary. Describing a kiss to your own brother was just too weird and what would be the point? Of course, she couldn't fault his assessment of Shad's character. It was too close to her own opinion.

"Don't worry, Gary"—she straightened up, egg in hand, and shrugged to fake a lack of concern "—I'm old enough to take care of myself."

But Shad's presence in the household and the experience of the first day did alter Charley's routine. In the mornings she splashed cold water onto her face until she was fully awake before she went downstairs dressed for the day. And she was the one who fixed breakfast.

Yet they were together often—working, sharing a meal or spending an hour or two in the evening in each other's company. Satellite TV was a pretty decent distraction, but she usually clicked onto a classic movie or a home-makeover show and skipped the nature channel. Too much mating. Way too much mating. With him on the same sofa she wasn't about to watch happy critters going at it.

The impact of Shad's ready smile didn't lessen with repeated exposure to it. In fact there were times when Charley felt her resistance was gradually being worn away. When his gaze would light on her with a glimmer of appreciation in their depths, she would feel a surge of satisfaction. Any direct contact with him, however accidental, would start a curious curling sensation in her toes. Those were the times when she wondered if she was waging a losing battle.

Less than a week after Shad had come to work for them, Charley was in the barn giving the horses their evening portion of grain. Outside she heard the rattle and roar of the tractor and mower signaling Shad's return from the hay field. She glanced at her wristwatch since Shad had told her at noon that he wouldn't be coming in until all the hay was cut. She had planned to serve supper at seven; an oven meal of ham, scalloped potatoes and baked beans since those dishes would be the easiest to keep warm if Shad worked until dark. As it was, by the time she finished with the evening chores and put the food on the table, Shad would have time to shower and clean up first.

When the horses were grained, Charley tossed some hay into the corral and checked the water in the stock tank. The bay gelding, Dollar, nuzzled her shoulder, trying to wheedle an extra portion of grain from her. Charley laughed and rubbed his velvet nose.

"Sorry, fella. That's all for tonight."

Slipping between the corral rails, she crawled through the fence and started toward the house. The grinding noise of a dead engine trying to be cranked to life attracted her attention. The sound stopped as she turned to locate its source and heard the tinny slam of a truck door. She changed her course, angling toward the machine shed where Shad was lifting the hood of an old pickup that had given up the ghost more than a year ago. She watched as he bent to examine the innards of the truck.

"It won't run." She approached him from the left, drawing his sideways glance.

"I noticed," Shad replied on a dryly amused note and went back to his inspection of the motor and its related parts. "Any objections if I tinker with it in my spare time?"

"Gary said it would cost more than it was worth to fix it," she warned. "He was going to junk it."

"I'll pay for whatever spare parts are needed." He straightened to close the hood. His face and clothes were dusted with hay chaff and dirt, perspiration caking his clothes to his skin. "I'm in need of transportation. If I manage to get it running again, you can sign the pickup over to me in lieu of a month's wages."

"But what will you do for money?" Charley frowned.

"I have enough cash to get by," he insisted and held out his hand to shake on the bargain. "Is it a deal?"

"Unless Gary has some objections, sure, it's a deal." Charley let her hand become lost in the firm grip of his. He held it a little longer than was necessary, his gaze locking with hers for a breath-stopping second. When he let go, she tried to defuse the suddenly charged atmosphere with a soft laugh. "You really want it?"

"Yeah. I do." His voice was low.

Suddenly she was all too conscious of his body

and the musky smell of him, intensified by the
heat of the sun. Charley thrust her hands into her
pockets and looked everywhere but at him.

"You know what they say . . ."

She was relieved to hear his usual casual tone
come back.

He shrugged when she looked at him and
smiled. "One man's junk is another man's trea-
sure, right?"

"Right."

"Were you headed for the house?"

She nodded.

"I'll walk with you."

He fell into step beside her as she started for
her original destination. Her heart began skipping
beats in schoolgirl fashion. It didn't resume its
normal pace until they parted company inside the
house. Shad went upstairs to shower and change.

Chapter Three

Farmers and ranchers just don't celebrate holidays or observe the Sabbath when there was work to be done in the fields or on the range. For a change, this Sunday in June was a day of rest on the Collins's ranch, except for the daily chores. The mowed hay in the fields was still too damp to be baled, none of the animals was sick, and no fences were down.

Charley headed out to the little community church in the mountains where she and Gary were members. Gary had refused to go with her, insisting that he wasn't going to ruin his one good pair of suit pants by cutting off one of the legs in order to put them on over his bulky cast. Shad had declined to attend as well, without giving a reason. So Charley had gone without them, leaving instructions for the roast in the oven.

When she returned a little after twelve noon, the food was done and the table was set. Gary freely admitted that the credit belonged to Shad.

The three of them sat down to a leisurely Sunday dinner and ate too much of it.

Not surprisingly, Charley didn't have any volunteers to help with the washing up. Shad disappeared outside and Gary clumped to the living room couch to lie down and take an afternoon nap. Even though washing, drying and putting away that many dishes probably counted as an aerobic activity, Charley still felt like a stuffed sausage. She went outside to walk off some of the feeling of fullness.

The serrated outline of the Sawtooth Mountains was etched sharply against the backdrop of a summer blue sky as Charley stepped from the front porch. She lifted her gaze to the distant peaks, a parade of rocky spires on the horizon. Their tops were crowned with snow while thick pine forests blackened their slopes. At their feet the lush, rolling meadows of the high country valley sprawled, crisscrossed with mountain-fed streams and dressed in the green of early summer. The Collins's ranch lay within the valley floor in the shadow of the Sawtooths.

A breeze, fresh with the scent of pines, swept across the ranch yard and playfully tugged at the fold of her wraparound skirt, like a child eager to have her follow. Charley smiled and did just that. The breeze brought her first to the corrals, where the horses trotted to the fence to see if she'd brought them any treats and stayed, crowding together and jealously vying for her attention.

After a little while she strolled away, keeping to the relatively smooth ground of the ranch yard, mindful of her dressy sandals. Shad was working on the old pickup truck, parked in the shade of the machine shed. Charley wandered over to see what progress he was making, if any. He was lying under the front of the truck, and all she could see of him was the denim-clad lower half of his body. It was a very nice view.

"Have you found out what's wrong with it yet?" Charley sidestepped the assortment of tools on the ground and stopped by the front fender.

"Yeah." Shad's voice was slightly muffled. "It won't run."

Charley countered with a laugh. "Told you so."

Lying on his back, he scooted out from under the truck except for one shoulder. Her pulse raced at the sight of his bare torso. His flatly muscled chest was all hard sinew and bone with a sprinkling of tightly curling black hair in a vee-shaped patch. The smearing stain of grease coated his large, work-roughened hands. There was an intensity to his look that made her catch her breath.

"Wish I'd listened." The lazy smile matched the mood of his drawling voice, while his very male interest was evident in his sweeping inspection of her. "Are you just going to stand there and be ornamental or will you pass me that wrench?"

Bending her knees, Charley stooped beside the assortment of tools and picked up a wrench. "This one?"

At his nod, she handed it to him and remained in her crouched position, half-sitting on her heels to peer under the truck to watch him as he worked. She was entranced by the rippling play of straining muscles as he labored to loosen an unseen bolt. She folded her hands across her knees, allowing the hem of her skirt to drag the ground.

Without pausing in his efforts, he let his glance run back to her for a brief instant. "Has anyone ever told you that you have beautiful legs?"

Since her skirt was hiding them now, Charley guessed that he must have noticed them before, when she was standing. Her legs tingled in delayed reaction, as if only now becoming aware of the stroking of his admiring gaze.

"Not lately." But she wasn't sure that anyone had ever told her that.

"It's a shame they spend so much time covered by a pair of jeans." Shad remarked. With the bolt loosened by the wrench, he spun it free with his fingers. "That part's done." The ring of accomplishment was in his voice as he wormed his way out from under the truck and passed Charley the wrench.

In reaching for it, she misjudged the distance and slid her hand over his dirt-and-grease-coated fingers. The contact left a smear of grime on the side of her hand. Charley didn't notice it until she had replaced the wrench. As she was straightening up, Shad was rolling to his feet in a move of superb coordination.

"Oh, hell. Do you have a rag?" she asked when she saw the black smear. "I got grease on myself."

"There's one on the left fender." He indicated its location with a wave of his hand.

As she walked over and picked it up, the breeze whipped a thick length of sandy hair across her face and into her eyes. Without thinking, she used her dirty hand to push it out of her eyes and unknowingly left a dark streak of grease across her cheekbone. When she could see clearly again, she began scrubbing her hand with the rag.

"You've smeared it on your cheek," Shad pointed out, smiling as he studied her.

"I did?" She lifted clean fingers to her cheek and they came away with traces of the dirty grease. When she tried to wipe her face clean with the rag, she only succeeded in spreading it.

"You'd better let me do it," he said and took the rag from her hand, encountering only hesitant resistance.

His sexy smile moved up to his eyes. He folded the cloth until he exposed a clean square patch. The task demanded that he stand very close to her. Charley felt the acceleration of her heartbeat as she lifted her face to his ministrations.

He wiped at the smear with firm, even strokes, taking his time to erase the smallest particle. She could see the black centers of his vibrantly blue eyes, half-closed as they looked down at her face. Her breathing was shallow, affected by his nearness and the raw, male vitality that flowed from him. Charley lowered her gaze, fighting the powerful attraction he exerted on her. The sight of his sun-bronzed, lightly furred chest was equally unnerving. When she looked up again, his gaze was centered on her lips with disturbing intensity. It produced an aching tightness in her throat.

Regardless of the way her body was reacting, she wasn't a giddy teenager and she knew the score. It didn't matter how it was added up, she would wind up being the loser in a romantic encounter with this man.

"Stop it, Shad." Her voice was low and husky from her effort at self-control.

"Stop what?" His look was alive with male interest, boldly sensual and disarming.

"Don't look at me like that." She kept her reply steady and faked a calmness.

"Like what?" He pretended an interest in her smeared cheek, but Charley was certain the grease already had been wiped away. "Like I wanted to make love to you?"

"You didn't say that." Charley tried to ignore the tumbling rush of her heart. "Or I didn't hear it. Or both."

"I want to, though. Does that bother you?" His mouth quirked in a very tempting smile.

"I'm not going to answer that," she replied and moved out of his reach. "I just don't want to get involved with you."

He made no attempt to get close to her again as he began wiping his greasy hands on the cloth. "Because I'm only passing through." He guessed her reason for backing off from even the possibility of an embrace.

"Aren't you?" She challenged him to deny it.

A hint of a frown flickered across his face as he half-turned away to throw the rag onto the truck hood. His split-second hesitation before answering caused Charley to hold her breath. But he gave her the reply she had initially expected.

"I'll be moving on sooner or later," Shad admitted without apology or any show of regret.

The ranch was nothing more than a temporary stop in his travels. She meant nothing special to him. He was attracted to her only because she was around and available. Charley had guessed all this but there was no satisfaction in having her suspicions confirmed. One foolish segment of her heart was wishing he had lied.

She longed for a glimpse of his averted face as the breeze rumpled his heavy black hair. When he turned his head to meet her look, she felt the throb of tension in the air. It was broken by the powerful drone of an approaching vehicle. They both glanced at the intruder on the scene as an SUV entered the ranch yard.

"Looks like you have a visitor," Shad remarked with cool indifference.

Charley recognized the late-model Ford Explorer slowing to a stop near the house and would have passed the information along to Shad if he had shown a speck of interest. But he turned his back to her, fixing his attention on the partially dismantled truck motor.

Her mouth was set in a taut line as she started forward to greet the stocky man climbing out of the cream-colored Explorer. She forced it into a curving smile of welcome when she came closer to him.

"Hello, Chuck," she greeted the owner of the neighboring ranch, her most patient and persistent admirer.

He took off his beige Stetson in a gesture of old-fashioned politeness. His white dress shirt emphasized the broadness of his thickening waist. A heavy silver buckle inlaid with turquoise protruded with his stomach. His face was ruddy from constant exposure to the sun except for a white streak across the top of his forehead where his hat had protected it. By no stretch of the imagination did he cut a dashing figure, but he was innately good and kind—and devoted to her.

Not that Shad was paying attention, she thought furiously.

"Hello, Charley. You look lovely today."

"Thank you." It was strange how a compliment from Chuck Weatherby meant nothing to her. Yet if Shad had told her that, she would have beamed like a fool.

"Am I interrupting anything?" he asked, then explained, "I was out for a drive and took the chance that you weren't busy to stop by to find out how you are."

"You aren't interrupting anything," Charley assured him. In fact she felt he couldn't have come at a better time. Shad's unexpected tenderness had almost made her give in. "I was just walking off my Sunday dinner."

"Who is the man you were talking to when I drove in? I don't think I recognize him." He frowned as he glanced in Shad's direction.

She followed his gaze and felt a surge of reluctant admiration at the sight of Shad's muscled physique. A sheen of perspiration made his hard flesh glisten like polished bronze in the sunlight.

Charley attempted to sound casual. "That's our new hired hand."

"He isn't local." Chuck gave her a questioning look.

"No, he isn't. His name is Shad Russell—from Colorado, originally. I think." She realized how little they actually knew about him, outside of his name and previous employers. All a rancher needed to know about a man was whether he could do the job—and Shad had proved himself more than capable. She hadn't even called the numbers he'd scrawled on the napkin because she'd chosen to trust him.

"You mean he's a drifter?" The disapproval of the breed was obvious in the tone of Chuck's voice. "What were you thinking, Charley? I thought you and your brother were going to hire someone local to help out."

"There wasn't anyone available," Charley explained with an unconcerned shrug.

"You didn't ask me." He gave her a reproving glance. "I could have spared one of my men to help you this summer."

"Then you would have been shorthanded, Chuck. No, this way is better." She turned down his belated suggestion, because she didn't want to be under any obligation to their neighbor no matter how well intentioned it was. She would have felt she owed him something even if Chuck wouldn't.

He didn't try to argue with her but his look narrowed on Shad with displeasure. "Your brother oughta give him hell, pardon my French."

"That's okay, Chuck. I've heard that word before. I even use it sometimes."

He didn't seem to be listening. "A man shouldn't take his shirt off to work when there's a woman present," he muttered. "It ain't proper."

"I imagine he didn't want to ruin his shirt with grease and oil from that old truck. Besides, it doesn't offend me." Charley was careful not to smile at Chuck's criticism, knowing that he had to be jealous of Shad's amazing body. Chuck insisted that he wasn't fat, it was just that his muscles had settled around his middle. But she doubted that Chuck had ever been built like Shad, even when he was younger.

"I still say it shows a lack of respect," he insisted stubbornly.

"Mmm. Well, it's getting warm out here in the sun." With a change of subject, she directed his attention away from Shad. "Let's go in the house and have a cold drink." As she started to move toward the house Chuck was quick to follow. "I know you want to chat with Gary while you're here."

"Yes, of course, I do."

His too-fast reply told her what she already knew. He hadn't stopped by to see her brother. It was her company he wanted.

"How is he?" Chuck asked.

"Much better."

Gary was sound asleep on the couch, snoring like he was sawing through a woodpile when they entered the house. Charley ignored Chuck's protests not to disturb him and shook her brother's shoulder to wake him. He stirred groggily, then saw their guest and pushed himself into a sitting position. Charley plumped some pillows and positioned them against the armrest to support his back so Gary could keep his broken leg stretched out on the couch.

Gary stifled a yawn with his hand and smiled sleepily at his neighbor. "What brings you here, Chuck?"

"Just wanted to see how you were getting along."

Chuck lowered his stocky frame into the armchair that matched the blue-flowered sofa.

"Oh?" Gary slid a knowing glance at Charley. "I thought it might have been my sister that you came to see."

She buried her brother with a killing smile. "I'm going to fix a cold drink. What would you like? Lemonade or iced tea?" Both men chose lemonade and she excused herself to go to the kitchen. "It'll only take me a few minutes."

As always happened whenever the two ranchers were left alone together, they became embroiled in a discussion of ranching, the livestock market, the effects of the weather, and this year versus previous years. It was something Charley had counted on and she wasn't disappointed when she returned to the living room to serve them their glasses of iced lemonade.

While they talked around her, she strategically placed coasters on the coffee table in front of the sofa so the walnut finish wouldn't be marred by water rings. Then she relaxed in the recliner with her glass of lemonade and raised the footrest. Good old Chuck didn't expect a woman to know a thing about the subjects they were discussing— sometimes she found it hard to believe they'd been born in the same century. But at least she wasn't obliged to take part in the conversation. Charley was content to sit in the chair and let the talk flow around her.

After about an hour the conversation digressed to the topic of politics, red states versus blue states, and how the government was going to hell, pardon Chuck's French. Charley daydreamed through most of it until she heard someone come in the back door of the kitchen. Aware that it had to be Shad, she stirred from the reclining lounge chair. Her movement attracted Chuck's attention and he shot her a questioning look.

"With all this dry talk, I thought you might like some more lemonade," she said.

He glanced at his empty glass and nodded. "Yes, I would."

"I'll bring in the pitcher." She quietly exited the room.

Shad was standing at the sink when she entered the kitchen. He turned sideways to glance at her as she approached. He had put his shirt on but hadn't bothered to button it or tuck it inside his Levi's. It hung loose, giving her a glimpse of his bare chest. Swinging back to the sink, he turned on the cold water faucet and let it run while he took a glass from the cupboard.

"I fixed a pitcher of lemonade," Charley said as she walked to the refrigerator.

"No, thanks. I prefer water." Shad filled a glass and drank it down, then turned to lean a hip against the sink counter and watch her. "Did your boyfriend come a-courting this afternoon?" He nodded in the direction of the living room.

"He isn't my boyfriend, but, yes, that's Chuck Weatherby from the next ranch," Charley admitted.

"If he isn't your boyfriend, it isn't from lack of trying," he said sourly and ran more water into his glass.

She didn't see any reason to argue the point. "You're welcome to join us."

"It's only a guess, but I'd say your friend wouldn't like it." His mouth slanted in a wry line. "So thanks for the invitation, but I think I'll pass."

Charley didn't try to change his mind because she knew he was right. His presence would irritate Chuck. With the pitcher of lemonade in hand, she returned to the living room. Stopping first near Chuck's chair, she picked up his glass to fill it with the lemonade. He tipped his head in her direction.

"Did I hear you talking to someone in the kitchen?" he asked.

"Yes. Shad came in for a drink of water," she admitted offhandedly. Replacing Chuck's glass on its coaster, she glanced at her brother. "More lemonade?"

"No, thanks," he said.

Charley refilled her glass, then carried the pitcher back to the kitchen. While she had been out of the room, Shad had slipped quietly out the back door. She glanced out the window and saw him crossing the yard to the machine shed. Fighting the twinge of disappointment, she returned the pitcher to the refrigerator shelf and rejoined Chuck and her brother in the living room. She quietly resumed her listening post in the recliner chair, playing the little woman for all she was worth.

When the cuckoo clock on the wall sang out half-past four, Charley sat up straight. "I didn't realize it was so late. It's time I started supper." She was politely hinting that it was time Chuck left, but her brother thwarted it.

"Why don't you stay and eat with us, Chuck?" he asked.

Charley could have screamed. She tried to catch her brother's eye but he wouldn't look at her. Meanwhile Chuck was silently debating whether or not to accept.

"No. I'd better be getting home," he said finally, and Charley nearly sighed aloud with relief. When he turned to look at her, she fixed a bright expression on her face. "I did want to invite you to have dinner with me Friday night."

"I don't know," she stalled, seeking an adequate excuse to refuse. "We'll be baling hay all this week. I'll probably be too tired. Besides, I don't like to leave Gary alone."

"Oh, please," her brother scoffed. "I'm not an invalid. All I have is a broken leg. You need to go out for an evening and enjoy yourself."

"But who would feed you?" she argued, wishing he would keep his mouth shut.

"Fix a casserole. Something Shad and I could warm up," Gary reasoned with a twinkle in his eyes.

"Seems like Gary's come up with a fine solution, Charley," Chuck inserted. "Will you come out to dinner with me on Friday?"

So much for making up her own mind. "Yes." Her tone was clipped as she gave in to the pressure.

A few minutes later, after Chuck had made arrangements to pick her up at six on Friday, he rose to leave. Charley walked him as far as the front door and watched him climb into the Explorer and drive away. She was fuming when she turned to confront her brother.

"You really were a lot of help, Gary. With a brother like you, I don't need enemies," she snapped. "I've done everything but beat Chuck over the head trying to make him understand that I'm not interested in him. Then you go and force me into accepting a date with him."

"Be practical, Charley." He tried to calm her. "He wants to take you out and you could use a break, so what's wrong with that? You're not committing to anything."

"I happen to like Chuck as a person," she retorted. "And I don't think it's right to lead him on in any way. It isn't fair to him." She turned on her heel and stalked into the kitchen, sorry that there wasn't a door to slam to vent some of her anger.

Charley was still seething when they all sat down to supper that night. The tension at the table was unmistakable. Sparks flew every time she looked at her brother. Shad eyed them both with a trace of humor.

"Is something wrong?" he finally asked.

Gary shrugged. "Charley's sulking because I forced her into accepting a date with Chuck this Friday. She hasn't been out of this house in weeks. I thought she needed to get away from here and let her hair down."

"I can't imagine letting my hair down with someone as conservative as Chuck," she retorted.

"Maybe not," her brother conceded. "But you haven't exactly had a flood of invitations for dates lately. And beggars can't be choosers."

Fire burned in the look she gave Gary. "You're

lucky I'm not sitting on the other side of the table, because I just might be tempted to rebreak that leg of yours."

"Nothing like sisterly love." Her brother grinned at Shad.

An angry sound of exasperated disgust came from her throat as she rose from the table to fetch the dessert. There were times when her brother was absolutely impossible. Tonight was one of them.

The week that followed was hectic, every minute filled from sunup to sundown. Charley fell into bed each night, totally exhausted, and dragged herself out of bed each morning. By Friday there didn't seem to be enough cold water to chase the sleep out of her eyes. Finally she gave up trying. She opened the bathroom door and walked straight into Shad.

"Oh." It was a soft sound of delayed shock as she found her arms resting against the solid wall of his chest. She swayed backward unsteadily, trembling from the unexpected contact with his warm flesh.

"Steady, girl." His hands closed on her shoulders to give her balance. There was a smiling light in his blue eyes as they ran over her upturned face. His look disturbed her with its caressing quality. "We've got to stop meeting like this." His drawling voice lowered its pitch to an intimate level. "Good ole Chuck might get the wrong idea if he found out about it."

Stung by his mockery, Charley broke out of his light hold and quickly sidestepped him. "Don't be ridiculous," she declared in a voice low with anger.

But he only chuckled. "I don't think it's funny," she said as she started toward her bedroom door.

His voice trailed after her. "Tonight's the big night, isn't it?"

She didn't think that remark was worthy of a response so she closed the door on him. Yet, in the quiet of her bedroom, the encounter outside the bathroom door started her thinking about how many things they shared besides a bathroom. They ate at the same table, slept under the same roof, drank from the same water jug out in the hay fields. She had spent more time with Shad under a variety of circumstances than she had with any other man in her life except for her brother. It was an unsettling discovery to realize how much he'd become a part of her life in two short weeks.

Chapter Four

Charley was ready promptly at six o'clock that evening when Chuck came to pick her up. She had left a casserole in the oven and salad fixings in the refrigerator for Shad and her brother to have as their evening meal. She was getting in the habit of cooking for them, which kind of scared her.

Men can cook, she reminded herself as she found a package of croutons from the shelf and threw it on the counter next to the salad bowl. Just show them where it says Open Here and explain about expiration dates. They will survive.

She thought about the perfect fried egg Shad had made for her as Chuck walked her to his SUV. It beat thinking about Chuck's approving glance sweeping over her. Charley felt uncomfortable in her long-sleeved dress. It was made out of a silky material, navy blue with white polka dots, with a wide matching belt at the waistline and a flared skirt. It was one of the most flattering dresses she owned, its dark color a complement to her honey-colored hair. She wasn't sure but she thought she might have chosen it out of spite, dressing with care simply because she had been maneuvered into accepting a date she didn't want.

Her big date with Chuck Weatherby wasn't the ordeal that Charley had pretended it was going to be. He was an undemanding companion and it was easy to relax with him. She would have enjoyed it more if she hadn't been aware that he wanted their relationship to become something more. If her conscience hadn't bothered her, it would have been a perfect evening.

After a long and leisurely meal at a restaurant in Ketchum, Charley wasn't surprised when Chuck suggested that he take her home. He wasn't the kind of person to stay out until all hours of the night, and with the exhausting week she'd had, she willingly agreed to his suggestion.

As they started out on the long drive back to the ranch Charley gazed out the window at the shimmer of stars in the night sky. They made the perfect backdrop for the magnificence of the moonlit mountain range. The combination of natural tiredness and the contentment of a good meal and pleasant company soon had Charley nodding off.

When she caught herself almost falling sound asleep, she sat up straighter in her seat and glanced self-consciously at Chuck, noticing his faint smile.

"I'm sorry," she apologized. "I didn't realize I was so tired." Her eyelids felt as if there were lead weights attached to them.

"Use my shoulder for a pillow," Chuck offered. "Otherwise you'll end up with a crick in your neck."

"Oh, I couldn't do that. The shift's in the way." She'd never been so grateful for bucket seats and huge ridiculous macho gearshifts in her life. She started to protest that she wouldn't fall asleep again when she was interrupted by a big yawn that refused to be postponed. She realized she was only kidding herself. She wouldn't stay awake for the entire ride. She slumped lower in her seat. Almost immediately her eyes closed.

"You realize that we should be driving back to our own home."

Uh-oh. Did that remark mean a discussion was looming about The Future of This Relationship? Charley stiffened and would have spoken, but he went on.

"No, don't say anything," he said. "I've heard it all before, but it doesn't change the way I feel about you, Charley. And I can't explain what it is that makes me so sure you'll wear my ring someday. It's just a feeling I have. I guess that's why I won't give up even though you've made it clear that I'm wasting my time." Charley didn't know how to fill the silence that followed his statement. After a few minutes he said gently, "Go to sleep."

When she finally closed her eyes, she didn't open them again until the Explorer slowed to a stop in the ranch yard. She sat up slowly, stretching her shoulders and blinking away the sleep in her eyes.

"Your brother left a light on in the house for you," Chuck observed as he turned off the motor.

Charley noticed it, too. "Why don't you come in for a little while and I'll fix some coffee?" she suggested.

He hesitated a split second, then accepted. "All right."

Before Chuck had a chance to climb out and walk around to her side, she had the door open and was stepping out. He waited for her with that old-fashioned politeness that she really did like and walked her to the house. The coolness of the mountain air was fresh and invigorating, chasing away the last remnants of sleepiness.

As she entered the house her gaze was automatically drawn to the lamp left burning. Shad was sitting in a chair beside it, illuminated by its pool of light. His large hands were busy with a shirt in his lap. He looked up when she entered, but Charley didn't notice. She was too busy staring at the glint of silver flashing in and out of the shirt material, certain her mind was playing tricks on her.

"I didn't expect you home so early," he said. "Gary went to bed about twenty minutes ago."

His voice broke the spell and she met his gaze, only vaguely aware that Chuck was standing beside her. "What are you doing?"

"A button came off this shirt. I'm sewing it on," Shad replied in a tone that indicated it was the logical thing to do. "There's plenty of coffee still hot in the kitchen."

"Thank you." She glanced at Chuck and saw him eyeing Shad with a measuring look. She realized the two men hadn't formally met. "Chuck, this is Shad Russell, our new hired man. This is Chuck Weatherby, a fellow rancher and neighbor."

"No, don't get up." Chuck waved him back into the chair when Shad started to gather his sewing together to stand.

"You two probably want the living room to yourselves," Shad said. "I'll finish this in my room."

"Don't bother," Charley said quickly. "Chuck and I will have our coffee in the kitchen." When she glanced at Chuck to obtain his consent, she noticed his expression appeared oddly tight-lipped. He was usually good-natured and easygoing.

"That will be fine," he agreed.

She started to suggest that Shad have coffee with them, then bit her tongue just in time. After another glance at Chuck, she moved toward the kitchen while he trailed in her wake. The coffee smelled hot and fresh as she took two cups from the cupboard and filled them with coffee from the pot. She carried them to the kitchen table where Chuck was sitting.

"Do you take cream or sugar?" She didn't remember.

"Neither." His expression appeared grim. "Does that man sleep here in the house?" His voice was pitched low so it wouldn't carry into the living room.

She was startled by the question and a little bit angry at the implication that Shad wasn't fit to live under the same roof. "Where do you think he sleeps? In the barn with the animals? He sleeps in the spare bedroom upstairs."

"I don't like it." He picked up the cup and stared into the black liquid.

"You don't have to like it as long as Gary and I are satisfied with the arrangements," she retorted.

"It's you I'm worried about, Charley," he explained. "It ain't right for a strange man to stay in your house."

"Maybe so, if I lived alone, but my brother lives here, too, in case you've forgotten," she reminded him somewhat acidly. "My reputation is hardly in jeopardy."

"I don't think you understand my concern." There was a wealth of patience in his voice. "You're a pretty young woman. The proximity of living under the same roof with you is liable to give the man ideas."

Living in the same house with Shad was giving *her* ideas, but she couldn't very well tell Chuck that. "Please," she said wearily. "I had a nice time tonight. I don't want to argue."

Pausing, he appeared to consider her request before he responded. "You're right," he agreed and pushed his cup aside without having taken a single sip. "Thanks for the coffee, but it's time I was getting home." As he stood up Charley started to do the same, but he forestalled her. "I'll show myself out."

Stopping at her chair, he crooked a finger under her chin and leaned down to kiss her good night. He wasn't totally inept. The pressure of his mouth was warm and ardent, but it left her unmoved. Charley saw the disappointment in his expression when he lifted his head and knew her response had been inadequate but she refused to fake what she didn't feel.

"Good night, Chuck," she murmured.

His smile was faintly sad as he left the kitchen. She remained at the table until she heard the front door close and his footsteps on the porch. She rose, leaving her own coffee untouched, and slipped her hand into the silken pockets of her dress to wander into the living room.

In the shadows near the front door she paused and listened to the car start and drive away. Her gaze was drawn to Shad, seated in the overstuffed chair. She watched him deftly ply the needle to make the last few passes to secure the button to the shirt material. Tying a knot, he lifted the thread to his mouth and bit it in two.

"I would have sewed that button on for you." Charley drifted out of the shadows. "You didn't have to do it."

"You've spoiled me enough already." He pushed the silver needle into the strawberry pincushion and returned it to her sewing basket by the chair.

"How?" She tipped her head to one side, her tawny hair spilling over one shoulder. She didn't recall going out of her way to do anything special for him.

"Doing my laundry, fixing all those delicious home-cooked meals, and keeping my room clean," Shad replied, getting to his feet in one motion.

She laughed softly and came closer. "That hardly constitutes being spoiled."

"Maybe not to some," he agreed with a slow smile. "How was your evening?"

"Fine." Charley gave a noncommittal answer because she didn't feel like talking about it. Aware of his penetrating gaze, she avoided it.

"Didn't he kiss you good night?" He sounded both curious and vaguely surprised.

She lifted her head, a little defiant. "Yes, he did."

Reaching out, he held her waist in his hands and maneuvered her into the lamplight so he could see her face clearly. The weight of his hands was heavy, holding her in place while his gaze wandered over her features.

"Funny. You don't look kissed," he said at last. The pressure of his grip increased, pulling her slowly closer to him. His eyes seemed to change color, growing darker and becoming sober. His mouth began a slow descent, stopping before it reached her lips. While the warmth of his breath caressed her skin, she drank in the intoxicating smell of him, a combination of aftershave, soap, and that scent that was his alone. "Chuck is a good man. He'd make a wonderful husband and a loving father for your children. He would be good for you, Charley. You really should marry him."

It wasn't at all what she had expected him to say. She flashed him a surprised and irritated look. "Everyone keeps trying to throw me at Chuck. First Gary and now you. What is this—a conspiracy?" she protested, pulling an inch or so back from his face to glare at him. "Everyone wants me to marry him, but no one bothers to ask me what I want."

"I think I know what you want." His gaze centered on her lips. The desire that burned in his eyes stole her anger. "I'm no good for you, Charley. We both know it. But it doesn't seem to matter, does it? It doesn't change anything."

"No," she whispered and stopped listening to her common sense.

His mouth came down those last few inches to settle onto her lips with tantalizing ease. A sweet rush of forbidden joy ran through her veins as her hands slid around his neck and she melted into his arms. A steel band circled her waist to press her tighter to his length while his other hand tunneled under the thickness of her hair to cup the back of her head.

The driving hunger of his kiss parted her lips, giving him access to her open mouth. She was caught in a whirl of sensation, all golden and consuming. Her sensitive fingers caressed his thick hair, over and over. She was crushed against the hard contours of his body, her flesh throbbing.

A tiny cry of intense longing broke from her when the hotness of his mouth moved to her throat and burned a nuzzling path to her ear. He tugged at an earlobe with his teeth and teased a hollow with the tip of his tongue. The roughness of his breathing was no more controlled than her own. He lifted his head, pulling away to create a small space between them while his hand absently rubbed the small of her back.

"Where do we go from here, Charley?" It was a low, husky query. "You tell me."

Unwillingly she opened her eyes and looked down the road. Eventually he would leave her. She knew it as certainly as she knew her own name. She pulled her hands from around his neck and pushed at his forearms to break his hold on her. It cost her a lot to deny him.

"We don't go anywhere from here," she said, "not together."

Shad accepted her answer with a silent nod. He raised a hand to cup the side of her face in his palm. A callused thumb brushed her lips, tracing their moist and swollen outline.

"At least now you look like you've been kissed." His mouth curved in a mocking line.

His hand fell away as he stepped back, setting her free. Charley hesitated uncertainly, then walked to the staircase. She paused at the opening to look back, but Shad was already disappearing into the kitchen. She slowly climbed the stairs to her bedroom.

The weekend came and went with Charley trying to pretend that nothing earth-shattering had happened and attempting to pick up the threads of her previously friendly relationship with Shad. He appeared to regard her Friday night answer as final, though she still saw the same look in his eyes: a mixture of desire and restraint that confused her. But he didn't make any overt moves. Charley was realizing that being with him every damned day was only increasing the sexual tension.

At least Gary was less irritable, probably because he'd mastered the use of his crutches. He could do anything and go anywhere on them. No longer housebound, he began doing some of the light chores such as feeding the horses, thus freeing Charley and Shad of that responsibility.

With the dawn of Thursday morning, Charley

awoke to discover a steady rain was falling. Doing ranch work was out of the question, except for the daily chores that Shad took care of. Charley spent most of the morning cleaning the house. The kitchen was the last room on her list. Gary was sitting at the table with his leg propped on a chair when she entered.

"Did you hear that?" he asked.

"Hear what?" She frowned slightly as she glanced at him, her mind busy trying to decide what to fix for lunch. Then, above the steady rainfall, she heard the sputtering cough of an engine before it caught and roared to life. Too preoccupied to understand the significance of that sound, she rummaged through the pantry shelves until Gary answered her.

"Shad's been working on that old truck this morning. Sure sounds as if he's got it running." He shook his head in wry amazement. "I didn't think he could do it. He's really something, isn't he?"

"Yes." Shad wasn't a subject she could comfortably discuss. He was becoming much too special in her life. She walked to the refrigerator. "How about cold roast beef sandwiches for lunch?"

"What you're trying to tell me is that we're going to have leftovers," Gary said mournfully.

"Oh, poor you," she teased him. "I want to clean the refrigerator this afternoon. We might as well eat what we have."

"Bring it on," he declared with a wave of his hand.

Charley began carrying the plastic food containers from the refrigerator to the table, an assortment of condiments and dressings, and a loaf of bread from the bread drawer. As she got out the plates and silverware the hum of the truck engine seemed nearer. She even thought she heard the tires splashing in the puddles of water. A horn blared right outside the kitchen door, causing her to jump. It sent out its summons a second time and Charley set the plates and silverware on the table and hurried to the back door.

Gary was a fraction slower, reaching the door after she had opened it. The truck was stopped just outside, the motor idling as steadily as a purring cat. Shad had rolled the window down on the driver's side and had an arm hooked over the frame. A hand was resting on the steering wheel. His rugged features were broken with a wide smile, his blue eyes dancing with a happy light.

"Hey, it sounds great!" Gary told him.

"Thanks!" But Shad's gaze was focused on Charley, disarming her with its cheerful persuasiveness. "What say we go for a ride, Charley?"

"I just put lunch on the table." She was well aware that the cold food could wait but heading out for a joyride alone with Shad probably wasn't the smartest thing to do. Still, his celebratory mood was catching.

"So?" he grinned. "Let Gary eat it." He glanced at her brother. "Promise you won't break your neck if we leave you alone for a couple hours."

"I promise," Gary said.

"Come on, Charley," Shad coaxed.

She glanced sideways at her brother, who smiled and gave an approving nod. "Go on."

Charley needed no second urging as she dashed

out from beneath the shelter of the overhang and into the raindrops. Shad leaned across the seat and opened the passenger door for her so she could climb right in.

"Are you sure this thing doesn't leak?" She was slightly out of breath as she slid onto the seat and closed the door.

"Does a Rolls-Royce leak?" He gave her a look of mock reproof for her lack of faith in the old truck. "Of course not."

As he shifted the truck into forward gear, a huge drop of water plopped onto the dashboard and they broke into laughter simultaneously. Charley reached out to wipe it away with the sleeve of her plaid blouse.

"A little water never hurt anyone," she assured him.

"That's what I thought." He sent a saluting wave to Gary standing in the back doorway and started the truck rolling forward. The windshield wipers swished back and forth, leaving spotty patches of water where the blades failed to touch the glass.

"You need new windshield wipers," she pointed out.

"But only when it rains," he countered with a wickedly teasing look.

"What do you think it's doing now?"

"That's liquid sunshine," he insisted.

As he turned the truck around in the yard and headed it down the lane, she felt the smooth acceleration of power.

"It really runs well," he said, "maybe better than it did before it conked out. But you tell me."

She had to agree, judging by the sound of the engine. "Yeah. You're right."

"All it needed was some loving attention and a few well-chosen words." He arched one dark eyebrow with amusement and Charley recalled a few times when she'd heard him cussing out a resisting engine part.

She laughed and lifted a hand to fluff the rain-dampened hair around her face. The dash from the house to the truck had left her only slightly wet. She would dry quickly.

"Now you have your own wheels," she declared. "When you finally leave, you won't have to hitch-hike. You can drive away in your own truck." Almost as soon as the words were out, she regretted them. Just knowing the day would come caused a twinge of pain in her heart. She wished she hadn't referred to it.

"That's right." Even the lightness of his voice sounded forced.

Leaning back in the seat, she let her head rest on the curved top and turned to look out the window. The mountains were shrouded in dark clouds, a gray mist hanging over the valley floor. The tap-tapping of the rain on the metal roof of the truck was a soothing sound.

"I love to ride in the rain," Charley said.

"So do I," Shad agreed and slowed the truck as they reached the intersection with the highway. There was no traffic in sight and he pulled onto the road.

"Where did you learn so much about fixing engines? I mean, my dad's generation was good at it but now that everything mechanical is computerized . . ." She trailed off, wondering what he would say. Shad's competence at so many things might mean that he had grown up poor, and got good at making do, because he'd had to. She didn't want to pry or make him uncomfortable, but she was curious.

Her question didn't seem to bother him. "I picked it up here and there, just like everything else."

Charley smiled at him softly. "Is there anything you don't know how to do, Shad?"

"Hmmm. Let me think. No." He looked over at her, returning her smile. "For example, a Mexican vaquero showed me how to braid and make cinch straps as soft as velvet when I worked on a ranch in Arizona. And an old-timer in Wyoming showed me a few tricks with a rope. I could go on all day but I'll spare you. Anyway, you can learn a lot of things if you keep your eyes and ears open"—he shrugged one shoulder in his easygoing way— "and—as long as you're not ashamed to admit that you're ignorant about something."

She hesitated before responding. It did seem to her like he wasn't making the most of his hard-earned knowledge of cattle raising, horsemanship and knack for fixing things. No matter what, ranching was a hands-on profession that still required those skills, and he was well suited for it. Exactly why he had remained a drifter was still a mystery to her.

"Haven't you ever wanted to be something else than what you are?" She faced his profile, her cheek resting on the back of the seat.

"Something other than a cowboy?" He shook his head. "No. Granted, the hours are long. Sometimes it seems that you get up so early in the morning that you're eating breakfast in the middle of the night. And the work is hard, sometimes dirty and smelly. The pay is peanuts. A guy could earn a lot more working in a factory."

"Not necessarily, what with foreign outsourcing and plants closing all over the country. Even union work isn't a sure thing anymore."

"Good point. Anyway, being a cowboy is a proud way to live."

There was an underlying emphasis on the last sentence, a sense of deep satisfaction and pride. Charley was moved by the force of his abiding love for his profession and hoped she hadn't given the impression that it wasn't a worthy one.

"Was your father a cowboy, too?" The question was personal but the closeness between them as they rode through the steady rain seemed to encourage intimacy.

"I really don't know." He spared her a glance, his expression thoughtful, then smiled absently and let his attention return to the highway. "I was abandoned as a child when I was somewhere around two years old. I don't remember anything about my natural parents. There weren't any papers left with me. I have no idea when or where I was born or what my real name is."

"I see," Charley murmured as a picture began to form in her mind. "This was in Colorado?" She remembered he had told her that was where he had been raised.

"Yes." The rain had become spotty and Shad switched off the windshield wipers.

"Didn't they try to find your parents?" It seemed incomprehensible to her that someone could abandon their child. She wondered what kind of people could do that, and knew the same thought had undoubtedly occurred to Shad. Such an experience had to leave a scar.

"They tried," he said, his expression suddenly impassive. "A service-station owner found me sleeping in a box when he opened up for business one morning. Not a clue to go on as to who left me there or why. The station had been closed and the video security camera was busted. I was put into foster care with the idea that my parents would come back to claim me but they never did." His voice was flat, almost a monotone. "I was shuffled from one home to another. For most kids, the system doesn't work. They end up homeless or worse when they're bounced out of it at eighteen."

Charley nodded, loath to ask for details. She read the newspapers like everyone else. She knew what he wasn't saying. "So you never really knew what it was like to have a family," Charley said. Moving on was what he knew and had always known from a very early age. There hadn't been a stable home in his life.

"No," he admitted, and sent her a smiling look that held no self-pity. "None of my foster parents ever mistreated me. They were all good to me but I was still an outsider. It wasn't until I was older that I discovered most children had parents and a family. When I found out differently, I was realistic enough not to cry about something I couldn't change. In some ways I was lucky because I was exposed to a variety of environments and lifestyles, learned a lot about people, and life in general."

"But it had to have an effect on you," Charley insisted.

"It wasn't all bad, Charley. I learned to be self-reliant and independent. I struck out on my own when I was seventeen," he explained. "Got a job herding sheep up in the high country of Colorado with a Basque shepherd as my partner. From there I went to work cleaning stables for a quarter horse breeder. Cattle were a sideline with him. That's where I started riding fence and working branding crews. I moved south after that—Arizona, New Mexico, Texas. I've seen a lot of country." His gaze made a sweep of the rugged land outside the truck windows. "But I guess I was mountain-bred. Look at that."

She glanced out the window and took a deep breath. It had stopped raining, leaving behind a world that had been washed clean. The air was vibrantly fresh, rushing into the cab through the now opened windows. The leaves of the trees had seemed to turn emerald green, while the pines took on a darker shade of green. The sun had broken through the clouds, a patch of blue showing in the sky. Against the backdrop of the wild mountains, a rainbow arched its multicolored promise.

"Everything is always so beautiful after a rain," Charley murmured with a trace of awe.

"Yes." But he was looking straight at her when he said it. The disturbing shadows in his eyes disrupted the steady beat of her heart.

She turned quickly to face front again and

fought the rush of wild longing that coursed
through her. The cab of the old truck suddenly
seemed very cramped. She was conscious of his
long, muscled thighs on the seat near hers and the
sinewy strength of his arms beneath the sleeves of
his shirt. It became difficult to think clearly in
such close quarters and Charley tried to concentrate on the passing scenery.

"Where are we going?" she asked as she tried to
recognize her surroundings.

"That's a surprise," Shad replied, deliberately
mysterious.

"Tell me where you're taking me," she insisted.
The game he was playing made her smile—somewhat reluctantly.

"Somewhere out of this world," he said with a
mocking grin and refused to tell her more than
that.

Charley sat back and stared into the distance.
Her mind raced in an attempt to guess their ulti-
mate destination. She made a lot of guesses and
discounted them all, no nearer to unraveling the
mystery than before. And Shad wouldn't help her.

Chapter Five

The highway swung along the foothills of the mountain range with the Snake River Plains spreading out flat on the other side. Charley was still in the dark about their destination until she saw the harsh, forbidding landscape ahead of them. Barren of plant life, it was a tortuous collection of volcanic rock and solidified lava.

"The Craters of the Moon, that's where we're going," she guessed accurately this time.

Shad chuckled and reminded her, "I told you it was someplace 'out of this world.'"

"That was a rotten clue and you know it." She poked her fist at his shoulder in a playful reprimand and laughed.

Slowing the truck, he turned into the entrance of the Craters of the Moon National Monument. The jagged rockscape flanked the road on either side of them. The colors varied from near black to a purplish gray. Shad stopped the truck in a small parking area along the side of the road.

"Come on," he said as he opened his own door. "Let's get out and walk."

Charley pushed her own door open and joined him by the front hood of the truck. Almost casually, he reached out and took hold of her hand to lead her onto the rough terrain. Charley didn't resist the warm grip of his hand as she followed him onto the uneven ground.

When the road disappeared behind them, an eerie silence seemed to descend. Shad paused in the center of the harsh landscape and Charley lifted her face to the slight breeze, pushing the hair back from her face and holding it there.

They were surrounded by cones and craters of volcanic rock. Long ago, massive underground explosions had created these weird formations and sent out the lava flows to create an island of rock crags in a land of grass and trees and earth. Its resemblance to photographs of the moon's surface was uncanny, so empty and lifeless.

Charley glanced over her shoulder at the mountain range on the horizon, needing the reassurance that this desolate landscape did not go on forever. When her gaze swung to Shad, his mouth curved in a smile of silent understanding.

"If a person ever wondered what it's like to walk on the moon, he'd have his answer here," he said.

"It's really strange. So quiet and so lonely." She looked around, seeing nothing but more sharp rock formations.

"There's the moon." With a nod of his head he indicated the pale white sphere in the daytime sky, its shadowy face barely discernible.

She moved closer to Shad, their arms brushing

against each other as she lifted her gaze to the heavens. When he released her hand, she missed the warmth of his touch, but his arm moved around the back of her waist, replacing one sensation with another.

"It makes you feel isolated, doesn't it?" He turned his head to look at her and Charley felt the first tremor of desire quiver through her at how close they stood. "As if we're the only people on earth, marooned here alone."

"Yes." Her voice was low and her monosyllabic answer concealed the stirring inside that his remark provoked. Being marooned with him was a heady thought. Just the two of them—with no possibility that he could ever leave her.

"Ever wondered what it would be like to make love on the moon?" His question robbed her of speech. She shook her head as Shad turned slightly to more squarely face her. He gathered her into his arms, fitting her soft curves to his male hardness and touched his lips to her forehead. "I have," he murmured, the warmth of his breath stimulating her skin. "It must be a unique experience."

With soft kisses he closed her eyes, bringing her to a whole other world of pure sensation. Her fingers curled into the hard muscles of his arms, clinging to him as she felt a strange weightlessness envelop her. While he explored the curve of her cheek and the corners of her lips, his hands roamed in exciting caresses over her shoulders and hips. He seemed to deliberately torment her with the promise of his kiss, but did not offer it.

The aching need that was building in her forced a soft moan from her throat. In answer to her wordless plea, his hard lips covered her mouth with bruising possession. The circle of his arms tightened, pressing her breasts, taut with desire, against the unyielding wall of his chest. Yet not even this closeness brought satisfaction and she strained to cross the physical limits of their embrace, to become part of him.

His mouth broke away from hers, his breathing labored and heavy. She could feel the pounding of his heart, thudding as quickly as her own. His eyes were half-closed with the weight of desire as he studied her face. He loosened his hold, bringing his hands up to curve them under the hair along her neck while Charley continued to lean against him, her legs almost too weak to stand without his support. His hands were restless, his fingers exploring the curve of her jaw and the pulsing vein in her neck.

"Your body feels so good against mine," he said huskily and lowered one hand to cup her breast. It swelled beneath his touch. "I want to make love to you, Charley. You know that."

His statement pulled away the veil she'd been hiding behind and she could see clearly. The one thing she had been so determined to avoid had happened despite her better judgment. She had fallen irrevocably in love with him.

"It isn't fair," she protested in a faint sob. "I want you so much, Shad."

"Charley?" Her name was a caress on his lips as he brought them down hard on her own, stealing what little vestige of control she had left.

The embrace would have ended in her total surrender if it hadn't been for the clatter of a pair of feet on the rocky ground. The approach of the intruder stopped the kiss before it reached the point where they both would have been beyond hearing a bomb explode. Shad lifted his head at almost the same moment that the sound ceased. As his arms loosened to let Charley go his frown turned into a lazy smile.

"Who are you?" he asked, and Charley wondered how anyone could resist his smile. Still a little shaky, she turned to see who Shad was talking to. A little boy, no more than six years old, stood poised in the shadow of a volcanic cone. His rounded blue eyes were studying them uncertainly. "I'll bet I know who you are," Shad stated. "You're the man in the moon, aren't you?"

The little boy laughed and nodded vigorously. "Yeah! How'd you know?"

Shad crouched down, sitting on his heels, to bring himself to eye level with the youngster. "Well now, I've always wanted to meet the man in the moon," he remarked and looked him over. "But I thought you'd be taller."

"I only look small," the boy said, his child's imagination liking this game. "I'm really bigger."

Charley could see that Shad was enjoying himself, too. He had a natural affinity with children, she realized. He would make a good father, she decided, and caught herself wondering whether his son would inherit those blue eyes and black hair. She squelched the thought, telling herself not to go there.

"I haven't had lunch yet and I'm starting to get

hungry." Shad tipped his head at an inquiring angle. "I don't suppose you'd tell me where you keep the green cheese."

"The moon isn't made of cheese," the boy said, scoffing at him for believing such nonsense.

"It isn't?" Shad looked surprised.

At just about that same moment, a woman's voice called anxiously, "Billy! Billy, where are you?"

The boy turned with a reluctant sigh and answered, "Here, Mom!"

A young woman in shorts and a knit top appeared a second later behind the cone where the boy waited. Her worried expression faded to exasperation as she found him unharmed. "Don't run away from your father and me like that ever again. What if you got lost?"

"But I didn't," he replied in a perfectly reasonable tone and turned to point to Shad and Charley. "They found me."

"You mean you aren't really the man in the moon?" Shad feigned a look of disappointment as he sent a brief smile at the boy's mother and straightened to his feet.

"No. I fooled you, didn't I?" The boy laughed.

"You certainly did," Shad agreed.

"I hope he wasn't a nuisance," the woman apologized and caught hold of her son's hand.

"Not at all," he assured her and sent a glance at Charley that contradicted his statement.

But the interruption had given Charley time to regain her senses. Shad's recognition of that fact flickered across his expression. Once they were alone, there wouldn't be a repeat of that embrace. The moment had passed when desire took over.

Falling in love with him hadn't changed the reality that he would leave her someday. It had now become a question of how much she would be hurt, and not whether she'd be hurt.

When the boy's father had joined his wife and son, Shad lightly took Charley's hand. In mutual silence they retraced their route to the parking area where they'd left the truck. After helping her into the cab, Shad walked around the hood to climb behind the wheel.

"Have you seen enough of the park?" He started the engine without looking at her.

"Yes." She made a show of glancing at her watch. "It's getting late. We'd better head back for the ranch before Gary starts wondering what happened to us."

Stepping on the accelerator, he turned onto the road and headed back toward the highway. "Do you want to stop somewhere for lunch?"

"I'm not hungry," she said quietly. "Are you?"

His gaze touched her, then moved over the sweet curves of her breasts. "Not for food," he replied and didn't need to add more.

As they neared the highway she forced her attention on the cross traffic. As soon as there was a break, Shad accelerated onto the highway.

During the next twenty or so miles they didn't speak at all. Gradually her tension ebbed away and Charley began to relax once again in Shad's company, her guard lowering. He seemed to sense the very moment it occurred, because he glanced over at her and smiled.

"So how did you like the Craters of the Moon?" he asked. There was nothing in his tone to make

Charley suspect she should read more into his question than what he had said.

"Very much. I haven't been there for a really long time but it's an amazing place." She didn't let her thoughts dwell on what had almost happened between them there. Combing her fingers through her hair, she looked out the window and sighed contentedly.

"What was that for?" His glance was curious.

"I guess it was an expression of pride in my home state." She shrugged, because she wasn't entirely sure what it had been. "Idaho has everything."

"Is that right?" His tone was faintly mocking.

"It's true," Charley insisted. "On the road toward Salmon, we have the Grand Canyon in miniature. East of here, there are sand dunes. And Shoshone Falls outside of Twin Falls, Idaho. The water there falls farther than the waters at Niagara Falls. There's the Snake River Canyon and the Salmon River of No Return. I could go on and on. Little Miss Tour Guide, that's me."

"I noticed," he chuckled in a way that gently teased her.

"Well, it does have everything." She laughed at her own enthusiasm.

"I wouldn't dream of arguing with you," he replied and reached out to link his fingers with hers. A warm tingle of pleasure ran up her arm at his gesture of affection and closeness. "Is there a reason why there has to be so much room between us?" Shad asked with a coaxing smile. "That's another great thing about an old truck. You can slide next to your honey on every curve."

Charley hesitated but the temptation to be close to him was too strong to resist. Besides, as long as he was driving, it seemed relatively safe. And there wouldn't be many chances to be near him.

"I suppose not," she admitted and wriggled her butt over to sit beside him.

Unlinking their hands, he put his arm around her so that she was snuggling in the crook of his shoulder with his hand on her waist. It was a natural, comfortable position and the warmth of his body was delicious.

"What's the longest you've ever stayed in one place?" Charley asked.

"Two years," he replied without any hesitation.

"Haven't you ever considered settling down?" There was a wistful quality to her question as she indulged herself in the ridiculous dream that she might be the one to persuade him to put down roots.

"Yes," Shad admitted. "I spent two years trying. That was five years ago when I was twenty-nine. I decided it was time I stayed in one place and build myself a home. So I bought a small ranch over on the Idaho side of the Bitterroot Mountains."

"You did?" Charley was surprised by his answer.

"Yes." And he went on to explain, "In the beginning, it was a challenge to fix the place up and bring the ranch up to its potential. I worked day and night at it, running new fence during the daytime and repairing the buildings at night."

"If you liked it, why didn't you stay?"

"Well, it was like having a new toy. When you first get it, you don't want to play with anything else. Later on, the newness wears off and you become bored with it. That's what happened to me with the ranch. Once it was up and running and on the verge of showing a profit, the yen to travel came back. There wasn't anything to keep me there."

"So you sold it and moved on," Charley said. A feeling of depression came over her.

"I moved on but I didn't sell it," Shad corrected her on that point. "A widower and his son manage it for me on a share basis. I have a small but steady income from it, which allows me to do pretty much what I please. It's a place I can go to when I'm too old to travel."

"Have you ever been back to the ranch since you left it?" she asked.

"No. But I was headed there when you walked into that café that day," his eyes sparkling as he cast a quick glance at her face. "I can't say for sure what made me change my plans that morning. I didn't need the money then so I guess it was the idea of having a honey-haired boss." Shad scoped out the empty highway in front of them and his rearview mirrors before he turned and bent his head to steal a kiss.

The sudden possession of his mouth caught her off guard. It took her a full second to recover her scattered wits. Her heart continued to trip over itself in an effort to find its normal rhythm.

"Eyes on the road, cowboy. Pay attention to your driving." Charley attempted to sound stern, but her voice was on the breathless side.

Laughter came from deep within his chest as his arm tightened around her, hugging her closer still. "You're a helluva woman, Charley. I've never met anybody like you. And that isn't a line," he informed her emphatically.

Charley fell silent, a faint smile on her lips as she savored his compliment and basked in the warmth of its afterglow. They passed through Ketchum and the turnoff to the skiing community of Sun Valley. The road to the Collins's ranch was not many miles away.

Eventually her thoughts returned to the one fact that she could never ignore for long. She found she had to ask him, "Why do you always have to move on, Shad?"

"I don't know." He seemed to consider her question with all the seriousness with which she asked it. "Maybe I was born with a wanderlust in my soul. When I was younger, I thought I would come to a place, look around and say to myself, 'This is it. This is where I'm going to stay.' But it doesn't happen like that. After I've been in new territory for a while, I start looking around and wondering what's across the river or over the next hill. It's taken me a while, but I've finally learned that there will always be one more river to cross."

His answer made it very clear to Charley that she was foolish to hope she could ever change him. She couldn't change herself. As much as she loved him she would never truly be happy traveling around the country. She would always be longing for a place to call home. It didn't seem fair. She felt the sting of tears burning her eyes and blinked to keep them back.

When they finally reached the ranch lane, Shad needed both hands on the steering wheel to make the sharp turn. As he removed his arm from around her Charley shifted to her own side of the truck. His frowning glance took note of the movement and the whiteness of her face.

"Why so quiet?" he demanded after several seconds had passed. "Is something wrong?"

"No. I was just trying to decide how I was going to keep from crying when you leave." The truth came out on a note of forced lightness.

It silenced him for a minute. "Charley, you do tempt me to stay." The very steadiness of his voice revealed that he meant what he said.

She laughed with a tinge of bitterness as the truck slowed down to enter the ranch yard. "Let's be honest, Shad. All I do is 'tempt' you, but you'll leave just the same."

The instant the truck stopped she reached for the door handle and climbed out of the cab. A door slammed behind her as she started for the house. Shad caught up with her before she reached the porch steps, his hand gripping her arm to turn her around.

"Charley—" He started to speak but she didn't want to listen to what he had to say.

"Just leave me alone, Shad. I'm not going to give you a chance to hurt me and I'm not going to let myself get attached to you." She stood rigidly before him, wary and defiant. "You said it yourself—you're no good for me." She threw his own words back at him and he recoiled from their sting, letting her go.

Her legs were shaking as she climbed the steps and crossed the porch to the front door. She wanted to run, but she managed to make a dignified retreat. Gary was just inside the door, leaning on his crutches. He knew her too well not to read what was written on her face.

"I heard the truck drive in . . . oh, Charley," he groaned in sympathy. "What have you done?"

"Made a fool of myself as usual. What do you think?" She tried to make a joke out of it and forced the look of longing out of her expression.

"If you had to fall for somebody, why couldn't it have been Weatherby?" She glared at him. "Okay, sorry, I didn't say that. But at least he would have caught you when you fell," Gary muttered sadly. "You knew right from the beginning that Shad was a drifter."

"I knew—and I tried not to care," she admitted, hanging her head in acknowledgment of failure. "But it didn't change anything."

Gary sighed. "Maybe I should have a talk with Russell."

"No. Just let it be," she said softly. "There isn't anything you can do to help me. I have to handle this alone, the same way you did," alluding to his broken engagement.

"I know that it hurts like hell, Charley."

"Yes, it does." Her short laugh was brittle. She turned away, feeling her composure start to crumble. "I have a headache. I think I'll go upstairs and lie down for a while."

"Is there anything I can bring you?" her brother offered.

"No." She hurried to the steps before she started crying.

* * *

There were times when Charley wondered if she would survive the next several days. Shad stayed clear of her and she could never seem to make up her mind whether she was happy or sad about that. He found a lot of reasons to ride away from the ranch during the day to check on the cattle or repair fences. Mealtimes were awkward and no one said very much. The evenings Shad either spent in his room or cleaning the tack in the barn or overhauling some piece of machinery.

She rarely saw him smile anymore. He remained aloof whenever she was around, always brisk and businesslike. Yet his constant avoidance of the issue only intensified the strain they were all under.

On Saturday Shad came to the house, quitting work early. He did no more than nod in Charley's direction before climbing the stairs to his room. When she heard the shower running in the upstairs bathroom, she went into the kitchen to peel the potatoes for their evening meal.

Twenty minutes later she heard him coming down the stairs—whistling. At the happy sound she pivoted around, facing the doorway when Shad walked through it. Freshly shaved with his black hair glistening, he was wearing a snow-white shirt and a leather vest. A pair of dark jeans, obviously new, showed off his narrow hips and long legs.

"Don't bother to fix any supper for me tonight. I won't be here," he said.

"Where are you going?" She could have bitten

off her tongue for asking such a nosy question. It really wasn't any business of hers what he did with his evenings, but it was too late. It had already been asked.

His mouth twisted into a rueful grin. "What does a cowboy usually do on a Saturday night? He has himself a steak dinner, romances the ladies, and gets drunk." Gary entered the kitchen in time to hear his answer and Shad turned to look at him. "What about it, Gary? Do you want to go with me?"

"You'll probably need me to carry you home," her brother said dryly. But he shook his head. "I think I'll pass. Can't go two-steppin' with one leg in a cast. No, I'm not ready to go out on the town."

"Have it your way." Shad shrugged indifferently. "See you later."

Charley turned to face the sink as he walked out the back door. From the window above the sink, she could see him cross the yard to the old pickup. There was a lump in her throat as she watched him drive out of the yard.

"Charley." Her brother spoke her name softly.

"I'm all right," she insisted, but was careful not to look at him. "It really doesn't make much difference, does it? When he leaves here, I'll be imagining him with some other woman so I might as well get used to it now."

"I wish you wouldn't be so hard on yourself."

"It would be worse if I pretended he was going to stay," she reminded him.

Chapter Six

After supper Gary helped her clear the table as best he could. Once in the kitchen, he propped himself against the sink, with the crutches under his arms for support, and washed the dishes while Charley dried them and put them away.

"How about a game of checkers?" he suggested when they were finished.

"I'm not really in the mood—" she started to refuse, then realized he was trying to be thoughtful and keep her mind off Shad and what he might be doing. She smiled quickly. "All right, why not?"

The first two games were close, although Gary won them both, but he was the better checker player, too. On the third, her concentration faltered and it was barely a contest. Her gaze kept straying to the kitchen wall clock as the evening crept by. Charley lost the fourth and fifth games, too.

When the sixth showed signs of turning into a rout, her brother grumbled, "I can't believe that anyone I taught to play checkers could play so badly."

"Sorry. Not your fault," she sighed. "I wasn't paying attention." Her glance darted to the wall clock.

"It's twenty-five minutes to ten," Gary said dryly. "The last time you looked it was twenty-seven minutes to ten."

"Sorry, sorry, sorry." She felt guilty because he was trying so hard to keep her entertained.

"And stop saying you're sorry." He flashed her an impatient look.

"I'm—" She had been on the verge of saying it again and caught herself just in time. They looked at each other and laughed, breaking the invisible tension in the air. "It's no use, Gary," Charley sighed. "I might as well admit defeat now. I can't concentrate."

"It's a losing battle, isn't it?" He dumped the checkers into their box, calling it quits.

"Yes, but it was a nice thought," she said as she pushed her chair away from the kitchen table.

"What are you going to do?" He put the lid on the box and handed it to her so she could put it away in the cupboard.

"I think I'll take a long soak in the tub—that man got under my skin," Charley said, giving him a self-mocking smile. "Let's see if bubble bath and a scented candle can cure what ails me."

"Have fun." Gary sounded doubtful. As he started to pull himself upright with his crutches he winced and turned white with pain, sitting back down again.

"What's wrong?" she said with instant concern.

"Nothing," he insisted. "I've just been sitting in

one position too long. It'll pass." He tried to stand up again and Charley could see that it hurt him but he finally managed to get upright.

"Are you sure you don't want one of those pain pills the doctor prescribed for you?" she suggested.

"No, it'll go away." But his jaw was clenched against the discomfort as he bit down hard.

"You won't make it easy on yourself, will you?" she chided him. "You have to tough it out."

His gaze flashed her a challenge. "Look who's talking." He reminded Charley of her own harshly realistic outlook.

"All right, I'll shut up." She started toward the stairwell in the living room. "If you need anything, call me."

"I will," he promised.

In the second-floor bathroom, she turned on the faucets in the tub and adjusted the water temperature until it was comfortably hot. She dumped in some bubble bath. On impulse she added an extra splash, giving in to a whim of self-indulgence. There had been enough misery in her life lately and she decided she deserved a little pampering.

While the tub was filling with water she went into her bedroom to undress and get her cotton bathrobe. When she returned, the bathtub was mounded with bubbles. She lit a scented candle and turned off the faucets. Then Charley piled her hair on top of her head, secured it with a clip, and climbed into the tub to stretch out full length, resting her head on the curved porcelain back. She closed her eyes and let the hot water and the fragrance of the candle soothe her inner aches.

After she had been in the tub barely ten minutes, she heard the thump of Gary's crutches in the living room below. The sound was followed by the opening of the stairwell door.

"Charley!" he called up to her, and she scowled at the interruption of her quiet bath. "Where are those pain pills from the doctor?"

She opened her eyes in surprise. His leg must really be bothering him for Gary to give in and ask for the pills. "They're in the medicine cabinet." She shouted the answer, and heard him thump away.

In a few minutes he was back, "Charley!"

"What?"

"I can't find them! What kind of bottle are they in?" His patience seemed to be running thin.

"It's brown! It's little! Make sure you get the right one—they all look alike," she called down and waited as he thumped off again.

This time he wasn't gone as long and his voice was decidedly more irritable when he called, "There are three bottles in the medicine cabinet and two of them don't have labels. How am I supposed to tell them apart?"

Charley sighed in mild exasperation. The pain he was in was making him act childish, but she couldn't very well not help him. "I'll get them!"

Climbing out of the tub, she grabbed a towel and dried herself hastily, and not very well. Her robe was hanging on the door hook. She slipped into it, wrapping the cotton material around her damp body and blowing out the candle before she hurried out of the bathroom to the staircase.

Once she was downstairs, Gary protested, "You could have told me what to look for. You didn't have to come down."

"Now you tell me," she retorted. Then she saw how white his face was beneath the tan and added in a gentler tone, "I don't mind. It's better than wondering if you took a pill from the wrong bottle."

With Gary following her, she went to the medicine cabinet in the downstairs bathroom and took out the brown bottle containing his medication. She didn't bother to point out to him that the other two brown bottles held generic aspirin and acetaminophen. She'd stashed them there so as not to have to go upstairs every time she needed to zap a headache. She gave him the prescribed dosage and a glass of water to wash them down.

"I'll help you into bed," Charley volunteered.

"My leg hurts too much to lie down."

"Listen, when those pills start to work, you'll be knocked out. And I can't get you into bed by myself so you're going there now," she ordered and Gary gave in.

By the time she got him settled, he was already beginning to feel the effects. She turned off the light as she left the room and went back upstairs to the bath she'd left. The bubbles had all dissolved and the water was barely tepid. Most of her enthusiasm for a long, luxurious bath had evaporated, too. She pulled the plug to let the water run down the drain. As it gurgled noisily, she scrubbed away the soap scum from the sides of the porcelain tub.

Once the bathwater was gone, she ran cold water out of the faucets to give the tub one final rinse.

Just as she finished, Charley thought she heard a noise downstairs. She stopped to listen, thinking maybe Gary was calling for her but there was only silence. Yet she was positive she'd heard something, so she went downstairs to check.

She tiptoed quietly into her brother's room. The outside yard light cast its beam through the window by his bed. Gary was sleeping soundly, his chest rising and falling in a slow, steady rhythm beneath the blankets. Reassured that he was all right, Charley slipped out of the room.

A flash of white in the living room caught her eye a split second before a low voice said, "Charley?"

She smothered her startled cry of alarm with her hand as Shad materialized from the shadows. Her hand slipped down to cover her rapidly beating heart.

"You startled me," she whispered.

"Sorry. I didn't mean to." He glanced beyond her to the bedroom door. "Is Gary all right?"

"Yes. His leg was bothering him earlier and he took a couple of pain pills. I was just checking on him to make sure he was okay," she explained. The initial surprise of Shad's sudden appearance in the house had gone. In its place was the sharp memory of where he'd been. "What are you doing back so soon?" Charley challenged in an icy voice. "I thought you were going to stay out until all hours of the morning."

"I was." His voice was low, unruffled by her tone. It was difficult to see his face in the shadowy dimness of the room. There weren't any lights on downstairs. What light there was came from the stairwell and outside. Yet Charley could feel the disturbing intensity of his gaze.

"Then what are you doing here?" Forced anger was her defense against him.

"After I had my steak dinner, I went to a bar. There was this drunk there . . ." His voice took on a different quality, gentle, almost caressing. "He kept singing 'Charley Is My Darling.' And I started wondering what I was doing in that bar when my Charley was here."

Her heart cried out for him, loving him all the more for saying such beautiful words, but it hurt, too. Charley turned her head away, closing her eyes tightly.

"You can skip the sweet talk, Shad." She fought for self-control.

"I'm telling you what I feel," he countered.

She tried to take the potency from his words with an accusation. "You've been drinking."

"Yes, I've been drinking," he admitted. As she started to walk away from him, he caught her wrist and pulled her around. She was in his arms before she had a chance to resist. "But I'm not drunk."

"Let me go, Shad." She tried to twist out of his arms but they tightened around her, holding her fast. The warmth of his hands seemed to burn through the thin material of her robe.

"Wow!" He spoke under his breath as he became suddenly motionless. An exploring hand moved over her hip. "You don't have anything on under this."

Aware of the imprint his body was making on

hers, her own senses echoed the aroused note in his voice. Yet she tried to resist it.

"Shad, don't," she protested.

But he merely groaned and rubbed his shaven cheek against hers, brushing her ear with his mouth. "It's no use, Charley. I've tried to stay away from you, but I can't."

His mouth rocked over her lips, persuading and cajoling, sensually nipping her lower lip until she was reeling. Restless male hands wandered over her back, caressing her. She was helpless against this loving attack.

"Do we have to deny ourselves?" Shad muttered thickly as her lips grazed along his jaw. "I don't see any reason to pretend I don't want you. Do you know what I mean?"

"Yes." The aching admission was torn from her throat, the ability to think lost. "I want you too . . . just as much."

It was the answer he had been waiting for as he swept her off her feet and into his arms. Her hands circled his neck while her mouth investigated the strong column of his throat, savoring the taste of him. He carried her to the couch and lowered her to the cushions while he sat on the edge facing her.

He leaned down to cover her parted lips with his mouth, his hard tongue taking total possession. Raw desire licked through her veins, a spreading fire that left none of her body untouched. His hands deftly loosened the buttons of her robe and pushed the material aside to expose her beautiful breasts.

Just as eagerly, her fingers tugged at his buttons.

When the last one was unfastened, Shad yanked his shirt free out of his jeans. She moaned softly as she felt the heat of his flesh beneath her hands. Her fingers moved over his flexed and rippling muscles, excited and stimulated by this freedom to touch and caress.

Forsaking her lips, his mouth began a downward path. Delighted quivers ran over her skin as he explored the sensitive cord in her neck and left a kiss in the hollow of her throat. Her fingernails dug into his flesh when his mouth grazed her breast, its point hardening with desire, luring his attention to it. Charley shuddered with uninhibited longing under the arousing touch of his tongue.

When she was weak with need, he returned to soften her lips with his kisses. "Tell me you want me, Charley," he begged. "I want to hear you say it again."

"I want you, Shad," she whispered against his skin. "More than that, I love you."

"I want you more than I've ever wanted any other woman in my life," he told her roughly.

"Stay with me tonight, Shad," she murmured. "Tonight and tomorrow night and every night of my life. I don't want you to leave me."

"You know I can't promise that, Charley," he muttered, brushing his lips over her cheek.

She knew. Her arms curved more tightly around him, fusing the warmth of his bare flesh with her own. "Hold me," she whispered. "Don't ever let me go." Her eyes were tightly closed, but a tear squeezed its way through her lashes. It was followed by more until Shad tasted the salty moisture on her skin.

"Don't cry, Charley." She felt the roughness of his callused hand on her cheek, wiping them away. "For God's sake, don't cry." His voice held no anger, only a kind of anguished regret.

"I can't help it." She honestly tried to check the flow of tears but it was unstoppable.

With a heavy sigh he eased his weight from her and sat up. She blinked and felt his hands closing her robe. Then he was leaning his elbows on his knees and raking his fingers through his hair to rub the back of his neck. Charley sat up, a hand unconsciously holding the front of her robe. She touched his shoulder, tentative, uncertain.

"Oh, Charley," he said, then turned to look at her. A dark, troubled light was in his eyes. "I swear to God I never meant to hurt you."

"I know," she murmured gently and a little sadly. "It isn't your fault. You didn't ask me to fall in love with you. Maybe if you had, I'd be able to hate you, but I don't."

She swung her feet to the floor and slowly walked to the stairs, leaving Shad sitting there alone on the couch. It was almost an hour later before she heard him come upstairs. He paused at the top of the stairs and Charley held her breath. Finally the door to his bedroom opened and closed. The tears started again.

Sleep eluded her. The hours that Charley didn't spend staring at the ceiling, she tossed and turned fitfully. By Wednesday morning the lack of rest began to paint faint shadows below her eyes. They didn't go unnoticed by her brother.

"You feeling okay, Charley?" he asked at the breakfast table that morning, studying her.

"I'm fine," she insisted.

"Well, you don't look so good," he concluded bluntly.

"Thanks," she snapped and paled under his scrutiny.

Gary's eyes narrowed suspiciously, but he made no comment. Charley knew that her brother probably guessed the cause of her sleeplessness, but there was nothing he could do about it.

When she crawled into bed that night, she expected it to be a repeat of the previous nights. She listened for the longest time, waiting for the sound of Shad's footsteps on the stairs. She dozed off without hearing, then awakened later and strained to hear sounds of him in the other bedroom— boots dropping on the floor, jeans flung across a chair. But there was nothing. Finally fatigue overtook her and she fell into a heavy sleep.

The buzz of the alarm clock was insistent, making her open her eyes despite her attempt to ignore it. She climbed wearily from the bed, irritated that the one time she'd managed to sleep, she had been forced to wake up. She dressed in her usual blue jeans and blouse and left the bedroom in a daze.

Charley barely glanced at the closed door of Shad's bedroom. She didn't know whether he was still sleeping or already downstairs. Not that it mattered, she told herself and entered the bathroom.

With her face washed and her teeth brushed, she lost some of that drugged feeling.

At the bottom of the stairs, Charley was shocked to find Shad sleeping on the couch in the living room. Too tall for it, he was sprawled over the length of the cushions with his feet poking over the end of the armrest. From somewhere, he'd gotten a blanket, which was loosely draped over him. She couldn't imagine what he was doing sleeping on the couch. She walked over to waken him.

Her hand touched his shoulder and he stirred, frowning in his sleep. The second time Charley gripped his shoulder more firmly and called his name. "Shad. Shad, it's time to get up."

He shrugged off her hand but he opened his eyes. They focused slowly on Charley's face as she leaned over him. He gave her a slow smile.

"Good morning." His voice was husky with sleep, its drawl thicker.

"Good morning." She wanted to ask him what he was doing on the couch, but his hand reached out to capture one of hers and pull her onto the cushion beside him.

"Don't I get more of a greeting than that?" Shad mocked and put his hand behind her neck to bring her head down.

Charley stopped needing direction when she neared his mouth. Her lips settled into it naturally and moved in response to his sampling kiss. She was breathing fast when she finally straightened. He started to shift his position and winced from a cramped muscle. The discomfort made him take note of his improvised place to sleep. He seemed to register vague surprise when he figured out that he was on the couch.

"Why are you sleeping here?" Charley finally asked her question.

"The mood I was in last night, if I had gone upstairs, I would have ended up sleeping in your bed." There was impatience in his expression as his hands settled onto the toned muscles of her upper arms and began rubbing them absently.

"Oh, Shad." She trembled with the quick onrush of desire.

"Yeah, you should say, 'Oh, Shad.' I don't think you know what you're doing to me," he muttered. "At this rate, I'm going to be sleeping in the barn next, just to keep my hands off you."

Neither of them heard the muffled thud of Gary's crutches. They were too engrossed in each other to pay attention to anything else. And they didn't see him enter the living room and stop to stare at them.

"What's going on here?" He frowned suspiciously, puzzled to see Shad using the couch for a bed.

Charley turned swiftly to face her brother but Shad was slow to let his hands slide from her arms, showing no signs of guilt.

"I was just waking up Shad," Charley explained, aware that her cheeks felt warm.

"What are you doing sleeping on the couch?" Gary ignored her to question Shad.

"All things considered"—his glance briefly touched Charley to indicate what things were considered "—it seemed like a good place to sleep last night."

Gary came farther into the room, his gaze not leaving Shad. "Are you fooling around with my sister?" he demanded.

"What a question," Shad said. "I can't say yes. I don't want to be beaten to a pulp by a guy on crutches."

"That's not an answer."

"Okay, then. No. So far my conscience has won. It's becoming more of a struggle, though."

"Really."

"Yeah." Shad sat up and tossed the covers aside. He still had his jeans on, Charley noticed with relief. But with his tousled hair and sleep-warmed T-shirt clinging to his chest, he looked anything but respectable. If her brother hadn't come in, she would have jumped him.

Charley avoided Gary's look at her and mumbled something about starting breakfast. The excuse made her sound like a TV housewife straight out of a 1950s sitcom but what the hell. June Cleaver got out of a lot of arguments by disappearing into her kitchen with a flounce of her apron, and Charley intended to do the same. Without the apron.

But the conversation between Shad and her brother didn't end with her departure. She listened to what they were saying, biting her lip in nervous anxiety.

"I don't want to see Charley get hurt," Gary began.

"If I didn't feel the same way, I would have been sleeping upstairs instead of down here," Shad replied with a flash of impatience.

"The kindest thing you could do is leave her

alone—" Her brother began to issue advice but Shad interrupted him before he had finished.

"Don't preach at me, Gary," he warned.

"I think you're forgetting that you work for me," Gary countered, reacting to the angry undercurrent in Shad's voice.

"You're right. There are a lot of things I've been forgetting lately," Shad declared. "Starting with not knowing why the hell I'm still here!"

Charley heard heavy strides cross the room and climb the stairs. It was several seconds before Gary entered the kitchen where she waited. His expression was grim.

"Why did you say those things to him?" She shook her head wearily.

"You're my sister. What did you expect me to do?" he argued.

"Shad isn't leaving, is he?" Although her voice was calm, there was fear in her eyes.

"I don't think so, not now at any rate," Gary replied and looked at her sadly. "Charley, you know he's going to leave sooner or later."

"Yes," she admitted. "But I don't want him to go now. Not yet."

The wooden posts rumbled in the back end of the pickup truck as Charley drove across the pasture to where Shad was running a new section of fence near the timberline. This last load of posts would take him to the end.

When he saw her coming he swung the posthole digger aside, letting it fall to the ground near the partially dug hole. With slow, energy-conserving strides, he walked to where she had stopped the truck. Charley was already out of the cab and lowering the tailgate.

As she grabbed for a fence post to drag it out of the truck Shad ordered crisply, "Don't be lifting those. I'll unload the posts."

"I can manage," she insisted. "I've done it before."

When she continued to pull the end of the post out of the truck bed, his gloved hand grabbed her arm. "I said leave it! I don't care what you've done before. As long as I'm here, I'll do the unloading!"

She had never seen that angry blaze in his eyes before or the uncompromising set of his features. He was almost a stranger to her. Charley let go of the post and Shad released her arm. She moved stiffly to one side.

"All right, I won't help, but you don't have to bite my head off!" she retorted.

He paused and leaned his hands on the tailgate, staring at the ground. When he lifted his head to look at her, much of the anger was gone but his expression was still tautly controlled.

"I'm not angry with you, Charley," he explained. "I'm angry with myself for letting this situation develop."

"You couldn't help it," she said, because it wasn't solely his doing.

"Maybe not, but it doesn't matter." He straightened, eyeing her steadily. "I can't ask a woman to share the kind of life I lead. It wouldn't be fair to her. It wouldn't work."

Charley didn't understand why he was bringing the subject up, unless—"Do you want me to go with you when you leave?"

"No." His answer was definite. "I'm telling you why I don't want you to come with me when I go."

He reached for a post and began sliding it out of the truck and onto the ground. Charley stood quietly beside the truck, letting no emotion show on her face as she watched him. When he had finished unloading the fence posts he glanced at her briefly.

"I'll see you at lunch," he said.

With a nod, she turned and walked to the cab and climbed in. There was a big emptiness inside her as she drove away.

Chapter Seven

It was nearly noon on Monday before Charley drove the truck into the ranch yard after taking Gary to town to his doctor's appointment. The doctor had decided to remove the cast a week early, so her brother was in a buoyant mood.

As she slowed the truck to a stop in front of the house she noticed Shad's saddle and gear sitting on the porch. Alarm shivered through her. Gary said something to her but she didn't hear him as she bolted from the truck and raced up the porch steps into the house.

Inside the living room, she stopped to face Shad. He was carrying his duffel bag. Her heart was pounding wildly in her ears as she stared at him for several long seconds, unable to speak.

Finally she said, "Where are you going?"

"Isn't it obvious? I'm leaving," he stated flatly. "You knew the day would come when I'd move on."

"You were going without saying a word. You

were just going to be gone when we came back," she accused in disbelief.

"It seemed the easiest way." His jaw was hard, all expression held tightly in check.

"But to go without even telling me good-bye . . ." She didn't understand how he could do that.

"You once told me that you were trying to decide how you were going to keep from crying when I left. At least give me credit for trying to spare you that," Shad said quietly.

"Don't go," Charley protested, trying hard not to plead with him.

"There's nothing you can say that will make me change my mind," he said firmly. "I should have left before now. I've waited too long as it is."

The screen door slammed as Gary walked in.

"Hello, Shad." His high spirits told Charley that he hadn't noticed any special significance in Shad's gear sitting outside. "As you can see, I've thrown away my crutches for a cane." Gary waggled it in the air. "They took the cast off today. Of course, Charley forgot to bring me some regular trousers so I had to walk out of the doctor's office with my pants leg cut off and my hairy white leg showing, but I feel ten pounds lighter." He paused, his glance lighting on the bag in Shad's hand. "Are you going somewhere?"

"I'm leaving," Shad repeated himself to her brother.

"Without letting us know?" Gary echoed her own words.

"Yes, and I've been all through that with your sister," he replied, irritated.

"This is sudden." Gary frowned and glanced at Charley, as if trying to figure out whether she'd known about this beforehand.

"You could have at least had the decency to give us a week's notice," Charley declared. "We would have had a chance to find someone to take your place. Gary has his cast off but it'll be a couple of weeks before he gets the strength back in his leg."

"That's true," Gary backed her up. "You're leaving us in the lurch. Charley can't possibly do all the work by herself and I'm not going to be that much help to her for a while yet."

Shad's mouth became compressed in a taut line as his gaze slashed from one to the other. "All right," he gave in reluctantly, suppressing his anger. "One week. I'm giving you one week's notice from this morning. If you haven't found someone to take my place by then, I'm leaving anyway."

"Agreed," Charley said.

After Shad had pivoted away and gone up the stairs to put his bag away, Gary glanced at her. "What did you gain out of that, Charley?"

"Time," she said quietly. "Time to hire another man. That's all."

Two days later Charley noticed that Shad hadn't bothered to unpack his duffel bag. His saddle and gear were stowed in the old pickup truck. When the time came, he would be gone in a matter of minutes. And that time wasn't far off.

The back door to the kitchen opened and Charley glanced over her shoulder to see Shad enter the house. Her initial rush of pleasure at seeing him faded quickly and she turned back to the stove to stir the tomato sauce in the pan.

"Lunch will be ready in a few minutes," she told him, trying not to let her mind make the count-down—only five more days, five more lunches to share.

"Have you found anyone to take over for me yet?" He came to stand beside her, his nearness disturbing her as always.

"No."

"Have you even made any inquiries yet?" Shad demanded with barely concealed impatience.

"I've been too busy," Charley replied.

He sighed heavily in disgust. "What are you trying to prove?"

"Nothing," she insisted.

"I meant what I said, Charley. I'm not staying one hour longer than my week's notice," he reminded her tersely.

"I'm aware of that," she murmured and closed her eyes as he walked away to wash up for the noon meal.

The following afternoon Charley was just leaving the house to help her brother with the evening chores when Shad drove up in his old pickup and stopped in front of the house. He walked right past her without saying a word and went into the house. Something about his purposeful stride made dread gnaw at her stomach. She waited on the porch. Within minutes he came out of the house with his duffel bag.

"What are you doing?" She stared at him, not quite accepting the evidence with her own eyes.

"This time I am leaving," he said and shouldered his way by her to descend the porch steps.

"But you can't," she protested. "You gave us a week's notice. There's still four more days left."

Opening the cab door, he heaved the duffel bag inside and turned to look at her. "Since you didn't seem to be in any great hurry to find someone to replace me, I took the matter into my own hands."

"What have you done?" There was little force behind her demand.

"I went to see your boyfriend this afternoon, Chuck Weatherby," Shad replied.

"He isn't my boyfriend," she said heatedly even though it was hardly important at the moment.

"I explained to him that I had to leave," Shad went on as if she hadn't interrupted him. "I asked him if he could spare one of his men to help you out for a couple of weeks until Gary can manage on his own."

"You didn't," Charley breathed.

"I did," he stated. "A man will be over first thing in the morning. I'm leaving now."

But as he turned to slide behind the wheel, Gary rounded the front of the truck, leaning heavily on his cane. The truck had blocked him from view when he crossed the ranch yard from the barns. He sized up the situation instantly.

"Guess you're going, Shad."

"That's right. Chuck Weatherby is sending over one of his men in the morning." His chin was thrust forward at a challenging angle, and he seemed prepared to argue if anyone wanted to.

But Gary had no intention of arguing. Instead he offered Shad his hand. "Thanks for all you've done. We couldn't have managed without you."

Shad's grim expression relented slightly, giving in to a slight smile as he shook hands with her brother. "Take care."

"Don't go!" Charley flew down the porch steps and stopped abruptly before she reached Shad.

"Nothing is going to stop me this time, Charley. Not even you." His eyes were hard points of blue steel, unwavering.

"You don't have to leave this minute." She was hurt and a little angry as she faced him defiantly. "You can at least stay long enough to hear what I have to say."

"It's all been said." He shook his head. "Nothing has changed."

"I know I can't persuade you to change your mind, but you can at least hear me out!"

"All right," Shad agreed, his mouth thinning. "Say what's on your mind and get it over with."

"You know I don't want you to leave but I'm not going to beg you to stay. So you don't need to worry that I'm going to cause an unpleasant scene." Her voice contained the hoarseness of pain, but it remained steady and forceful. "I just want you to know that I've figured out a few things about you, Shad Russell."

"Such as?" His attitude was one of almost cynical indulgence.

Charley was stung by the way he appeared to be enduring these last few minutes with her.

"Such as the reasons why you never stay in one place." Her throat muscles were so tight it was hard for her to breathe. "It isn't because you have this itch to roam, like you pretend."

"Is that right?" He openly mocked her.

"Yes, that's right. Because if you stayed in one place, you might start to care for someone. And when you care for someone, you have to make a commitment. You don't want to see what's on the other side of the hill. No, you're afraid of being responsible for someone other than yourself. You don't know how to be a friend, so you won't take a chance and find out!"

"Are you finished?" He didn't appear to have heard a single word she'd said. She was almost crying with frustration.

"Not quite!" Her voice was raw and husky. "I love you. And if you had an ounce of sense, you'd stay right here and marry me. But you don't so you're going to do what you always do—move on down the road." She paused to take a breath. "There's just one more thing I want to say."

"That's encouraging," Shad murmured dryly.

"If you leave now, I won't be waiting for you if you decide to come back!" Her voice was breaking, her control cracking. "I mean it, I won't wait. I'm not going to pine my life away for a fool-hearted man like you, Shad Russell!"

"Are you finished now?" he asked.

"Yes!" Charley choked on a sob and swallowed it before it escaped to humiliate her. Her hands were clenched into tight fists at her side while she stood tall and unmoving before him.

There wasn't a word offered in farewell as Shad turned and climbed in behind the wheel of the pickup. His gaze didn't stray to her when the motor grumbled to life. There wasn't a look or a wave as the truck pulled away from the house.

"I won't wait for you, Shad!" Charley cried again.

Gary limped over to put an arm around her shoulders in silent comfort. Silent sobs began to shake her shoulders as Shad circled the ranch yard and headed down the lane to the highway.

"The stupid jackass! Hasn't he ever seen any movies? Doesn't he know that he's supposed to turn right around and come back to me?" She sobbed in a crazy kind of anger.

Seconds later the truck disappeared from sight. Soon she couldn't even hear the sound of its motor. Burying her face in her hands, she started crying. Gary turned her into his arms, hugging her close while his chin rubbed the top of her head.

"I'm sorry, Charley," he murmured.

She leaned on him, unable to stop the flood of tears. Sobs racked her shoulders, tearing her apart. There was no relief from the pain inside.

"Come on, Charley. There's no point in standing out here," Gary urged. "Let's go in the house."

She let herself be turned toward the porch, leaning heavily on the support of his arm. Too blinded by tears to see where she was going, she let Gary lead her. She stumbled up the steps and across the porch floor to the door, the retching sobs continuing to tear at her chest. Inside the house he guided her to the sofa and sat down with her.

"That's enough, Charley." Her brother betrayed his inability to handle her tears. "Crying isn't going to help. If you keep this up, you're going to make yourself sick."

Pulling a handkerchief from his pocket, he tried to dam the flow of tears by awkwardly dabbing at her eyes. In self-defense, Charley took the hankie from him and honestly tried to stop crying. The sobbing was reduced to painful, hiccuping breaths.

"That's better." There was relief in his voice.

But it wasn't, not really. It was all on the inside now, all the pain and the heartache. She sat up, sniffling loudly, and pressed her lips tightly together to stop her chin from quivering. Her fingers twisted into the handkerchief, wadding it into a tight ball. Then she noisily blew her nose and sniffled some more.

"Damn him!" She swore at Shad, her voice taut and laced with pain.

"Now, Charley," Gary attempted to soothe her, but she shrugged away from his comforting touch.

"How could I be so dumb?" She bounded to her feet and began pacing the living room. She switched from cursing Shad to berating herself. "I should have had more sense than to fall in love with him. I must have been crazy."

"You aren't the first person to make that discovery," Gary advised and studied her worriedly. Her lightning changes of mood left him confused and uncertain how to react.

"He told me—he warned me that he'd be moving on, but I thought—" She stopped, closing her mouth at the knife-sharp surge of pain. When she continued there was a betraying quiver to her voice. "I thought he'd love me so much he'd change his mind."

"You'll get over him, Charley—in time," he comforted.

She turned on him in a blaze of anger. "No, I won't! I won't get over him—not ever! I'll never stop loving him—not even when I die! I'll come back and I'll haunt him!" she declared.

"You don't know what you're saying." He looked at her uneasily.

"Yes, I do," Charley insisted and spun away. The beginnings of a sob started again and she pressed the balled handkerchief against her mouth and sniffed in a breath. Her eyes were watering again, blurring her vision. "Do you think he'll come back, Gary?" The question was barely above a whisper. When he didn't answer, she pivoted around to face him and repeated it. "Do you?"

He tried to squarely meet her gaze and failed. "I don't know."

"But you must have an opinion," Charley insisted. "Do you think he'll come back? Not right away, maybe, but someday?"

Her brother clasped his hands together and studied them, taking his time before answering her. Finally he lifted his head and shook it sadly. "I don't think he'll come back, Charley. Shad couldn't have made it any plainer that he wanted to leave."

She swallowed in a breath, feeling the last hope die with Gary's answer. She looked away, blinking at the hot tears scalding her eyes. "I would have gone with him if he'd asked me," she said hoarsely. "I would have lived out of the back end of that truck. It wouldn't have mattered—just so long as I could be with him." Even as she made the statement, she knew that she was ranting like a hysterical teenager. There wasn't anything romantic or wonderful about living in a truck. But she couldn't seem to stop it. "He never asked me, Gary. Not once."

"Maybe that's best," he suggested tentatively.

"The best thing would have been if I had never hired him in the first place," she retorted. "I knew the moment I saw him that he was just passing through. I should have told him to keep traveling. I guess that's what he did," Charley said with a bitter laugh. "The only problem is he walked all over my heart as he was leaving. Does that sound too much like a cry-in-your-beer country song? I don't care."

"You do, though. Don't blame yourself for that. Falling in love is just too damn easy sometimes, Charley."

"I guess I should just say good riddance and get over him."

"That's right," Gary was quick to agree. "The sooner the better. Shad isn't the kind to ever settle down. He'd always be wandering off someplace. A leopard can't change his spots."

"I don't want a leopard. I want Shad." She switched sides again, and Gary rolled his eyes without letting her see. "If he was going to leave, why didn't he go before I fell in love with him? Why did he stay so long? He said he didn't want to hurt me. For someone who didn't want to, he certainly did a bang-up job!"

"You're just torturing yourself with all this talk, Charley." Gary used the cane to push himself to his feet. "Look, let me fix you some coffee. You need something to settle your nerves."

A truck drove into the ranch yard. When Charley heard it she pivoted toward the door, her heart leaping into her throat. She glanced wildly at her brother. She felt dizzy with hope.

"Do you think it's Shad?" she whispered. "Maybe he's come back . . . maybe he's changed his mind and finally realizes how much he cares."

Outside the engine died and a metal door was slammed shut. Charley rushed toward the front door, her feet hardly touching the floor. When she saw the man walking toward the porch, the world came crashing down around her. She sagged against the door frame, her spirit broken by abject disappointment. She turned away and leaned her back against the wall, her eyes tightly shut.

"It's Chuck Weatherby," she informed Gary in a painful whisper, and pushed away from the wall, putting distance between herself and the front door. "I don't want to see him or talk to him. Send him away—please."

On the far side of the room, she stopped and listened to Gary limp to the screen door. There was no creaking of the hinges so she knew he hadn't opened it to invite their neighbor inside.

"Hello, Chuck." She heard her brother greet him. "What brings you over this way?"

"Afternoon, Gary." The greeting was returned as Chuck's footsteps stopped on the porch. "Your hired man stopped over to see me earlier this afternoon. He said he was leaving and wanted to know if I could loan you one of my men for a couple days. I told him I could, but I thought afterward that maybe I ought to check with you."

"That's good of you, Chuck," Gary said. "Russell

did leave and, uh, we could use an extra hand around the place for a few more days."

Listening to Chuck's steady voice started Charley to thinking. She wiped away the last traces of tears on her face and took a deep breath. Taking a determined hold on her emotions, she turned toward the door and tilted her chin a fraction of an inch higher.

"Gary, why don't you invite Chuck in?" she suggested in a loud voice.

Her brother cast a puzzled look over his shoulder. His glance seemed to demand that she make up her mind. Scowling at her so Chuck couldn't see, he shifted to one side and pushed the screen door open.

"Come in, Chuck," he invited.

"Thank you." As the rancher entered the house he removed his hat and ran a hand through his auburn hair. "Hello, Charley." He nodded respectfully toward her and smiled. "I just came by to—"

"Yes, I heard," she interrupted him. "Gary and I appreciate your helping us out this way. We know it's difficult to spare a man at this time of year."

"You know that any time I can help you out, all you have to do is ask," he insisted and moved slowly across the room toward her. "It's a shame that Russell just decided to up and walk out without giving you any notice. I warned you all along that he wasn't the kind of man you could depend on. I'm surprised that he stayed as long as he did."

"Yes, well . . ." Her voice wavered as she faltered over the words. She had to pause and take a deep breath before she could continue. "We'd hoped Shad would stay longer."

Chuck's gaze narrowed on her face, noticing her red and swollen eyes and the stiffness of her walk. "What's wrong, Charley? You've been crying."

Glancing at her brother, she attempted to change the subject. "Weren't you going to put some coffee on, Gary? You'd like a cup, wouldn't you, Chuck?" she offered with forced brightness. "I think there's some apple pie left from lunch."

"Yes, that would be fine." Despite his affirmative reply, the rancher hadn't been distracted. He looked at her with curiosity.

"So you do want me to put some coffee on?" Gary asked as if he half-expected Charley to change her mind.

"Yes," she nodded and her brother started for the kitchen. "I'll dish up the pie while you fix the coffee." When she took a step to walk past Chuck, he caught her arm and stopped her. He made a closer study of her tear-washed face.

"You going to tell me what happened?"

She flashed a glance after Gary but he'd already disappeared into the kitchen. With a sigh, she met Chuck's steady look. "No." That was all she wanted to say. She knew he would see through any excuse she made.

"I'm guessing it's because that Shad fellow left." He released her arm.

Hanging her head, Charley nodded, "Yes."

For a minute there was only silence following her admission. Then she sensed the growing anger that filled the rancher. It seemed to flow from him in waves. It was strangely more comforting than any kind words would have been.

"I knew something like this would happen the

minute I laid eyes on him," Chuck muttered savagely. "Men like that just can't do right."

"It's all right, Chuck." But she was deeply moved by his anger, which put all the blame on Shad and none on herself. His loyalty was unshakable.

He turned to her, his mouth tight. "Somebody should teach him a lesson. He deserves to be strung up by his heels for hurting you."

"It wouldn't change anything." Her eyes misted over with tears, all the hurt rising to the surface again. It didn't matter what anyone said about Shad, she still loved him.

"I passed him on the lane when I was driving in here," Chuck said. "He can't have gone far. If you want, I'll go get him and bring him back here."

"No." Pride stiffened her shoulders. "If he doesn't care enough to come back on his own, then I don't want him. I don't want any man that I have to drag to the altar."

Her reply stole his sense of outrage on her behalf. He breathed in deeply, his expression turning sad and grim. "Charley, I don't know what to say except . . . I'm sorry."

"So am I." Her faint laugh was just short of a sob.

"I'd like to get my hands on that guy for five minutes," Chuck muttered under his breath. "I'd teach him a thing or two about hurting people."

Gary hobbled into the living room and paused, glancing from one to the other and guessing at the conversation. "Coffee's done. Should I pour it?"

"Will you be staying for pie and coffee, Chuck?" Charley asked, giving him the option to refuse now that he had learned how she felt about Shad.

"Of course," he said, studying her quietly, "if you're sure I'm welcome."

"I'm sure," she nodded, then deliberately put on a cheerful smile. "You've always been a good friend, Chuck, a very good friend. That hasn't changed."

Just a flicker of regret showed in his ruddy features before his expression turned impassive.

"I hope you know that you can call on me whenever you need anything," he replied, not referring to his own deep affection for her. But his meaning was clear.

Charley didn't reply to that. Instead she glanced at Gary. "Let's all go into the kitchen."

All of them went through the motions as if this was an ordinary afternoon. While Gary poured the coffee, Charley sliced the pie into servings. Chuck started a conversation about ranch work to ease the stilted silence.

The pie was consumed and a second cup of coffee downed before Chuck sat back from the table. "That pie was delicious, Charlotte." He rubbed his expanding stomach.

"Would you like another slice?" she offered.

"No thanks, my supper's already spoiled," he said. "Speaking of which, it's time I was getting back to my place." He stood up, hitching his trousers higher around his middle. "Ray will be over first thing in the morning."

As he turned to leave, Charley came to a decision and stood up. "Chuck?" She waited until he glanced at her. "There's a dance next week in town. I wondered if you would like to take me."

"I—" He stared at her for a stunned instant, not quite certain he had heard her correctly. "I'd like that fine, Charley."

"Good," she said with a decisive nod. "I'll be ready around seven."

"I'll pick you up then." He was smiling as he pushed his hat onto his head and walked into the living room to the front door.

When she heard the door slam and his footsteps on the porch, Charley turned back to the table. Gary was staring at her with a dumbfounded expression. He shook his head as if trying to figure it all out.

"Charley, are you all right?" he asked, combing his fingers through his hair. "What am I saying? You're not all right. That's obvious."

"Why?" She looked at him calmly, a calmness born of a new purpose.

"I don't understand you. You're not making sense," her brother declared. "Not an hour ago, you were crying your eyes out over Shad, shattered by a broken heart. I just heard you asking another man to take you out. What's going on?"

"I told Shad I wouldn't wait for him and I meant it," she replied.

"Oh, Charley," he moaned in dismay. "You don't know what you're doing."

"Yes I do," she insisted and started to clear the table.

"No, you don't. You're making a big mistake," he warned.

"No, I'm not." She set the stack of dishes down. "The way I see it I have two choices. I can either grow old and lonely waiting for Shad to come back, which he never will, or I can marry someone else and have a home and a family."

"You aren't serious?" Gary stared at her. "Are you saying that you're going to marry Chuck?"

"Why not?" Her hands were on her hips in mute challenge. "He's a good man, solid and dependable. You've said so. Shad even said Chuck would make a wonderful husband for me. He couldn't have a higher recommendation than that, could he?" There was more than a trace of sarcasm in her voice.

"That's no reason to marry a man." Gary shook his head at her reasoning.

"Listen, Gary"—her chin quivered slightly—"chances are I'm never going to love anybody the way I did Shad again. So I might as well marry someone I like and respect. Chuck might not win any prizes, but he is nice."

"Okay, maybe there is some logic in what you say," he conceded. "But don't rush into anything on the rebound, Charley. Don't marry the guy for spite. Promise me."

"I promise," she agreed.

Chapter Eight

For the next two months, Charley managed to stay busy. There was a lot of work to be done on the ranch that occupied her time even though Gary had fully recovered from his broken leg. She continued to see Chuck in her free time, more frequently than she ever had before.

On the outside she appeared cheerful and fun-loving. But it was only on the outside. She worked a lot, played a lot and laughed a lot—trying not to feel the enormous emptiness inside. Where her heart had been, there seemed to be one big, hollow ache. It throbbed through her with a never-ending rhythm.

She never stopped thinking about Shad or remembering their brief time together. Every time a vehicle pulled into the ranch yard she held her breath, hoping, even when she knew it was useless. When she looked through the mail she wanted to see his name in the upper left corner of some envelope, someday, but she never heard from him—not a word.

Sometimes Charley would gaze at the ragged line of the Sawtooth Mountains and wonder where he was and what he was seeing. She would close her eyes and picture him as clearly as if he was standing in front of her—his thick, pitch-black hair, his bold blue eyes always glinting with lively interest and his lean, handsome features. A tear would slide down her cheek, leaving a hot trail to remind her that the pain of losing him hadn't eased.

Charley wiped another tear from her cheek and turned away from the mirror. With a determined effort she shook away the hurt and fixed a smile on her mouth. Her shoulders were straight and square and her step was light as she walked out of her bedroom into the upstairs hall. She made it a point not to glance at the spare room to the right of the stairs, passing it on her way down.

Gary was entering the house by the front door when she emerged from the stairwell. He paused at the sight of her all dressed up, his glance warm with brotherly appreciation for the results.

"Do you like my new dress?" She did a slow pirouette to show it off. The plum skirt flared, then swirled against her legs when she stopped. "Impulse buy. I couldn't resist it."

"It's beautiful," he assured her.

"I thought so." Charley glanced down to check the fit and smoothed her hand over the waistline, enjoying the feel of the velour fabric. "Do you think Shad will like it?"

"Shad?" Her brother's reply was low and sadly questioning.

Her head jerked up as she realized what she had said, her pretense shattering for an instant before she recovered.

"That was a slip of the tongue," she insisted with forced lightness. "I meant Chuck."

"It was a slip of the truth," Gary corrected.

"That's beside the point." Charley couldn't argue with him. "So do you think Chuck will like me in this?"

"Yeah," he agreed dryly. "But you could wear a burlap bag and Chuck would say you look beautiful. He's crazy about you."

"Well, this is hardly a burlap bag." She glanced at her watch. "I'd better get my coat. He'll be here shortly to pick me up."

"Where are you going?" Gary watched her walk to the coat closet.

"We're going to Twin Falls for Sunday dinner and maybe an afternoon movie." She removed her suede coat with its fur collar from the hanger. "There's a salad in the refrigerator and you can grill yourself a steak."

"What time will you be home?"

"I don't know," she replied, folding the coat over her arm. "It might be late. We have a special occasion to celebrate today."

"Oh?" Gary lifted an eyebrow and frowned. "What's that?"

"It isn't every day that a girl gets herself engaged." She managed a smile. Not a triumphant one, but a smile all the same.

Her brother looked unhappy. "I suppose Chuck proposed to you again."

"No." She shook her head. "As a matter of fact, he hasn't even brought up the subject of marriage these last two months. Usually he would have mentioned it a half dozen times. But if he doesn't propose to me today, then I'm going to ask him."

"Charley," he sighed. "You may be able to kid yourself but you can't kid me. Shad might be out of your sight, but he hasn't been out of your mind for a single minute."

"I won't deny that, Gary." She couldn't because it was true. Drawing a deep breath, she steadily met his gaze. "But if he hasn't missed me by now, then he never will."

"Are you being fair to Chuck?" he reasoned. "Pardon me, that was a rhetorical question. You aren't. Don't you think it's wrong to marry him when you're in love with someone else?"

"No, I don't think it's wrong—not if Chuck wants to," Charley replied. "As long as we both go into marriage with our eyes wide open, we can make it work."

"Maybe. Maybe not."

"It's my life," she reminded him. "And our decision."

"And I'm just supposed to stand by and say nothing?" he asked incredulously. "You're rushing into something you aren't ready for, Charley. And you're doing it because you've been hurt. Stop and think."

"I have. I've thought it all through very carefully. I know what I'm doing even if you don't think I do."

A car drove into the yard as Charley finished. She steadied the foolish leap of her heart. "Chuck's here," she said and walked over to kiss her brother on the cheek. "I'll be home tonight sometime."

A grim resignation kept him silent until she reached the door. "I only want you to be happy, Charley," her brother said.

"I know." Her mouth twisted into a rueful smile before she pushed open the door and stepped outside to meet Chuck coming up the walk.

"Hi!" She adopted a bright, lighthearted air as she paused at the top of the steps. Slipping into her coat, she breathed in the crisp autumn air. "It's going to be a beautiful day," Charley declared.

The serrated peaks of the mountain range were cloaked with snow, standing out sharply against a turquoise blue sky. On the slopes the dark green of the pine forests ringed the white mountain crests. Stands of aspen groves shimmered gold in the bright sun.

"We'd better enjoy it," Chuck replied. "Winter won't be long in coming."

Charley pulled her gaze away from the mountains that had called to Shad and insisted he come see what was on the other side. As she looked at Chuck, his freshly scrubbed appearance reminded her of a little boy all slicked up in his Sunday best. It was strange how Shad seemed so much more a man in her eyes even though Chuck was the older of the two. Yet Chuck looked at the mountains and resisted their beauty. His outlook was more practical. Winter was coming and Charley wanted in out of the cold.

"Are you ready?" He paused at the bottom of the steps and studied her closely when she continued to stand on the porch.

After a second's hesitation she started down the steps. "Yes, I'm ready." She reached out to take his hand. For a second she allowed herself to wonder if she wasn't selfishly reaching out for the comfort and warmth he offered without considering that she was depriving him of something he needed in return.

It was easy to relax in Chuck's company and she made it a point to enjoy herself, although she acted happier than she truly was. They had many mutual friends and shared interests, incidents to recall and a background in common. With Chuck she was comfortable. He was an old family friend, solid and reliable, someone she could respect and trust. He was also staid and unexciting, able to arouse her affection, but not her passion. But Charley refused to consider any of those things.

Chuck treated her to a big Sunday dinner, a full-course meal complete with soup, salad and entree. When Charley attempted to beg off the dessert, declaring she couldn't eat another bite, he became insistent.

"Have some ice cream," he said. "There's always room for that." When she shook her head to refuse, he glanced at the waitress. "Bring her a chocolate sundae."

"Chuck," she protested, "I'm stuffed, honestly. Besides, a chocolate sundae has about nine million calories. Are you trying to fatten me up for market?"

"That's exactly what I'm doing," he admitted. He smiled at her, but the smile didn't quite reach his eyes. "You've lost weight lately. You could do with some extra pounds."

What he didn't mention was why she had lost weight, but it didn't need to be said. Both of them knew the cause: Shad. Even that veiled reference was enough to make Charley end her protest. The weight loss was one of the reasons she had bought the new dress. Most of her clothes didn't fit her properly anymore.

"All right, you've twisted my arm." She forced out a laugh and glanced at the waitress. "One chocolate sundae, please."

As the girl left, Chuck eyed Charley with approval. "You're finally showing some sense."

"Am I?" she replied. "I probably won't be able to move after eating that."

After dinner their plans to see a movie were postponed by mutual agreement. There was nothing playing at any of the theaters that particularly caught their interest. When Charley suggested that they walk off some of their dinner, Chuck agreed.

Hand in hand they strolled along the business district and gazed into shop windows at the merchandise displayed. They stopped now and then to look and admire and wander on.

Charley pointed at a window. "Would you look at that? Christmas decorations!" she exclaimed in disapproval. "Halloween isn't even here yet. Christmas is starting earlier every year."

"Do you mean you haven't started your Christmas shopping yet?" Chuck teased as they continued on to the next shop.

"No. I wait until the last week, then I run around like a maniac trying to buy everything at once." She smiled at herself. "To me, that's the Christmas spirit."

The next shop was a jewelry store with a display of wedding rings. Unwillingly Charley paused to look. The thought of exchanging vows with anyone but Shad made her feel a little sick. But she had made her decision earlier, and she wouldn't retreat from it. The smile on her lips felt brittle when she glanced at Chuck.

"If you're interested in buying something for my Christmas stocking, one of those rings would be nice," she prompted him.

He eyed her warily, not sure whether she was serious or just joking. In his uncertainty, he chose the latter. "I suppose that would be an example of good things coming in small packages."

"Yes, it would," she said, then realized he wasn't going to take the hint. Good old Chuck didn't exactly appreciate subtleties, although her remark had been anything but subtle. Maybe he hadn't picked up on it because she had rejected him too many times in the past. Hesitating, she gathered her resolve. "You once asked me to marry you, Chuck, and I turned you down. I'd like you to ask me again."

There was a long, silent moment when she thought he was going to refuse. When he looked away, avoiding her gaze, Charley was sure of it.

"You're still in love with him, aren't you?" He stared into the jewelry store window.

The question hurt as much as her answer. "Yes." Through the glass she saw him close his eyes, and knew it was painful for him to hear, too. "But that doesn't necessarily mean I can't grow to care for another man." Charley didn't try to pretend to Chuck that she loved him.

"I've never stopped loving you, Charlotte." He continued to stare into the window. "And I've never stopped hoping that you'd get over him and turn to me. But you're not over him."

There wasn't any way she could argue with that so she didn't even try. "I wasn't expecting that answer. Used to be that you were the one who wanted to marry. Now it's me." She smiled at the irony of the situation and Chuck finally turned to look at her. Her smile faded into a serious expression. "I would be proud to be your wife, Chuck. And I'll be a good one, too. I'll make sure that you're never sorry you married me."

After considering her words for a minute, he reached inside his coat pocket and took out a jeweler's ring box. He held it in his hand, studying it. "I bought this for you three years ago and I've been waiting all this time to give it to you, wondering if the day would ever come when you'd accept it."

"Chuck," she whispered and felt empathy for all he'd gone through.

"Every time I've seen you, it's been in my pocket ... just in case," he added with a tentative smile, then paused to nervously clear his throat. "Will you marry me, Charley?" He looked into her tear-filled eyes. "I mean, Charlotte. I guess I should be more formal, huh?"

"That's okay. Charley or Charlotte. I'm still the same person." *Not since Shad came into your life.* She pushed the unwelcome thought away. "Anyway, the answer is yes." Her voice wavered on the answer and she tried to pretend it wasn't caused by reluctance. It had been her decision.

His hand trembled as he opened the box. Her left hand felt as cold as ice when she offered it to him. She flinched inwardly as he slid the fancy ring onto her fourth finger. It felt strange. *That's because Shad didn't give it to you.*

"I had to guess at the size," Chuck explained. "It's loose." His glance held a silent apology.

"That's all right," Charley assured him. "It can be made smaller." As a dutiful bride-to-be she was obliged to admire the engagement ring. A cluster of small diamonds surrounded a center stone. It was a more elaborate ring than she would have chosen for herself, but she wouldn't hurt his feelings by saying so. "It's beautiful, Chuck."

"I hoped you would like it."

When she saw the way he was looking at her, she realized he expected something more in the way of a reaction than just words. She made the initial move to kiss him and sensed his disappointment at her lukewarm response to the pressure of his mouth. It was something she was going to have to work on, but she was confident that in time she would find some pleasure in his embrace.

Drawing back, he smiled at her. "You don't pick the best places to ask a man to propose to you," he chided. "This happens to be a public street, in case you haven't noticed."

If it had been Shad kissing her, she would have been oblivious to the passing traffic. With Chuck, she was conscious of it—as he was. She tucked her hand inside the crook of his arm so they would start walking again.

When she glimpsed their reflections in the glass panes of a storefront, she thought they made an incongruous pair. But perhaps they didn't. They were both in love with someone who didn't love them.

"I was thinking that maybe we could get married after the first of the year," Chuck suggested. "Things are slower on the ranch during the winter. It would be easier for me to be away. We could go somewhere warm for our honeymoon. Acapulco, maybe."

For a minute she almost panicked, feeling that she was being rushed. She steadied her nerves and smiled a tremulous agreement. "Um, yeah. That'd be okay—I mean that would be great. And winter is as good a time as any."

"I'm glad you agree. I know there's probably a lot you have to do—" he began.

Charley quickly interrupted him. "I'd rather not have a big wedding. Just the family and a few close friends." She couldn't take the hypocrisy of a large church wedding with hundreds of guests. "Do you mind?"

"I don't mind," he assured her. "As a matter of fact, I wasn't looking forward to the idea of wearing a tuxedo. But I know women like all that stuff."

"Not this woman," she corrected. "I just want a simple ceremony."

The Explorer was parked just ahead of them. Chuck paused. "I was just thinking."

"About what?" She cast him a sideways glance.

"I know it's probably old-fashioned, but I was just thinking that maybe I should take you home so I can speak to your brother."

"Oh, I don't need his permission," Charley smiled. "But we can go if you want."

She felt a vague reluctance about facing her brother. She was having enough second thoughts of her own without hearing again about his misgivings. Now that the ring was on her finger and the engagement was an accomplished fact, Charley was frightened by what she had done. Her only consolation was that the alternative—being alone —was more frightening.

When they returned to the ranch, they found Gary in the machine shed fixing the spare tire for his truck. He seemed surprised to see Charley home so early.

"I didn't expect you until tonight," he commented.

"No movies playing that we wanted to see," Charley replied.

"Actually"—Chuck cleared his throat, his normally ruddy complexion turning redder—"we came back because . . . I asked Charley to marry me and she accepted. We wanted you to be the first to know."

His expression seemed shadowed as Gary turned his accusing glance on her. "I didn't really think you'd do it." Feeling the full weight of his disapproval, she inwardly flinched.

Chuck missed his meaning and laughed. "Neither did I. I've been asking her for so long that I couldn't believe it when she indicated she would accept." He sobered under Gary's cold glance. "Since you're the man of the family, so to speak, I thought it was only proper if I—"

"Guess you're going to ask my permission," her brother growled.

"Yes," Chuck hesitated, looking momentarily baffled.

"Damn it!" Gary swore. "I knew Charley wasn't responsible for her actions, but I thought you'd have more sense than to make such a fool move, Chuck."

"Stop it, Gary," Charley protested in a furious whisper.

"I'd love to stop this ridiculous marriage before it happens!" he snapped.

"I'm sorry that you disapprove," Chuck murmured.

"For God's sake, Chuck, open your eyes!" her brother insisted. "She's still in love with Shad. Can't you see that?"

"Yes, I know," the older man admitted grudgingly. "We discussed it."

"Are you prepared to live with a woman who's in love with someone else?" Gary challenged. "To sleep with her, knowing that she's imagining another man in your place?"

"Whoa! That was totally out of line!" Her temper flared at last.

"No, it isn't!" Gary countered, matching her fire. "It has to be said. Chuck has a right to know what the hell he's letting himself in for. It's something I don't think either one of you have faced!"

"We have," Chuck asserted.

Gary glanced from one to the other, then released a long, weary breath. "I guess there isn't anything else I can say then, is there?"

"We haven't set a date for the wedding," Charley said. "But it will be sometime after the first of the year. I'd like you to give me away, Gary."

"You know I will." A look of resignation spread across his face. "But I still think you're making a mistake. I'm sorry."

"It's going to be a simple wedding with only a few guests, nothing elaborate." It seemed safest to discuss the wedding plans. There could be little argument about the details.

"That's a blessing," Gary muttered.

"It's really your blessing we want," Charley said.

"You have it," he sighed heavily. "I wish you both all the happiness in the world. But that doesn't change the fact that I don't believe you're going to find it together."

"Thanks anyway. Sorry to throw you for a loop, Gary. We kinda sprang this on you. Maybe we shouldn't have." Chuck put his arm around her as he spoke but the way he said the word *we* made Charley wince inside.

"Don't thank me." Gary shook his head. "I probably should be trying to pound some sense into your heads."

"I'd like to have an informal get-together here next weekend and invite some of our friends so

Chuck and I can announce our engagement," Charley explained. "Is that all right with you?"

He gave her a baffled look. "Since when are you so considerate? Did you see that *Stepford Wives* remake or something?"

"I told you we didn't go to the movies. Maybe I should just wallop you," she hissed.

"Now, honey," Chuck said.

Charley removed his arm from around her waist.

"Go ahead," Gary replied. "I mean, you can have all the parties you want. I doubt if I'll feel like celebrating. Excuse me"—he brushed past them—"I'm going to the house and wash up."

When he had gone, Charley murmured, "I'm sorry, Chuck."

"He made it pretty plain what he thought of our chances, didn't he?" He sighed.

"Don't pay any attention to him," she insisted.

"That isn't easy."

"Staying for supper?" she asked, not wanting him to leave in this mood.

"No, thanks. I'd better be getting back home." He kissed her cheek before he took a step away, then paused. "Do you know that I always expected this would be the happiest day of my life? But right now I don't feel happy. Not at all."

"It'll be all right," she whispered, trying to convince herself as much as him, but Chuck didn't seem to hear her as he walked away.

Chapter Nine

Altogether, eight couples attended the engagement party in addition to Gary, Chuck and Charley. She brought the chairs in from the kitchen so there would be a place for everyone to sit in the living room, but most of them were standing and talking. The kitchen table became a buffet table, holding the refreshments—an assortment of chips, sandwiches and cheeses. A variety of soft drinks provided setups and Chuck had brought a case of beer.

On the surface the party appeared to be a success, but it was proving to be more of an ordeal than Charley had expected. Seemed that she and Chuck had been talked about as a potential couple for years, since they lived right next to each other and all, yet everyone seemed amazed by their engagement. Every time she turned around, a different friend proclaimed surprise.

This time it was Betty Todd. "I just can't get over it!" she declared in a voice that always seemed one degree too loud. "I never dreamed you two would actually become engaged."

"As you can see, that's exactly what we've done," Charley assured her with a stiff smile.

"Let me look at your ring." She grabbed Charley's hand and turned and twisted it to watch the flash of light from the diamonds. "It must have cost Chuck a fortune. Did he say how much he had to pay for it?"

"No. And I didn't ask him. I didn't think it was any of my business." And it certainly isn't any of yours, she felt like adding.

"You should get it insured, Charley," Betty advised her. "It's so loose. Why, what would happen if it slipped off and you lost it?"

"We're having it made smaller so that won't happen," she explained. "Chuck's taking it into the jeweler's next week."

"You and Chuck." Her friend returned to the same theme, marveling, "Isn't it something after all this time?"

"I don't see why it's such a surprise to everyone," Charley declared at last.

"You've been kind of going together for years, right?" Betty paused for dramatic effect. "And there were rumors flying around that you were having an affair with that hired man you had working here."

Charley blanched. A hand touched her shoulder and she turned with a start.

"Hi, sis," Gary said, a smile masking the alertness of his gaze as it traveled over her pale face. Then he shifted his attention to the other woman. "Hi, Betty. I think Glenda wanted to talk to you.

She's over there with Sue and the others." He gestured toward a group of women.

"Ooh, Glenda always has the best gossip. 'Scuse me."

As the woman crossed the room Charley sipped at the glass of fruit punch in her hand. "Good timing, Gary."

"I thought you looked like you needed rescuing," he murmured. "Where's Chuck? I thought he'd be with you."

"He's right over there, talking to Clyde Barrows." She nodded to the trio of men only a few feet from her. "We aren't a pair of giggling teenagers who are inseparable."

"I know. That's what worries me," her brother replied dryly.

"Please, Gary, don't start," Charley protested in a weary tone.

"Sorry. This is a party, isn't it? How's your drink? Would you like another?" he offered.

"No," she refused even though the ice cubes had melted and turned the drink watery.

The front door opened and closed, letting a draft of cool night air into the room. Thinking one of the guests had stepped out for some fresh air, Charley absently glanced toward the door. She looked straight into a pair of glittering blue eyes. Shock riveted her to the floor.

She was hallucinating. Her mind was playing cruel tricks on her. It couldn't be Shad.

Yet he was crossing the room, walking directly toward her. Dressed in a white shirt and a black quilted vest, he was just too damned solid and real to be a mirage. Joy soared through her at the sight of him, lifting her to the heights of fool heaven.

She couldn't help herself. Her shining gaze wandered over the heavy blackness of his hair and his handsome, utterly masculine features, so tanned and vigorous. When he stopped in front of her, it was his eyes that captivated her. The smoldering intensity of their blue light was breathtaking.

"Hello, Charley, my darling." The lazy drawl of his low voice was a caress, touching her and assuring her of his existence.

"Shad," she whispered.

His glance impatiently swept the gathering of people only just beginning to notice his presence. "It looks like I'm crashing somebody's party. What is it? A birthday celebration?" His glance returned to Charley. His question brought her sharply back to reality and she had to lower her gaze. Shad looked beyond her. "Is it yours, Gary?"

"No, it isn't my birthday," her brother replied and left the explanation to Charley.

"You're certainly looking fit since the last time I saw you. How's the leg?" Shad made the polite inquiry of her brother but a hard edge began to underscore his voice.

"Good as new." Gary kept his responses short and to the point, inviting no further discussion of the subject.

"Is this all the welcome I get, Charley?" Shad's voice came back to her, low and demanding, rough with frustration. "I know I hurt you when I left but—aren't you glad to see me?"

Tears were in her eyes when she lifted her gaze.

All the bitterness of the past two months was in their pain-filled depths. There was frustration, too, that Shad should return just when she had reconciled herself to never seeing him again—when she had promised herself to Chuck and accepted his ring.

"Why did you wait so long to come?" she accused in a hoarse whisper. Her throat was as raw as her feelings.

"Because I was stupid and blind." His look became warmly possessive as he brought his hands up to grip her shoulders.

His touch opened an emotional wound so deeply painful that she started trembling. She loved him so much—too much. But the misery of the past two months was suddenly gone and every nerve in her body became sensitive to him. She ached to be held in his arms and feel the healing strength of his kisses, but . . . There was another man's ring on her finger. Charley clutched her drink glass with both hands to keep from returning Shad's caress.

"It took me a while to realize it was your voice I heard whispering in the breeze, calling to me," Shad murmured. "You were the shining warmth I felt when I walked in the sunlight. There was nothing over the next hill that was better than what I'd left behind. The best thing in my life had already happened to me and that was you. Anything else would only be hollow echoes of what I'd known. I was surrounded by emptiness, Charley, and the bittersweet memories of you."

"Quite a speech, Shad." She closed her eyes

tightly, but the tears squeezed through her lashes to run down her cheeks.

"I mean every word."

She just looked at him, mute. Trouble was, she knew he did.

"You have every right to be angry," he went on. "You told me how it would be before I left, and you were right. I can't live without you, Charley. You are my life."

Opening her eyes, she blinked through her tears to see the confidence in his expression, the loving fire of his blue gaze. There was a movement beside her. She half-turned and recognized Chuck's blurred form.

"Shad, this isn't a birthday party." Her voice was husky with the pain of her announcement. "We're celebrating my engagement to Chuck. We're going to be married."

She felt the stillness that rocked Shad and drained the color from his face, leaving him white beneath his tan. His surprise was so total that she felt a surge of anger. She hadn't heard a single word from him in all this time. Yet he had come back, fully expecting her to forgive and forget because he naturally assumed that she still loved him. Just for a second, she hated his male ego. Really hated it. But not him.

"I told you I wouldn't wait," was all she said. Lashing out at Shad would only give her so-called friends something more to talk about.

His hands fell from her shoulders and he turned his head away but not before she saw the desolation in his eyes. Charley almost cried out, but

Chuck touched her arm and took the glass from her trembling hands before she dropped it. The movement pulled Shad's gaze to Chuck.

"Congratulations." His voice sounded choked as his large hand reached out to shake Chuck's. "I think you know you're a lucky man."

"Yes, I am." Chuck sounded gruff and defensive.

Shad's troubled gaze slid back to her. "I guess I deserve this," he said in a low murmur. Charley couldn't speak. She could only look at him in mute misery. "He'll be a better husband for you than I could ever be. I told you before that I thought he was a good man for you."

"Yes." She remembered it too well. Shad had advised her to marry Chuck.

He didn't take his darkly haunted eyes from her face, but he addressed his next request to Chuck. "Do you have any objections if I kiss your fiancée? Just one last time."

Shad's odd but politely phrased request must have assured Chuck that there was no threat, because he gave his permission. "I don't mind."

Her handsome cowboy stepped forward and cupped her face in his hands, his thumbs lightly stroking her cheeks. A moan came from her throat, so soft that it was barely audible; a tiny cry of utter longing. He brought his face closer to hers, his gaze seeming to memorize every feature.

"No one will ever love you as much as I do, Charley." His low drawl was so quiet only she could hear what he was saying. "I don't have to travel over the next hill to know that. It probably doesn't mean anything to you but I'm not drifting anymore. I've crossed my last river."

Her breath came in a sharp gasp, then his lips were trembling against hers, moving over them softly. She swayed against him, her hands spreading across his vest. A raw hunger claimed him, hardening the kiss with its fierce urgency. Charley responded to its demands, aware only of her deep, abiding love for him.

"Just a damn minute—I thought you meant kiss her on the cheek," Chuck said indignantly.

Shad broke their embrace, letting her go abruptly to turn away. He muttered an emotional, "Take care of her," to Chuck and left a dazed Charley standing there to watch him stride across the room and out the front door.

"Are you going to let him walk away?" It was Gary who prodded her into awareness.

"What else can I do?" She turned her tear-filled eyes onto her brother.

"You love him, Charley. Damn it, go after him," he declared impatiently. "Don't stand here crying!"

"Was this your idea?" she demanded, remembering how determined her brother had been to put a stop to her marriage to Chuck. "Did you ask Shad to come here tonight? Did you do this?"

"If I had known how to get ahold of him or where to find him, I would have dragged him here, willing or not," Gary admitted. "But I didn't. He came back to you on his own. That has to prove something to you. Are you going to let him leave?"

Her gaze rushed to the front door where Shad had gone. She longed to run after him but she hesitated, twisting the diamond on her finger. She looked at it, trying not to feel the weight of her promise to Chuck, a man so unswerving in his loyalty.

"You want to go to him, don't you?" His sad voice spoke to her.

"Chuck." She turned to him, an aching regret sweeping through her at the defeat in his expression. "I don't want to hurt you."

"I guess I always knew it wasn't meant to be for us. I've just been kidding myself, pretending that you might care for me someday." His mouth twisted in a rueful line as he bent his head.

"I'm sorry," she said, and meant it.

He was shaking a little as he took her left hand. "I put this ring on your finger and I'll take it off." It slipped off easily at his touch. "You're free, Charley. Go to him. He's the one you want."

Charley wanted to thank him, but Gary was already pushing her toward the door. "Hurry up before he leaves."

She started out at a walk. Before she had taken three steps, she was running. Distantly she heard the astonished murmur of voices from the guests, but she was past caring what anybody thought as she raced out the door and into the night.

At the top of the porch steps she paused to search the shadowed yard of parked vehicles for Shad. There was a second of panic until she noticed a dejected figure leaning against the cab of a pickup, an arm hooked over a side mirror for support. She flew down the steps and through the shadows toward him.

"Shad!"

He stiffened at the sound of her voice and

turned to face her, his posture rigid. She stopped short of him, able to make out his features and the pain carved in them. Love kindled a fire that sent its warm glow through her body.

"I don't know where you think you are going, Shad Russell." She was smiling as she wiped away the moisture on her cheeks. "But this time, you aren't leaving without me."

"Charley." He took a step forward and stopped.

She guessed the cause for his hesitancy and explained, "Chuck has the ring. The engagement is off. You're the only man I love—the only man I have ever loved."

With a shout of delight Shad swept her into his arms, lifting her into the air and whirling her around. She was laughing with free-flowing happiness when he finally stopped. For a breathless moment they both looked at each other.

When his mouth settled onto hers, his kiss wiped out all the pain and confusion. Now there was room only for the boundless joy they found in each other, together at last.

Ending the kiss, Shad kept his arm around her as he opened the driver's door of the truck and gave her a push. "Inside," he ordered.

"Where are we going?" Not that it mattered as long as they were together.

"We're going across the state line into Nevada and find ourselves the first preacher who will marry us," he stated as he climbed behind the wheel once she was in the cab.

"If that's a proposal, I accept." Charley laughed. Reaching in the side pocket of his vest, he took out a small box and dropped it into her lap as he started the engine. "Got a ring for my best girl. Hope you like it."

She opened it and drew a breath of delight. It was a simple diamond solitaire set in a wide band of gold. "It's perfect. It's beautiful. I love it." Her arms went around his neck as she placed a big wet kiss on the corner of his mouth.

"Careful, I'm driving," he warned with a laugh, and kissed her lightly on the lips before negotiating the truck through the parked cars. "Aren't you interested in where we're going after we're married?"

"Where?" If it was to the ends of the earth, she'd follow him.

"To my ranch near the Bitterroots. I've spent the past two weeks fixing the house and remodeling the kitchen for you. New everything. Cost a mint," he said. "But if you don't like anything, you can change it."

"We're going to have a home?"

"I told you. I've crossed my last river." He stopped the truck to take her in his arms and tell her how much he loved her without saying one more word.

DAKOTA DREAMING

Chapter One

Edie Gibbs stared at the check in her hands. Her mind refused to assimilate the number of digits in the dollar figure. She lifted a hand to touch her fingertips to her temple and let them glide into her soft brown hair.

"I . . . I don't think I understand, Mr. Wentworth." At last she found her voice and looked up at the lawyer sitting in the wing-backed chair that had been her late husband's favorite. "When you called and asked to discuss my financial situation, I thought—" A bewildered laugh escaped her throat. "It took all of our savings to pay the funeral costs. And here I've been worrying how I was going to earn enough money to keep the house. I thought you were going to tell me about a monumental pile of debts. But this?" Her confused hazel eyes sought the attorney's face as she clutched the check. "Is it real?"

"Yes, it is." The gentleness in his expression said he was pleased his news was good.

"But I didn't know Joe had any insurance." Edie held on to the slip of paper that represented so much money. "We talked about it a long time ago, but we couldn't squeeze the premium payments into our budget." Which raised another question in her mind. "Where did Joe get the money to pay them?"

"I was just coming to that." He opened the briefcase sitting on his lap and took out a sheaf of papers.

"May I look at that, Mom?" Her daughter reached over to take the check. Edie barely looked at the pony-tailed girl seated on the couch before her attention was claimed by the documents the attorney was handing her. She glanced through them, but the legal jargon was beyond her comprehension at the moment.

"What does all this mean?" Again her hazel eyes darkened with confusion.

"I believe your late husband did a lot of tinkering in his workshop," he began.

"That's an understatement," Edie declared with a rueful sigh. "Joe spent nearly every spare minute he had in his workshop. He'd come home from the garage, shower, eat and disappear into the shed until it was bedtime." There was nothing malicious or resentful in her statement. It had been too much a part of their married life together. "He loved working there. That was his escape."

"It was a profitable escape. In with those documents are patent registrations, some of which your late husband was able to sell to auto manufacturers in Detroit," John Wentworth explained.

"Patents?" Edie was beginning to think she

would never escape this whirl of confusion. None of this was making any sense. "Joe didn't even have a college degree." Something he had been very self-conscious about. He'd settled for a job as an auto mechanic, saying that people would always need their cars fixed, no matter what shape the economy was in. He'd made a good living, but he'd always said his job was nothing to brag about.

"Nonetheless," the lawyer began.

"He tried. He got online whenever he could— there's a lot of sites for what he was interested in. I know he picked up the basics of mechanical drafting and engineering but . . ." Edie let the sentence trail off.

"Whatever your late husband lacked in formal education, he more than made up for in natural inventiveness," the attorney assured her. "The royalties off these patents will provide you with a very comfortable income for a good many years, Mrs. Gibbs. Plus I have a national firm negotiating to purchase the rights on two more of his patents."

This was more than she could take in. The silence from her daughter and stepson indicated they, too, were finding all this hard to believe.

"I don't understand." She shook her head, the softly curling length of her brown hair barely brushing her shoulders. "Why didn't Joe tell me . . . tell us about these patents?"

"I really can't answer that," John Wentworth sighed. "I know he seemed very self-conscious about his inventions, as if they were a fluke. He was determined that no one should know about them."

"And the money from these patents went to pay the premiums on the insurance policy?" Edie had to be sure she had the facts. Although she'd managed the household account, Joe had handled most of their financial paperwork, and he simply hadn't told her everything. She'd signed their tax returns year after year without really reading them closely.

"Some of it, yes," the attorney nodded. "And he saved the rest. Obviously he wanted you to be taken care of in the event anything happened to him. It was almost as if he had a premonition." He removed another set of papers from his briefcase and handed them to Edie. "These are a summary and a projection of your annual income under the present agreements."

He leaned forward to go over them with her. Edie listened and followed his moving finger down the list, but it was all a haze, something not quite real. She had been so braced for bad news that being presented with a pot of gold was something that seemed too good to be true.

Edie was pale. Her face, usually animated with an irrepressible zest to meet life and its problems head-on, was blank of expression. She was slim and looked slimmer dressed mostly in black, but she seemed too young to be a widow, the attorney thought—or to have a grown daughter for that matter. Either way, this very attractive woman was not at all the way he had pictured Joseph Gibbs's wife. He noticed the stunned look in her large eyes.

"Let me make a suggestion, Mrs. Gibbs," he said. "I'll leave these papers for you to look over. You can call me in a couple of days. I'm sure you'll have some questions, and I'd be happy to discuss your financial future, possible investments, that kind of thing."

"Okay. But give me a few days to think about it," Edie agreed a little numbly and belatedly started to rise.

"Um, I'll walk Mr. Wentworth to the door, Edie," her stepson volunteered. Jerry stood up, shoving his hands into the pockets of his jeans. His awkward politeness reminded her with a pang that he was the man of the house now.

"Thanks, Jerry," she said softly. "I will call you, Mr. Wentworth," she added.

Good-byes gotten over with, the front door was opened and closed, but Edie still felt stunned by the unexpected turn of events. At the sound of approaching footsteps, she lifted her gaze from the papers in her hand.

"Did you know about this, Jerry?" It was possible since her stepson had often helped Joe in his workshop on weekends. She looked at him curiously. His youthful face looked a lot like his father's, with the same steady and reliable expression. Except his blue eyes often held the twinkle of humor, his mouth smiled easily, and his sandy brown hair was shaggy in a carelessly attractive way.

"He explained what he'd learned from the online sites once in a while, and I remember once he was trying to modify an emission-control device and a couple of other things, but no"—he shook his head and paused by her chair to take the papers from her hand and leaf through them—"he didn't tell me anything about patents. Inventors are pretty secretive, I guess. They have to be."

"You'd better take this check, Mom." Alison

shoved it into her hands. "I can't believe we have so much money. Last night I couldn't sleep, worrying that I might have to sell one of my horses. Now . . . we could buy a whole stable full and not put a dent in that check."

"I was afraid we'd have to sell off some of the acreage," Edie admitted. "Alison, you were great about helping with the horses we boarded to keep ours in hay, not to mention the vet bills, and the mortgage payment on this place, the utilities, groceries—oh, geez. It was almost too much."

"You don't have to worry about that now, Edie." Her stepson said the very thought that was echoing through her mind.

"I know," she murmured. "But why didn't he tell us? Why didn't your father tell us?"

"Dad . . . was too easygoing," Jerry said without criticizing. "You always were the battler in this family, Edie. You managed the money and kept the bill collectors at bay during the hard times. Remember that time I got picked up for drinking on my sixteenth birthday? You were the one who went to bat for me with the judge."

"I managed the household money, yeah. But he did our taxes—I was usually too busy. I didn't really know what was coming in. But what has that got to do with this?" she argued. "Think of how much money it cost him for this insurance policy. We could have used that money . . . or some of it. We could have taken a vacation or bought a new car," she added, remembering the succession of clunkers Joe had kept running.

Jerry shook his head. "Edie, just before I went

into the marines, Dad sat me down for a talk. Not that he was ever much of a talker." His voice was carefully controlled. "He told me that the one thing he had always regretted was marrying my mother when he was just sixteen. He got his high school diploma because his parents pushed him, but I was born the month after he graduated. He wanted to make sure I wouldn't do something like that. He told me how much he loved me and Mom but that he'd had to abandon his dreams." Jerry sat down in his father's chair and leaned forward, clasping his hands together in a thoughtful attitude.

"That was one reason he was always so determined that the two of you had a chance at life." Edie knew that story, and she was warmed by the memory of how profoundly her late husband had meant it. "He told me that, too."

"What he probably didn't tell you," her stepson continued, "was that he felt guilty for marrying you."

"Guilty?" She was startled. "Why?"

"After my mother died in that car accident, Dad didn't know how to cope with raising a kid on his own. Then he met you, Edie, and you hadn't even turned twenty-one. He said he stole your dreams, too. Right away you had a child to raise, debts to pay, a living to earn and no time to be young and in love."

"But Joe needed me. So did you," Edie protested. "I never felt that I missed anything."

"It always bothered him that the two of you never had a honeymoon," Jerry added.

"We had a honeymoon, a belated one," she insisted. "Don't you remember that camping trip we all took to the Black Hills?"

"What kind of honeymoon is that?" Alison laughed affectionately. "You had two nosy little kids along. Not exactly romantic."

"Joe wasn't a very romantic person," Edie admitted. It was the truth, and she didn't feel she was being unkind to his memory to say so. His other qualities had more than made up for his lack of sentimentality. Anyone who had ever known Joseph Gibbs had loved him, herself included. Honesty about his faults wouldn't diminish what he'd been.

"To answer the question that started all this," Jerry said, "I think Dad did what he did, and the way he did it, because he wanted you to be able to have your dreams, Edie, if anything ever happened to him."

The telephone rang and Alison bolted from the couch. "I'll get it!" As she raced to answer it, she ignored the extension in the living room in favor of the privacy of the kitchen phone. "Could be Craig." The quick explanation was tossed over her shoulder.

Edie watched the slim, long-legged girl sprint from the room. "She hasn't heard from him since the funeral," she murmured to Jerry, referring to the boy Alison had been dating steadily since spring graduation, Craig Gurney.

"She won't, either." His face wore a very adult expression, revealing all of his twenty-four years of experience and more. "Commitment issues."

"Huh?" Obviously her stepson knew something neither she nor Alison did.

"The word's out. Since Alison won't fool around, Gurney's looking for a girl who will," he said grimly. "Good riddance, if you ask me, but please don't tell her what I said. I don't think Alison realizes how much guys talk."

"I won't."

"And let me know if Craig tries to see her again. I want to talk to him if he does."

It didn't take much reading between the lines to guess what Jerry would talk to him about. He'd been very protective of Alison since the day Edie had brought her home from the hospital. Rivalry between them was nonexistent. Alison idolized her older half brother, and Jerry had long ago put his baby sister on a pedestal. Their closeness had always been a great source of pride and pleasure for Edie.

"Mom?" Alison stuck her head around the kitchen door. "It's Mrs. Van Doren." She wrinkled her nose in dislike. "She wants to know how soon you can have her sofa and chair reupholstered. I explained about Dad's funeral and all. To hear her talk, you'd think Dad picked a terribly inconvenient time to die—the old prune face."

Edie smothered a sigh of irritation and tried to remember how much work was left on the items. "Tell her I'll have them finished by Friday."

"Okay." Alison disappeared behind the door.

Reupholstering furniture in her home had been one of the ways Edie had supplemented their income. Joe's salary had covered their necessary expenses. What with the house, the garden and taking care of the horses they boarded on the acreage, even with Alison and Jerry helping after school, it hadn't been feasible for Edie to have a job in town.

"There's something I didn't make clear when we were talking a minute ago about the money Dad left you," Jerry said. "He left it for you, Edie. Not for me or Alison. You're the only mother I've ever known. I mean, I don't call you mom, but you are. I don't want you to think that we need any of that money . . . or should have any of it."

"But—" She attempted a protest.

But Jerry interrupted, "No arguing. You're only thirty-eight, Edie. Got your whole life ahead of you yet. And, um, you're really pretty. My friends even say so."

"Really? Which ones?" Edie smiled at him.

"That's classified information."

"You're very good for my ego, Jerry." Edie would have continued, but he wouldn't let her.

"Dad wanted you to have it. I know I speak for Alison when I say that we want you to have it. We know how much you've sacrificed for us. How long has it been since you bought a new dress?" he challenged.

"How long has it been since I needed a new one?" she joked, because her husband hadn't been the type to party or go out for an evening, even if they could have afforded it. He preferred a home-cooked meal to any restaurant fare.

"With that money"—he gestured toward the check in her hand—"you can buy yourself a whole new wardrobe, travel, have fun, do anything you want." As he was making the statement, Alison reentered the living room in time to hear it.

"There's something else you can do, too, Mom," she inserted, pausing to sit on the arm of Edie's chair. "I was thinking about it in the kitchen after I hung up from talking to Mrs. Van Doren. You could open up your own upholstery shop, go into business for yourself. Everybody around here knows how good you are at it."

Own her own business? Edie considered the idea, then dismissed it with a slight shake of her head. "I don't think so. That would mean having a shop in town and spending most of the day inside when I'd rather be outdoors. As for traveling, there's always the Discovery Channel."

"Mom!" Alison glared at her. "You can't just sit around and watch that Australian guy wrestle alligators. You should go someplace."

"But—" Edie sighed and shut up, because how much fun would it be to sightsee alone? The memory of their one and only camping trip to the Black Hills of South Dakota and the instantaneous love she had felt for that Indian land came back to her. She doubted she would feel like that about Europe, or anywhere else in the world.

"It isn't anything you have to decide now," Jerry reminded her.

"No. And I don't intend to make any decisions right now." She smiled firmly.

"No need to," Jerry declared, and pushed his lanky frame upright. "It's just about chore time so I'd better get back to the farm." Since he had returned home after his tour of enlistment with the marines, Jerry had worked for a large, corporate-owned farm with an enormous acreage of crops as well as a cattle feedlot operation.

"I'm glad you could get time off from work to come over while the attorney was here," Edie said.

"Yeah, well, it was too wet to be in the fields today anyhow, so—" He shrugged away the rest of the sentence.

"Speaking of chores"—Edie glanced at her daughter—"we have some horses that need to be grained."

"And stalls to be cleaned." Alison grimaced. "I'd better go change clothes."

"Me, too," Edie agreed, glancing down at her dark dress.

Jerry had started toward the front door. "I'll probably be over Sunday, unless we start haying."

"Sunday dinner will be at one o'clock, as always," Edie told him before she followed Alison up the stairs to the bedrooms on the second floor.

After the front screen door slammed shut, the engine of Jerry's pickup roared to life in the yard of the old farmhouse. Edie paused at the open door of her daughter's bedroom. She watched for a silent second as Alison dragged a pair of worn blue jeans and an old shirt from her closet. It didn't seem possible that Alison would be eighteen in two short months.

"Did you want something, Mom?" Alison glanced up to see her standing in the doorway.

"I was just wondering—" she began, and changed to a more direct approach. "Do you want to go to college, Alison?"

"Nope. You know I don't." She widened her brown eyes in mock exasperation.

"I know we talked about it before you graduated, but," Edie paused, "I want to be sure you refused because you didn't want to go and not because you knew we couldn't afford it. With the insurance money—"

"Uh-uh," Alison interrupted firmly. "I'm not college material. Look at my grades. Besides, I'm like my dad. Home and family mean everything to me."

"Okay, but you could still get an education. Don't say no just yet. Those aren't mutually exclusive goals, Alison." Edie was immediately defensive, because she knew too well how much Joe had wanted to do better for himself and his family.

"That depends," Alison said. "I know why Dad never said anything about those inventions of his. He didn't want people to treat him like someone he wasn't. He was just a mechanic—a good one, but just a mechanic. He wasn't ashamed of it, and neither am I."

"There was more to him than that, obviously. That doesn't explain why he didn't tell us." Edie returned to the question that kept nagging her.

"He just wasn't ready to. Probably didn't want us to get our hopes up, either. And he didn't want to get a reputation as a nutty inventor if his gizmos never sold."

"But they did sell. And he made money from them."

"Well, then, he just didn't want to be the center of attention, I guess."

"Yes, I suppose you're right," Edie sighed, accepting the odd logic of her daughter's explanation. Alison was right about being like her father.

In a town the size of this small Illinois community, Joe's inventions would have been big news. And Joe was fundamentally shy and not always sure of himself. Funny, he hadn't even been able to cope with raising a small boy on his own, yet he had been such a strong, stalwart man in many ways.

"Look at me. I'm good with animals—breaking and training horses and stuff," Alison continued as she untied her wraparound skirt, tossed it on the bed and tugged on her jeans. "I know you said I could be a vet someday, but it's about a hundred times harder to get into a veterinary college than a medical school. You know that."

"Yeah. I do. And I know there aren't very many veterinary colleges and there's a lot of competition."

"Tell me about it. Every horse-crazy girl and sick-of-shoveling-it farmboy wants to be a DVM. But the ones who get in are in the top one percent of their class."

"Okay, okay. We've been over this. Sorry. I wasn't trying to put my expectations on you."

"You meant well. But, between the money I got from selling Fiesta's colt and what I'll be able to save working as a ranch hand this summer, I'll be able to pay for that horseshoeing course this fall. Then we won't have the expense of shoeing our horses; plus I can make extra money by shoeing the horses we board."

"One thing is certain. I don't think we'll ever be without horses," Edie said with a wry smile.

"Yeah," Alison agreed, and looked up to reveal the impish twinkle in her brown eyes. "We're both horse crazy. Dad loved them, too," she added, a faint sadness touching her smile before it brightened. "Even if we never could get him to climb on one."

"True enough. But he was so proud of your riding and everything you did." Edie fell silent for a moment. "And he would've told you the same thing: don't say you'll never go to college."

"Uh-huh. You'd better hurry up and get changed, Mom." She leaned against the single bed to pull on her boots. "I want to work Fiesta's filly at halter, and I'll probably need your help at first."

"I won't be a minute," Edie promised and moved away from the door to her own room.

It was funny how young Alison seemed to her, yet she'd been close to that age when she'd married Joe. Edie walked to the closet to remove her old clothes. Now there were only hers on the shelves and hangers; she had given all of Joe's good clothes to the church. Not that he'd had many, since he'd rarely worn anything but garage overalls. He hadn't hung them in the closet they shared, of course—their faint greasy odor lingered on everything. Jerry had taken them away to spare her that task.

While she dressed, her gaze strayed to the framed photographs on the dresser. One, the most recent picture she had, was a picture of the four of them taken ten years ago at Christmas. Everyone was smiling except Joe, whose face was in the shadow of the Christmas tree. The second and third frames held yellowed photographs of her parents and her two brothers, and her grandparents. Their deaths when Edie was only four were a tragedy still talked about in the small Illinois community; almost an entire family, save Edie, wiped out in a single wrong move on an icy road. Her uncle and aunt had raised her with their children, treating her on an equal basis with her cousins, yet Edie had never felt that she truly belonged to their family.

In the spring of her senior year in high school she'd met Joe. At almost the same time, her uncle had announced that they would be moving to California where he had been transferred with a promotion. Edie hadn't wanted to go. And the more she saw of Joe and five-year-old Jerry, the more she realized how much they needed her . . . and how much she needed them. In his quiet, old-fashioned way, he courted her for almost two years, wanting her to be sure she knew what she was getting into, and in the end she'd said yes. With joy.

All in all, she'd had a good life and a good marriage. She didn't regret it.

The next three months were an adjustment period for Edie as a single woman again. Although she was used to running the household since Joe had so often been preoccupied, with his work or projects, there had always been the comforting knowledge that she could consult him when a problem arose. Now virtually everything was up to her—from what time to get up to what to fix for dinner.

There was one major decision Edie had postponed making—what to do with the money. She

Zebra Contemporary

had discussed it with John Wentworth, the attorney. And as soon as various friends and acquaintances learned about it, they volunteered suggestions. To this point she had spent only a tiny fraction of it since she had continued to live on the strict budget they'd had before. Nearly all of it had been safely stashed in a mutual fund with a healthy rate of return, waiting for her decision.

One thing kept running through her mind whenever she thought about how she should use it. Jerry's comment that Joe had wanted her to have her dreams kept echoing back. At first she had dismissed the possibility because, on the surface, her dream seemed ludicrous and impractical. Although she never discussed it with anyone, not even the kids, the idea kept coming back. Each time she found more and more reasons that made it seem plausible.

Finally Edie realized that she had to sound out her idea on Jerry and Alison. She needed their reaction to her proposal. Without their support, she wouldn't be able to achieve her goal. The opportunity came on Sunday when Jerry arrived to have dinner with them.

Having set the platter of roast pork on the table, Edie sat in the chair opposite Jerry, at the head of the table. She waited until Alison had offered the blessing and the food was being passed around.

"Mmm, you outdid yourself today, Edie," Jerry declared, sniffing appreciatively. The fragrant aroma of the sage dressing accompanying the pork permeated the air. "After a week of eating what comes out of the tin cans Chuck opens, this is heaven."

"Hey, is it true that Craig is going out with Chuck's sister?" Alison demanded.

Jerry gave his half sister a sidelong glance, then nodded. "Yep." He helped himself to a heaping mound of mashed potatoes.

"I thought so." It was a somewhat choked response that Alison tried to hide.

"I was cleaning a closet this week and ran across a couple of boxes pushed way to the back. You'll never guess what I found in one of them," Edie stated, and didn't make them ask. "Old snapshots of our trip to the Black Hills. They're on the buffet table behind you, Alison."

The distraction worked. Alison reached back to remove the packet of photographs from the bureau top. "Pretty good pictures for a non-digital camera," she remarked after she had glanced at the first couple of snapshots. "How old were we, Mom? Oh, Jerry, look at this one!" She laughed and instantly handed it to him.

"I think you were eight and Jerry was fourteen," Edie replied.

"You were a bean pole then," Alison teased her brother.

"You were pretty skinny yourself," he retorted good-naturedly.

"Look! This is really a terrific picture of the four faces at Mount Rushmore!" Alison handed him another. "Here's one of the buffalo herd!" As she continued to pass the snapshots on to him, Jerry would sneak a bite of food and set his fork down in time to take the next one she handed him. "We had so much fun on that trip," she sighed.

"Do you remember this, Edie?" Jerry handed her one of the pictures, amusement in his eyes. "You were trying to cook hamburgers on an outdoor grate. They kept breaking in half and falling through onto the coals."

"And Joe kept rescuing them," Edie remembered.

"Gritburgers," he said. "You said they were good for our character."

"Definitely not one of my more memorable meals," she agreed with a laugh.

"Would you just look at that country? Isn't it beautiful?" Alison murmured as she handed Jerry a photograph taken of the wild, rolling landscape. "Do you remember how we all started dreaming about owning a ranch there someday? Even Dad?"

"Do I remember!" Jerry nodded. "We planned how many acres we were going to have, how many head of cattle, how much hay ground we would need for winter feed, how many horses we should have. Dad and I were going to get the software to figure it all out. Our virtual ranch."

"You called it our Dakota dream ranch, didn't you, Mom?" Alison remembered with a faraway look.

"It doesn't have to be just a dream ranch," Edie said carefully. "We could have it now."

Alison stared at her for a long moment. "We could, couldn't we?" she breathed.

Edie turned her gaze to the young man seated across from her. Astonishment was written in his features. He set his silverware down again, the food on his plate forgotten as he searched her face.

"You're serious about this, aren't you?" His response was almost an accusation.

"Yes." She was holding her breath.

"Do you know how much a ranch out there would cost?" Jerry's voice held a note of disbelief.

"I have a pretty good idea," Edie said, looking to Alison for support.

"We can afford it."

"Even after the down payment there'd be enough money left out of the insurance to buy some stock and have a year's working capital." Edie had already done some rough figuring in her head. "And there'd still be some income from the patents besides that."

Jerry obviously found it difficult to argue. He shook his head and glanced at the photographs scattered across the table amid the bowls of food. "I guess finding these pictures made you think about it."

"No. I went looking for them, because I remembered what you said about Joe wanting me to use the money to fulfill my dreams," she explained. "Except this isn't just my dream. It was *our* dream. Yours, Alison's, Joe's and mine."

"I think it's the greatest idea I've ever heard," Alison enthused.

"All right." Jerry was still thinking, mulling it all over. It was what Edie wanted him to do. "You can afford it. And it is something you've wanted. But how on earth are you going to go about it? What do you know about running a ranch?"

"A lot. It takes basic common sense," Edie reasoned. "And I'm not completely without experience. I was raised on my uncle's farm. I've hayed, driven tractors, doctored sick animals, and done a hundred other things. I've certainly had a lot of experience mending fences, and I've been riding horses since I was five." She looked at Jerry, who was tearing a roll into small pieces and not eating it. "Of course, none of that means I can handle the operation of a ranch by myself."

"I'm relieved to hear you admit that." Jerry leaned back in his chair, a vaguely mocking smile on his mouth.

"However"—Edie paused for effect—"I think I might know where I can get qualified help." She glanced at her daughter. "There's you, for instance, Alison. Now that you and Craig are finally through, you might consider coming with me. Between the two of us, we have delivered our share of foals, including the breech birth Fiesta had this last time. Cows can't be that much different. Besides, you have enrolled in that horseshoeing course, a skill that will definitely come in handy on a ranch."

"I'll pack tomorrow, Mom," Alison promised.

"What about you, Jerry?" Edie glanced at her stepson, who was the big question mark in her mind. "You're the one with the experience. You've worked practically every summer on the farm with that feedlot operation. You have all the firsthand knowledge about cattle. And you can walk me through the computer program for the business end of it."

"Yeah. You'll pick it up quickly." He leaned back in his chair and looked at her without saying more.

"Is there someone special here you wouldn't want to leave?" Since he had moved out she knew very little about his social life, except that he dated, but she didn't know of any girl he was seeing exclusively.

"Nope. There's no one special," he admitted, and Edie could see he was weakening.

"There is one thing I would want clear from the very start," she said. "This is going to be a family ranch, especially if we are all working for it. We'll all have an interest in it and a share of the profits, if there are any.

"Thanks to your father, I don't *have* to do anything. It's what I want and what I think is fair. The two of you are going to work just as hard as I am to make the ranch successful. What's your answer, Jerry? Do you think you'd like to go into partnership with me and Alison?" she challenged.

He shook his head and smiled crookedly. "It's so insane it just might work, do you know that?"

"That's what I thought!" Edie laughed, unable to check the flow of happiness at his easygoing answer.

"We're really going to own a ranch." Alison said it aloud as if she needed it repeated to believe it.

"First things first." Edie sobered. "First we are going to have to get in touch with a real-estate company to find out what's on the market. We agree on South Dakota, right?"

"How else are we going to have a Dakota dream ranch?" Jerry said.

"And we aren't going to jump at the first place that's up for sale, either," she insisted. "We aren't in any hurry, so let's find the right ranch for us, agreed?"

Both nodded.

"What about this place?" Jerry wondered.

"We'll sell it," Edie decided. "Of course, that means the house and barn are going to need a fresh coat of paint. The fences, too."

"We'd better not put it up for sale until we're fairly sure we've found a ranch," Jerry cautioned.

"Yes, otherwise we'll have to find a place to keep our horses until we move," Alison agreed, then asked, "We are taking our horses, aren't we?"

"Definitely." Jerry nodded and glanced questioningly at his half sister. "Didn't you say that buckskin you bought last winter would make a good roping horse?"

"I think so. Try him out this afternoon and see for yourself," she suggested.

"I'll do that."

Alison rose from her chair. "I'm going to get a paper and pencil so we can make a list of all the things we need to do."

Jerry pointed to the next room. "Don't forget the computer. We can do the initial search on-line. Not as if there's a land rush on in the Dakotas. A lot of folks in the heartland are selling out and moving on. It's freakin' cold up there in winter and it's tough to make a living year-round."

Edie looked at her departing daughter, then at her stepson. "Think we can?"

"Worth a try."

The warm look in his eyes reassured her instantly.

Chapter Two

Needless to say, the Gibbs family's decision was a hot topic in the local diner. Everyone for miles around discussed it over coffee and pie. No one quite believed that they really intended to go through with it.

It wasn't easy to carry out their plan, either. To begin with, there weren't many ranches they wanted to buy in the Black Hills region of South Dakota. At first, everything seemed too expensive, too large or too small. But Edie persisted in trying, and with her in charge, Jerry and Alison kept busy.

The quarter horses Alison had trained for the show ring and speed events were retrained for working use. Two of the five horses had to be sold when they proved too nervous and unsuitable. In addition, Alison completed her horseshoeing course while Edie and Jerry studied up on ranch management, cattle and land use. If the locals didn't take their plans seriously, no problem. The Gibbses did and that was what counted.

Four months from the Sunday when they'd made their decision and begun the plans, the real-estate agent called to tell Edie about a ranch that had just come on the market.

The owner, an elderly man, was being forced into retirement by an injury. Everything about the ranch sounded ideal, from its total acreage, the amount of pastureland and hay ground, and ample water supply, to the financial terms of the sale. Leaving Alison behind to look after the horses and the house, Edie and Jerry flew to Rapid City for a firsthand look at the operation.

The real-estate agent met them at the airport and drove them out to the property. Snow covered the land, hiding more than it revealed as it followed the curvature of the hills and dipped into gullies. Dark green pines dotted the winter landscape. Driving into the ranch yard, Edie viewed the outbuildings with their snow-covered roofs and drifts banked close to their walls. There was no movement, no sign of stock, but smoke curled out of the chimney of the house to wind a white trail against a startling blue sky.

"The buildings look rundown, don't they?" Jerry said to Edie.

"Let's hope their appearance is deceiving," she replied in a low voice. "They must be structurally sound or they would have collapsed."

The tires crunched in the snow as the real-estate agent slowed the car to a stop in the center of the yard. Switching off the engine, he glanced at them. "Up for a walk outside? Anson Carver, the owner, is on crutches, so we'll have to show ourselves around."

"Sure," Edie agreed.

She buttoned up her fleece-lined suede parka as Jerry stepped out of the car and pulled his cowboy hat low on his forehead. Edie discovered why when she slid out next and a stiff wind blew its icy breath over any exposed skin. Bareheaded, she turned up the fleece collar of her coat and buried her hands in the warm pockets.

They tramped around and through the ranch buildings. As Edie had suspected, the barns and sheds were soundly built, but there were boards and windowpanes that needed replacing. The sliding track for the barn door had broken, and another side door was precariously hinged. The signs of repair they did see were the lick-and-a-promise kind. Even the corral and holding pens of the feedlot were constructed out of an assortment of materials—boards, wooden posts, split rails—whatever was handy and the right length at the time.

Trying to hold the front of his topcoat shut against a tugging wind, the agent produced an aerial photograph of the property and oriented them to their location so he could point out boundaries and landmarks. The picture had been taken during the summer, so it was difficult to compare it with the wild and rolling terrain blanketed with snow.

They wandered farther out from the ranch yard into the near pasture. The snow was nearly to the top of Edie's insulated boots. A thin crust on the top crunched with each step. Jerry paused to sweep away a patch of snow with his boot. Beneath the snow was a tangle of long, yellow grass frozen together in thick clumps. The agent was busy extolling the merits of the place, stressing its untamed natural beauty.

"Untamed, huh?" Jerry said under his breath. "That's another word for natural disaster."

It took a few pointed questions from Edie regarding more practical matters, such as how many head of cattle they could expect the land to support, before he realized she would not be swayed into buying a place merely on looks.

When they turned back toward the ranch yard, Edie moved to the fencerow where a strip had been partially cleared of snow parallel to the line. She slipped on a patch of ice and grabbed for a post to keep from falling into a drift. Instead of supporting her, the wooden post gave under the pressure of her grasping hand. Jerry's quick reflexes kept her from stumbling to her knees.

"Must be rotted through at the base," he murmured grimly under his breath and ran a calculating eye along the fence line.

Edie knew what he was thinking. The entire property would probably need new fencing. "This place needs a lot of work."

"You can say that again," Jerry agreed before they caught up with the agent.

The house was in no better shape than the rest of the buildings. It was a one-story, rambling affair that'd had rooms added on with no attempt to adhere to design. White paint was chipped and peeling away to expose gray boards. A knock on the door brought a summons to enter. The interior of the house was as cheerless and dingy as the outside. After the brilliance of the bright sun glaring off white snow outdoors, it took Edie a moment to adjust to the gloom.

The front door had opened directly into a living room where an old woodstove was giving off waves of heat. The sudden change in temperature made Edie's chilled skin tingle with needle-sharp pain. The cold had nipped her cheeks red and made her facial muscles stiff, while the wind had tousled her chestnut hair into casual disorder. She paused inside the door to unbutton her coat and smooth her hair, not wanting to track into the house with her snow-wet boots on. The real-estate agent didn't appear to suffer from any such compunction and walked to a corner of the room where an old man sat in an armchair with one plaster-cast leg propped on a footstool.

"Hello, Mr. Carver. I'm Ned Jenkins from the real-estate office," the agent introduced himself. "I called you this morning to let you know I was bringing these people out to look at your ranch."

"I remember," the old man's gruff voice answered; then he turned his keenly piercing gaze to the pair standing by the door. He waved an impatient hand for them to enter the living room. "Come in. I don't intend to shout across the room to carry on a conversation with you."

"Let me take off my boots first so I don't track," Edie said and bent to unfasten them. A puddle of dirty water was already beginning to form on the floor around her feet.

"Take them off if you've a mind to," the old man scoffed, "but a little water and mud ain't going to be strange to this floor."

Regardless of his lack of concern, Edie went ahead and removed her boots, and Jerry did likewise. She set them neatly against the wall before crossing the room in her stocking-clad feet to meet the present owner.

Aware that Jerry was a step behind her, Edie stopped in front of the old man's chair. Age had wrinkled his sun-browned face and thinned his hair until there were only wispy gray tufts atop his head. Disabled and probably living alone, he obviously didn't bother with things like combing his hair.

The real-estate agent did the honors. "Mr. Carver, this is Mrs. Edie Gibbs from Illinois. Mr. Anson Carver, the owner of the property."

"Hello, Mr. Carver." Edie was a little surprised by the firmness of the grip of the withered hand that clasped hers.

"This is her son, Jerry Gibbs."

"How do you do, sir?" The crispness of Jerry's acknowledgment hinted at the years he'd spent in the military.

"Your son?" Anson Carver's sharp gaze swung back to her, sweeping her from head to foot. "What did you do? Have him in high school?"

At first Edie was taken aback by the blunt question. Then a rueful smile slanted her mouth. "Jerry is my stepson," she admitted.

"Where's your husband? How come he sent you instead of coming himself?" the old man demanded.

"I lost my husband eight months ago, Mr. Carver. I'm a widow," Edie stated in a voice that invited no sympathy.

She wished she hadn't unbuttoned her parka even before he made his next remark. "Face like that, figure like that . . . you won't be a widow for long."

Somehow, Edie wasn't shocked. Mr. Carver was just a little too eccentric and too lonely to bother with conversational niceties, but there was no help for that. "I believe you are flattering me." She smiled it away.

"At my age I don't have to say things I don't mean. In fact, I can say a lot of things I do mean." His smile indicated that he derived tremendous pleasure from doing just that and shocking people in the process. Definitely an irascible old coot, Edie decided. "Pull up a chair and sit down. I'm getting a crick in my neck looking up at you," Anson Carver ordered.

The agent brought a straight chair over for Edie to sit on while Jerry got a chair for himself. It was too hot this close to the woodstove to leave her coat on, so Edie took it off and draped it on the chair back.

"So you came out here to look at my ranch," the older man declared in a gruff challenge. "What do you think of it?"

Edie took a breath, then told him, "Honestly?"

"Yeah."

"Mr. Carver, you've let it go to hell."

Her candor startled him. With a frown he grumbled, "The place got too big for me to handle alone. Either that or I got too old. I admit it needs fixing up here and there."

"Here and there?" She lifted an eyebrow. The heavily ribbed, biscuit-colored pullover she was wearing with her brown corduroy slacks gave Edie a very earthy and countryish look. "Your buildings are in need of repair. I doubt if there's a section of fence on the property that doesn't need to be replaced. And who knows what other things the snow is hiding? It's going to take a lot of labor and material to bring this place up to par."

"In other words you think I'm asking too much for the ranch?" he bristled.

"Yes, I do."

"I suppose your husband left you a bunch of money and you've decided to invest it in a cattle ranch." He sounded faintly contemptuous, but Edie had faced that attitude many times in the months since they'd made their decision. "Who's gonna run it for you?"

"Nobody's going to run it for us. We're going to do it ourselves," she said, nodding toward Jerry to include him.

"Do you think you can handle it?"

Edie shrugged. "We'll do a better job than you have lately."

"You're pretty frisky for such a slip of a gal. If push came to shove, you'd do some shoving yourself, wouldn't you?" He grinned unexpectedly. "What do you think this place is worth?"

Edie told him and added her terms. They haggled back and forth for several minutes. Every time the real-estate agent tried to make a relevant point, the old man told him to shut up. They went through a rapid series of compromises until the last difference in their two positions was settled.

"Lady, you drive a hard bargain, but you just bought yourself a ranch." The man extended his hand to shake on the deal. He sliced a piercing look at the agent. "Did you make a note of all the terms so we can draw up an agreement?"

"Yes, sir. I—"

"Fine. Start writing it up." Anson Carver was quick to dismiss him from the conversation. Now he was directing his attention to Jerry. "You look like you got a head on your shoulders, boy. Do you think you and your stepmomma can handle this place?"

"I do or I wouldn't be here," Jerry said with a smile. Not a big one, but it was a smile.

"Got any more like him?" Anson Carver shot the question at Edie.

"I have a daughter. She's looking after our place in Illinois while we're here."

He rested his head against the chair back for a moment. "I'm glad someone like you is buying the ranch. I didn't want to see it gobbled up into somebody else's holdings," he explained absently. "I've lived in this house seventy-two years. It's good to know that somebody will be living in it when I'm gone."

"Where will you go, Mr. Carver?" Edie asked.

He pursed his lips, puckering them as if there was a bad taste in his mouth. "I'm moving to my grand-daughter's in Deadwood. She's got a room all fixed up for me, she says."

"You'll always be welcome to stop by," Edie stated.

His gaze swung to her, a look of gleeful mischief in his eyes. "A widow and two kids," he chuckled. "I'd love to see his face when he finds out!"

"Whose face?" A frown flickered across her forehead.

"It's a private joke." He didn't explain. "You won't understand until after you've lived here for a while. At my age there are few pleasures left in life that I can enjoy. But to know that I'm the one to show the he-bull in these parts that he can't have everything the way he wants it gives me a lot of satisfaction. Mind you, it's nothing personal, but I'll have many a laugh over this once I'm safe in Deadwood."

"Does it have something to do with the ranch?" Edie persisted, puzzled by his answer and certain that he intended her to be.

"You aren't going to have any problems you can't handle," he assured her. "When do you want possession?"

Edie glanced at Jerry. There were a whole lot of things that had to be done in Illinois—put their house and acreage up for sale and pack. Plus there was all the legal paperwork involved in buying this place.

"The end of March? What do you think?" she asked.

"Sounds good to me." Jerry nodded. "Spring will be breaking. That gives us a little over two months."

"Would that suit you, Mr. Carver?" she asked.

"Fine. Make a note of that, Jenkins," he ordered. "While he's writing all this down, why don't you go in the kitchen, Mrs. Gibbs, and fix us some coffee? I would, but"—he thumped the plaster cast on his leg—"I don't get around too good." He pointed to a hallway behind him. "It's that way."

"I don't mind at all," Edie said, and rose from her chair. Anson Carver was a dinosaur, but he was a funny old dinosaur. And he'd agreed to a fair price for a place he'd lived for most of his life.

As she left the room she heard Jerry ask, "When we were walking around outside, I didn't see any sign of livestock. Don't you have any?"

"No. When I got laid up, I didn't have any way of looking after them. And I never could keep good help on the place. So I asked . . . my neighbor to round up anything that moved and sell it."

Edie couldn't help thinking it was comforting to know they would have the kind of neighbors who were willing to help out in time of need.

Everything seemed to fall into place after that. Within a month after they had listed their Illinois property for sale they had a buyer. All the legal paperwork for both the sale of their property and the purchase of the ranch was completed in two months. During the last week there was a string of farewell parties for them.

Edie was aware that many people thought she was being disrespectful to Joe's memory by selling the home where they had lived and moving away. But Joe had made this chance possible. She was convinced it would be a greater injustice to him if she didn't take it.

Happy was an inadequate description of the way she felt. She was excited, eager, looking forward to this new life and its challenges. It seemed like an adventure. She wanted to laugh aloud for no reason at all. Since she was alone in the cab of the rented U–haul truck, she did.

A series of signs were tacked to the row of fence posts along the highway. Edie read them with quick glances and reached for the mike of the CB radio temporarily mounted on the dash. It had been one of the going-away presents, and it was easier than using a cell phone, especially up this way, where the service wasn't too dependable.

"Breaker one-nine. This is Dakota Dreamer in the rocking chair, talking to Pony Girl up there at my front door." Sounding like a remake of *Smokey and the Bandit* was kind of fun. She could see Alison in the car ahead of the truck.

"You've got the Pony Girl. Come back," Alison responded.

"Did you read those signs we just passed? Come back."

"I must have missed them. What did they say this time?" her daughter asked.

"Quote unquote. 'You are entering God's country. Don't drive through it like hell,'" Edie told her.

"Yeah, so ease back on the hammer, Pony Girl," Jerry joined their radio conversation. "Your back door has a load of dog meat, in case you've forgotten. Slow it down." He was bringing up the rear of their small caravan in his pickup truck, pulling the horse trailer loaded with their horses and gear.

"My foot got heavy, Leatherneck. I'm easing it back," Alison replied.

"Hey, Pony Girl," Jerry called her back. "If you see a rest area, pull over. I want to check the horses."

"That's a ten-four," Alison agreed.

Then the radio went silent for a while in Edie's cab except for the chatter of other CBers some distance away. Her gaze strayed to the rolling landscape of the South Dakota prairie. Its flat appearance was deceptive as its grassy sod undulated toward the horizon. Trees, mostly cottonwoods, clustered wherever there was water. With a magic all its own, there was a timeless quality about this open expanse of land stretching endlessly into the beyond. Patches of snow could be seen in shadowed ditches, an indication that winter hadn't released its grip on the land.

After traveling almost a full hour, Edie saw the dark mass looming on the horizon. Her mouth barely curved as she recognized it, her pulse quickening in a surge of excitement. Again she reached for the CB mike to share her discovery with Alison and Jerry.

"Breaker one-nine. Come in, Pony Girl and Leatherneck. Do you see that on the horizon?" she asked.

"Where?" Alison came back. "You mean that mass of clouds? I hope we aren't in for a storm."

"Those aren't clouds," Jerry corrected. "That's the Black Hills. Now you know how they got their name."

"Hey, roadside tables just ahead. Looks like there's room for all of us to park," Alison informed them. Edie saw the turn signal blinking on the car ahead of her and flipped hers on.

When the rental van filled with their furniture and belongings was parked and the motor switched off, Edie grabbed her parka and the thermos of coffee from the passenger seat. Alison was already standing by the roadside picnic table, stretching and arching muscles cramped from long hours of driving. Yesterday they had started out at daybreak and continued till dark, crossing from Iowa into Nebraska. Now the Black Hills dominated the horizon, rising above the prairie. The pine-covered slopes gave the deceptive impression of darkness that had earned the landscape its name. Their ranch, their new home, was on the western edge of this sacred Indian land within the national forest.

"We don't have far to go now," Edie declared as she joined Alison by the picnic table. A cold wind tried to slide its icy fingers inside the collar of her jacket, but Edie fastened the top button to keep it out.

"Mmm, coffee." Alison took one of the cups and held it while Edie filled it half-full. "I wish I could have gone with you guys to see the ranch."

"Don't expect a picture postcard," Edie cautioned. "The place is rundown and needs a lot of work to put it in shape."

"I hope there's enough coffee there for me." Jerry paused beside her, wearing an insulated vest over his plaid flannel shirt, but otherwise coatless. He rubbed his hands together to warm them as Edie poured him a half of a cup of coffee, too. "The ranch may not look like much, but we know for sure it isn't worthless," he said, picking up the conversation where Edie had left off.

"What?" At first Edie didn't follow his meaning. Then she remembered with a nod of her head. "You mean that offer."

"Yes." He sipped at the hot coffee. "We could have sold the place for a handsome profit even before we'd signed the final papers to buy it."

"Did you say profit? Maybe we should have," Alison suggested.

"Where would we have gone?" Edie reasoned. "Our place was already sold. We had to move. Who knows how long it might've taken to find another ranch that was right for us? Can you imagine how much we'd have to pay to board our horses?"

"I suppose you're right," her daughter conceded.

Edie knew why Alison was having doubts. The answer was simple—Craig Gurney. He had managed to turn up at every farewell party given for them. It was to Alison's credit that she had treated him coolly in the beginning, but Craig's persistence had her weakening toward the end.

"Speaking of horses"—Jerry paused to drain the last of the coffee from his cup and hand it back to Edie—"I'd better check on them."

Edie watched him for a second, then turned, a light of anticipation in her eyes. Tomorrow they would be riding the horses on their very own ranch, exploring the property. Her mouth opened to share the thought with Alison until she saw the wistful, faraway look in her daughter's eyes as she looked back at the road they had traveled.

"Are you sorry we left, Alison?" Edie asked gently.

It was a full second before Alison blinked and let her gaze refocus. "I . . ." she began uncertainly, then finished with a sighing, "No."

Masking her relief, Edie offered, "More coffee? There's only a little bit left in the thermos."

Alison held out her cup in silent acceptance. "Mom, were you, uh, experienced when you married Dad?" she asked thoughtfully.

Craig Gurney had to be responsible for that question, Edie thought as she replied, "No."

"What I meant was . . . were you a virgin?"

"Oh. Yes, I was."

"You didn't . . . anticipate your wedding or anything like that, did you?" Alison persisted.

"No." A smile twitched at the corners of Edie's mouth. Her daughter's polite euphemisms were pretty funny in this day and age. But asking your mother a question like that couldn't be easy. "But it isn't easy to anticipate anything when you have a five-year-old boy along to chaperone on all your dates."

While taking a sip of coffee, Alison was overcome by a laugh. She choked and sputtered, and coughed out the laugh. "I'm sorry." Her eyes were brimming with tears and shining with laughter. "But for a second I was trying to visualize Dad sweeping you off your feet. And he just wasn't the type," she declared. "I can't see Dad ever tempting any woman into a sinful situation."

"Well, no," Edie agreed, smiling with her daughter, knowing Alison wasn't criticizing Joe. "He was pretty old-fashioned about stuff like that. I thought he was sweet. I really liked him."

"Well, yeah. And Dad was good-looking in his own way," Alison recalled. "But he was never an exciting kind of man. I don't mean he was dull. I used to get so exasperated with him when he'd forget your birthday that I wanted to bat him over the head. One time I told him that instead of kissing you on the cheek when he came home, he should take you in his arms and do it properly. Of course, he didn't take my advice," she sighed in a gentle way to indicate it hadn't mattered.

"Joe wasn't very demonstrative, but he was a good man—the best." There was a tiny catch in Edie's voice. While her late husband hadn't been a passionate man, he had made her feel good—needed, wanted and loved.

"You miss him, too, don't you, Mom?" Alison said softly.

"Yes. It isn't so bad during the day because he was usually at work. In the evenings he was usually in his workshop. But when I wake up in the night and he isn't there to cuddle up to, that's when I really miss him," Edie admitted, looking away.

"Do you think you'll get married again, Mom?"

The question jerked her chin up. After a startled second had passed, Edie took a deep breath and answered. "Your father hasn't even been dead a year. I'm certainly not looking for a replacement."

"But if you meet someone," Alison persisted.

"If I met a man that I thought I could love and who could love me, I would consider it." What else could she say? She saw no point in pretending that it might not happen. Her life certainly was far from over.

"They say that every man makes love differently, that just because you've been to bed with one man doesn't mean the feeling will be the same with the next. It has to do with the chemistry, I guess," Alison said vaguely.

"*They* say that, do they?" Edie mocked, amused

by her daughter's voice-of-experience air. "I'm afraid I wouldn't know about that."

"Oh, Mom!" Alison blushed and laughed.

Edie joined in. "I hope you don't object if I don't bother to check *their* theory to see if it's true or not."

"I'll disown you if you do." Alison continued to laugh.

"Hey! Come on, you two!" Jerry shouted from his truck. "Let's get on the road. We still have a ways to go and a lot of unloading to do before nightfall."

"We'll be right there!" Alison called back, and handed the plastic coffee cup to Edie. "I think he's trying to tell us to hurry up," she grinned.

"You could be right." Edie stacked the cups inside one another and screwed them onto the thermos.

Jerry was in his truck with the motor running by the time Edie crawled into the cab of the rental van. She warmed up the engine and waited until Alison had pulled onto the highway before falling in behind the car. Jerry was right. They did have many more miles to go, and the last stretch would be on gravel roads.

Chapter Three

Stopped in the ranch yard, the three of them were slow to step out of their individual vehicles. When they did, they gravitated toward each other, unconsciously solidifying into a united front.

"It looks worse, doesn't it?" Edie murmured.

Without the pristine whiteness of snow cover, the ramshackle condition of the ranch stood out against the stark background of brown grass and craggy hills. The buildings were weathered and gray, the patchwork repairs telling their own tales of shoddy workmanship. The corral behind the barn looked incapable of holding a newborn calf. The house had four different colors of shingles on its roof.

"This is it?" Alison's skeptical expression revealed her opinion.

"I warned you that it needed work," Edie reminded her.

"I thought you meant a face-lift, not major surgery," she replied with faint disgust.

"The first thing we have to do is fix that corral, so we'll have somewhere to unload the horses," Jerry said with his usual practicality.

Glancing at the sun dipping toward the western horizon, Edie added, "We'd better all help if we want it done before dark."

They practically rebuilt the corral before they were finished—replacing this post, bracing another, ripping out rotting boards and tearing barn stalls apart for replacement boards. When they were finished it was almost twilight. The end result didn't look any more attractive than the previous corral, but they knew it was sturdy.

The temperature was dropping with the setting of the sun. Although the hard labor had all three of them perspiring, Edie felt the clammy chill setting in. Jerry was maneuvering the horse trailer into position to unload with instructions from Alison. Edie glanced toward the bleak exterior of the house and the soot-blackened chimney on its roof.

"You two unload the horses. I'll see what I can do about getting a fire started in the house," she said, and received an acknowledging wave from Jerry.

Without the clutter of Anson Carver's worn furniture, the interior of the house was more depressing than the exterior. The cold, dreary emptiness of the rooms was not welcoming. To make matters worse, when Edie flipped the light switch to chase away the gathering shadows, nothing happened. It was the same with every light switch in the house, which meant they had no electricity. And it was too late to call the power company.

Sighing, Edie walked back outside to the rental van for the battery-operated flashlight. Somewhere, packed neatly away in boxes, there were candles and a hurricane lamp. With her luck, Edie was positive they would be in the last box she searched.

The beam of the flashlight gave off enough illumination for her to check the woodstove to be certain the damper was open before she lighted it. When the fire was blazing strongly, she left the living room to check out the rest of the house. What she found made her spirits sink even lower. Cobwebs, dust and dirt coated everything. So much for her new beginning on her dream ranch. Her mouth twisted in irony.

The front door opened and she heard the sounds of different footsteps, heavy and light, echo in the house. "I'm starving," Alison said. The comment was followed immediately by, "Mom? What's the matter with the lights?"

She stepped into the hallway to flash the beam toward them. "We don't have any electricity. There must have been a mix-up."

"Oh, please!" her daughter exclaimed in disgust. "Now we'll have to stumble around in the dark to unload everything. What about something to eat?"

"There's cold cuts and bread. And peanut butter. We won't starve," Edie said briskly.

"Want me to bring in the cooler and groceries from the truck?" Jerry asked.

"Yes, and all the cleaning supplies, too," she added.

As Alison walked down the hallway illuminated by the flashlight beam, she ran into a cobweb.

"Ugh!" She wiped it off her face with an expressive grimace of distaste. "This place is filthy!"

"I noticed," Edie said dryly. "I'm afraid all we're going to accomplish tonight is scrubbing out the bedrooms so we'll have a place to sleep."

It was nearly midnight before all three bedrooms were cleaned, the bedroom furniture unloaded from the van and the beds made. Alison unearthed the candles and kerosene lantern, which helped. They were not only without electricity, but also without hot water. None of them relished a cold shower no matter how dirty they were, so Edie warmed a pail of water on the woodstove. They washed the worst of the dirt off and tumbled into their beds, too exhausted to care.

The next morning they unloaded the rest of the furniture from the van. Edie left Alison and Jerry at the ranch to finish cleaning the house and arranging their belongings while she drove the rented truck into town to return it and find out what the problem was with the electricity. She expected to be finished by noon and made arrangements with Jerry to pick her up at the grocery store.

It was almost three o'clock before she met him. What groceries they needed he had already bought and stacked in the front seat of the cab.

"I was beginning to wonder what had happened to you." Jerry took one look at her seething expression and tried to hide a grin. "I don't think I'll ask what kept you."

"I've been getting the royal runaround," she snapped, and crawled into the cab of his truck, pushing the grocery sacks out of her way and still fuming. "I kept getting shoved from one person at the power company to another. First they tried to tell me that we hadn't requested service."

"Did you show them a copy of the letter we sent?" Jerry started the motor and reversed away from the curb into the street.

"Yes." Edie glared out the window at the boardwalks shaded by jutting overhangs of western-styled buildings. "Then they tried to tell me we hadn't made a deposit. Don't think I've ever met such incredibly ignorant and uncooperative people in my life."

"I guess you got it straightened out. You're not the kind to give up easily."

"No, I'm not. We're supposed to have the electricity connected late this afternoon." She leaned back in her seat, rubbing her forehead where it was pounding. "I treated myself to a manicure just to get my hands clean." She waved her polished fingernails under his nose. "What do you think? Beautiful, huh?"

"Wow." He grinned. "What do they call that color?"

"Ruby Red Temptation, if you really want to know."

"Just right for ranch work. What about the rest of you? Are we going to have hot water?" Jerry teased.

"They'd better have it turned on. I want a shower tonight." She closed her eyes and tried to will away the angry tension. "Meanwhile, back at the ranch . . . how's everything going?"

"Okay. I left Alison cleaning the kitchen and swearing a blue streak," he answered.

Edie opened her eyes and gave him a weary look. "I hope she has it finished before we get back so we don't have to help."

"Right!" Jerry tipped his head back to laugh in hearty agreement. "I don't want dishpan hands."

Edie closed her eyes again and let the rhythm of the rolling wheels on the pavement soothe her into relaxing. When Jerry made the turn onto the gravel road, she opened them to study the scenery racing by the pickup window. Tall ponderosa pines hugged the edges of the road to form a green corridor. Here and there they thinned out to make a meadow of yellow grass. The winding gravel road alternated between sun and shadow. Beyond the pine branches there were glimpses of high mountains, granite rock interlacing with trees. A valley opened up, grassy and serene.

"Even with all the unexpected problems, I'm glad we're here," Edie murmured.

"So am I. None of us thought it was going to be easy. But we know all about work." Jerry slid her a smile. "We've never been afraid of it, and there's more reason than ever not to be now."

"That's true." She laughed softly. They had a ranch to build and a future to think about.

"Tomorrow we'll have to ride the perimeters and check the fences."

For the rest of the drive they talked of the things that needed to be done to prepare for the purchase of stock cattle as well as some yearling calves for fall sale. When they arrived at the ranch, Alison met them at the door, demanding to know where they had been. Edie and Jerry exchanged a silent look of amusement. They knew Alison was in an evil mood because she had been left to finish the cleaning alone, and they knew how much she detested housework. As Edie was relating her tale of battle with the power company, the lights came on. Alison forgot her bad mood to join in the cheers for Edie's triumph over the utility company's screwup.

With the house in a semblance of order and as clean as the dingy place could ever be, the three went out to briefly exercise the horses, then brushed them down and grained them for the night. At six-thirty they sat down for the first home-cooked meal they'd had in three days.

"Did you hear a car door slam?" Alison asked, and cocked her head to listen before helping herself to a second portion of macaroni and cheese.

"If you turned that radio down a notch, we might be able to hear ourselves think," Jerry suggested dryly.

"It isn't that loud," she protested, but reached behind her to turn down the volume of the radio on the kitchen counter.

Instantly there was a loud knock at the front door. Edie frowned in surprise and started to get up. "Who could that be?"

"I'll get it." Jerry waved her into her seat. "It's probably that real-estate agent checking to see how we've settled in. Wasn't his name Jenkins?"

"I think so," Edie agreed as he left the room. The lights flickered overhead, and her mouth thinned into an angry line. "Or maybe it's somebody with the utility company. If I have to raise hell, I will."

She emerged from the kitchen as Jerry opened

the front door. Edie could tell by the reserved tone of his greeting that her stepson didn't know the person calling.

A pleasantly deep male voice responded, "Good evening. I'd like to speak with Mrs. Gibbs if she's free."

There was an impersonal quality to the request, yet it carried the crispness of authority. Edie noticed the way Jerry unconsciously squared his shoulders and stood a little straighter, as if he was facing a commanding officer.

"If you'll step inside, I'll call her." Jerry swung the door wide to admit the man. As he pivoted, he saw her in the hall. "Edie, there's a man here to see you."

Curious, she moved forward. The man was tall, over six feet. She knew that because he had to remove his hat and duck his head to walk through the front door. He was wearing a beat-up-in-all-the-right-places leather jacket that emphasized the breadth of his shoulders and his narrow hips. Western-cut jeans flared slightly over his boots.

Her first impression of the stranger reminded her of a range bull, all leashed power and raw virility very clear in the way he carried himself. She tried to remember what she knew about them as she looked at him. Proud ... rugged ... dangerous when riled and implacable in the face of danger. Even the most powerful predators would veer away from a range bull.

And Edie found herself treading warily in his presence. When her gaze skimmed his rough-hewn features, there was nothing in the thrusting power of his jaw and chin, the slightly crooked bend of his nose or the firmly cut line of his mouth to change her initial impression. The flecks of iron in his shaggy dark brown hair were a sign not of encroaching weakness, but of maturity, of a man in his prime. Or maybe her opinion had been influenced by the hardness of the iron gray eyes that took note of her approach.

Her smile was pleasant enough when she stopped in front of him. It was only natural, Edie supposed, to feel intimidated by his size. She also understood why Jerry had felt the impulse to snap to attention, but she suppressed it. Here she was the one in charge. The fact remained that although this stranger was standing in her living room with his hat in his hand, there was nothing humble about him.

"I'm Edie Gibbs," she confirmed her identity. "You wanted to see me?"

The mocking glint that flashed in his eyes gave Edie the impression that he wasn't impressed by her in the least. His gaze started at the top of her head and slowly worked its way down.

First Edie realized that she hadn't combed her hair since coming into the house from exercising and caring for the horses. The soft, curling length of her golden brown hair was undoubtedly wind-blown and tousled. His inspection of her face made her conscious that she wore no makeup; even her lipstick had worn off at the supper table. It took every ounce of willpower not to moisten her lips when he studied their contours.

His silent appraisal continued its downward progress, reminding her of the boy's flannel shirt she wore, a size too small. In consequence the plaid material was stretched tautly across the rounded fullness of her breasts, the buttoned front gaping slightly.

Oh, hell. She stood a little straighter. A man like this knew what was underneath a woman's clothes. Yet that thought didn't make her feel any less uncomfortable.

Then his gaze was skimming her faded denims, hugging tightly to her hips and shapely thighs before running stovepipe straight to her boots. He even took note of the scuffed and weathered toes, permanently stained with mud and manure.

When his metallic gaze returned to her face, the tour of inspection hadn't taken more than twenty seconds, but it had seemed like an eternity to Edie. Should she tell him that she hadn't been expecting visitors? Why bother? He should have expected to find her still in work clothes from doing ranch chores. Edie held her tongue. She wasn't about to defend the way she dressed in her own home—not to a complete stranger.

"*You're* the widow?" The inflection in his husky voice smoothly demanded verification.

It had been an exasperating day. Her irritation raced through nerve ends that had only begun to recover. His casual question set her teeth on edge. Admittedly she was on the wrong side of thirty, but it didn't mean she had to be dumpy and plain, or clad in black with smelling salts at hand.

"Yes, I am." The faint note of belligerence in her answer didn't appear to register in his expression. She lifted her chin to an angle of controlled challenge as her smile lost its warmth. "You have the advantage. You know who I am, but I don't know who you are."

"Will Maddock." He didn't extend his hand in greeting. "I own the Diamond D Ranch."

Edie guessed she was supposed to be impressed, but since she had never heard of it—or him—she simply filed the information away in her mind.

"The Diamond D?" Jerry spoke up. He had been standing to one side. "I saw that brand on some cattle on my way into town this noon. They were in a pasture next to our property."

At the sound of Jerry's voice, Will Maddock had turned his head to subject her stepson to his appraisal. He measured Jerry with a practiced eye, noting his lanky but solidly muscled frame and the shadow of a man's beard on his cheek, not the peach fuzz of a boy.

"You own the land next to ours?" Jerry questioned.

"Yes." It was a simple, straightforward answer.

"Then you're our neighbor," Edie said.

The iron-hard gaze swung lazily back to her. "Yes."

She stifled the resentment that she had begun to form against him. Will Maddock was obviously calling to welcome them to the area, a gesture of polite friendliness that shouldn't be brushed off just because she'd had a bad day. Possibly Will Maddock was the same neighbor who had rounded up and sold Anson Carver's livestock when the old man was laid up. He struck her as the kind of man you'd want on your side if you were in trouble. She definitely wouldn't want him as an enemy.

"Pleasure to meet you, Mr. Maddock." She extended her hand in belated greeting.

He glanced at her, hesitated, then accepted the gesture. When his work-roughened hand closed around hers, Edie experienced a tremor of surprise. She had always thought Joe's hands were large, but her hand felt like a child's against Will Maddock's. It was such a strong, capable hand, and it didn't need to assert its strength by crushing her fingers. There was the firm warmth of its clasp; then her hand was released. A little overwhelmed by the discovery, Edie didn't notice that Will Maddock hadn't said he was pleased to meet her.

Instead she turned to introduce Jerry and caught sight of Alison, who had slipped unnoticed into the room. "This is my stepson, Jerry Gibbs, and my daughter, Alison. Mr. Will Maddock."

Jerry stepped forward to shake hands with him, but Alison simply smiled and nodded from across the room. It was part of her natural reserve when meeting strangers, not caused by shyness.

Remembering her manners, Edie spoke for them all. "Won't you sit down, Mr. Maddock? Let me take your coat."

He accepted the invitation to have a seat but refused the second suggestion. "No, I won't be staying long."

He did unbutton the leather jacket to let it swing open before sitting in the armchair that had always been Joe's favorite. But Edie never remembered Joe ever filling it the way this man did. In fact, it took on the appearance of a throne. Again Edie felt a little flicker of resentment that she had to suppress.

"We just finished supper. We were about to have some coffee when you arrived." She told the white lie out of a sense of courtesy. "Care for a cup?"

"No." His iron-flat gaze made a pointed glance toward Jerry and Alison. "I'd like to speak to you in private, if I may."

The skin along the back of her neck prickled, irritated by the polite phrasing. His whole attitude left Edie with the feeling that he belonged here and they didn't. And worse, that he was used to giving orders and expected them to be obeyed as a matter of course.

"What about?" She sat down on the flowered sofa and leaned against the cushions to indicate that she wasn't intimidated. And, just in case he cared, that she was the one in charge around here.

"This ranch."

"Really? Well, this is a family holding, Mr. Maddock," Edie informed him. "Alison and Jerry are directly involved in all phases of it. There's no need for them to leave. In fact, since it's the ranch you want to talk about, they definitely should stay."

Briefly she wondered what he wanted to talk about. There had been no mention of a boundary dispute. Perhaps he was going to complain about something.

"A few weeks ago I made you an offer for this ranch," he began.

"That was you?" she asked and sat up straighter. "We did receive an offer on the property, but we didn't bother to inquire who made it since we weren't interested in selling it."

"The real-estate agent told me you turned it down, even though it meant a quick and handsome profit," Maddock admitted. "I'm here to raise my offer by fifty dollars an acre."

Edie raised an eyebrow in surprise, then glanced at Jerry and Alison, who were exchanging a glance of astonishment. "That's a generous offer, Mr. Maddock, but we're not interested in selling it."

Impatience hardened his features. "Let's not waste time, Mrs. Gibbs. Just tell me how much you want."

If she'd felt the slightest temptation to consider his offer before, she didn't now. "I told you, we aren't interested in selling."

"Everyone has a price," he replied bluntly. "You can use the money to buy a ranch somewhere else—one that isn't as rundown as this one."

"Maybe so. But you seem to want it very badly," she murmured. "Why is that?"

"It joins my land," he said as if that was reason enough.

"Do you plan to own every ranch that joins your land, Mr. Maddock? That would take longer than a lifetime," she taunted.

His hard gray eyes turned to cold steel. "It took years of neglect and abuse to let this place get in its present condition. I don't intend to stand idly by and let it go from bad to worse while a trio of greenhorns amuse themselves by playing cowboy."

Incensed by his swift condemnation—after all,

he knew nothing about whether they could run a ranch or not—Edie rose from the sofa. When Will Maddock stood up to face her, she felt like a banty hen tackling a silver-tipped grizzly.

"Is that right? You haven't even bothered to ask about our qualifications or experience, although it isn't any of your business." She was controlling her temper with an effort, speaking sharply and concisely.

"I know how much work it's going to take to whip this place into shape again."

"We aren't allergic to work. Guess what. We've done it all our lives," Edie said indignantly as Jerry and Alison moved over to stand beside her, uniting again.

"You're talking about backbreaking hours of hard, physical labor. I don't doubt the boy will do his share, or try. But two females?" His gaze flicked over them dismissively.

"Don't underestimate us," Edie insisted tightly. She raised a hand to push her hair back from her face, a sure sign she was angry. Her stepson noticed the gesture and moved closer to her. Will Maddock noticed it, too. Ruby red fingernails and all.

"Nice manicure, Mrs. Gibbs," he told her. "But that polish will chip off soon enough. Ranching isn't gardening, you know. You'll be too exhausted to eat and too tired to sleep. And that's just the beginning."

"We aren't made of glass."

"You'll find out." There was a hard sureness in his voice.

"Don't be too sure, Mr. Maddock," Edie replied,

and refrained from jamming her hands in her pockets, not wanting to show any weakness in front of him.

An expressionless smile slanted his mouth. "I'm sure of one thing, Mrs. Gibbs—one way or another you're gonna sell to me before the year is out."

"That sounds like a threat." She tipped her head back to challenge the man towering in front of her.

"I don't waste time with threats. You aren't hurting anyone but yourself by being stubborn, Mrs. Gibbs." He put his hat on and pulled it low on his forehead. "Let me know what you want for the ranch when you're ready to sell."

He started toward the door. After a second Edie followed him. "It's a pity that you didn't buy the place from Mr. Carver since you want it so much."

Pausing with his hand on the doorknob, he gave her a sidelong look that was shadowed by the brim of his hat. "I was out of the states when he put it on the market; otherwise you wouldn't be here."

He left without saying anything more. At the sound of an engine starting up, Edie's knees began shaking. She hadn't realized how emotionally tense she had been.

"What a psycho!" Alison declared. "Sell me your ranch or I'll shoot your dog. Is everybody around here like that?"

"No. Of course not. We don't have a dog and he didn't say that," Edie said distractedly. "Anyway, we aren't selling. Not to him. Not to anyone."

"That's who Anson Carver was talking about," Jerry mused, staring thoughtfully in the direction of the car.

"When?" Edie demanded.

"When he said the 'he-bull' wasn't going to get what he wanted," he answered with a faint smile deepening the corners of his mouth. "I'll bet you Maddock tried to buy this place from Carver half a dozen times and Carver wouldn't sell."

"Why wouldn't he sell?" Alison frowned. "Obviously our friendly neighbor would have paid more money for the ranch. Look what he's offered us!"

"I don't know. Carver mentioned a couple of things," Jerry remembered. "He didn't want the ranch gobbled up in a bigger one, which Maddock's obviously is. And he was glad we were going to be living in this house. Maddock would probably have torn it down or abandoned it."

"You could be right," Edie murmured. The old man had been cantankerous and stubborn. She doubted that he'd sold the ranch because he needed the money, so his decision to sell to them might not have been dictated by price.

"This house is a dump and an eyesore. I don't blame Maddock if he wanted to tear it down. I wish we could," Alison muttered.

"We can fix it up," Edie sighed, because she couldn't agree with her daughter more. "But we have a lot of work ahead of us. Maddock was right about that," she finished on a bitter note.

"You've had a rough day, Edie. Why don't you go take a shower and relax?" Jerry suggested.

"What about me?" Alison protested. "I'm turning into a prairie Cinderella. This place totally sucks."

"Turn the radio on and prop your feet up. I'll

do the dishes," Jerry volunteered. "Maybe your mom'll give you a manicure. Got any nail polish, Edie?"

"Nah. They made me surrender it at the state line. Womenfolk in South Dakota ain't allowed no fripperies and foolishness. And they ain't allowed to talk back to the men neither."

Her remark got a laugh from Jerry and Alison, and helped dispel the tension of Maddock's unexpected visit.

"You're more than a match for him, Mom," Alison said. Jerry nodded his agreement.

Chapter Four

The next morning they were up with the sun. After packing sandwiches for lunch and a thermos of coffee, the three saddled up their horses and rode out to inspect the property and its boundaries.

The tour around the perimeter of their ranch took the biggest share of the day. They made two discoveries, one of which Edie had already suspected. There wasn't a section of fence line that didn't need to be repaired or replaced.

It was the second discovery that came as a surprise. Their ranch was bounded on three sides by Diamond D land, something Edie had noticed when she'd looked at the map of the property. But the lay of the land made it seem like Maddock's ranch practically surrounded theirs. There was a stark contrast between his neat, precise fencerows running at right angles to the drooping and tumbledown excuse of their fences. Their meadows abounded with thistles while his were thick with nutritious grasses.

The differences didn't need to be pointed out. But it was clear that Will Maddock had cause to regard Anson Carter's ranch as an affront to his own. There was more work to be done than they had imagined.

That night it was decided that Jerry would go into town the next morning and order the barbed wire and new fence posts while Edie and Alison explored the interior of the ranch property. They needed to learn where the best grazing lands and their water sources were.

No matter how much riding Edie had done in the past, none of it had prepared her bones and muscles for an entire day and part of a second in the saddle. By midday she was so stiff and sore she wanted to cry. And she knew that Alison, a much more experienced rider, was suffering, too.

The Dakota hills bore no resemblance to the Illinois landscape where they had ridden before. Here there were deep ravines to be descended and climbed, the horses plunging and rearing to claw their way up, rocky slopes to be negotiated, the horses' iron shoes slipping and stumbling over stones and clear, cold streams to be crossed, the horses splashing the icy water onto their legs. Seldom was there time to admire the view. Daydreaming was usually punished by a low-hanging limb that the unwary rider didn't see in time to duck.

One such branch came damn close to decapitating Edie. "Damn!" she swore under her breath as her hat was knocked off.

"Are you playing at cowboy?" Alison teased and leaned way over to pick up the hat without dismounting from the black mare.

"If you want me to laugh, don't repeat what Maddock said" Edie retorted with a weary grin.

"I'll remember that," Alison laughed, and returned her mother's hat. They had ridden almost to the crest of a ridge. Alison reined her mare in a half circle to traverse the last few yards. "Mom, look!" She pointed toward the valley below. "There's cattle down there. Do you see them?"

When they rode down to investigate they discovered a dozen head of Hereford cattle grazing in the tall grass of a meadow. The Diamond D brand was burned on their rusty red hips.

"What do you suppose they're doing here?" Alison asked.

"Eating our grass," Edie retorted and sighed. "They probably wandered through a break in the fence. We'd better drive them back."

"Our first cattle drive . . . and it's somebody else's cattle." Alison sent her a laughing glance. "Too bad Jerry isn't here. We could outnumber them."

Herding the cattle back to the boundary fence was a welcome change of pace. After an initial reluctance to leave the lush grass of the meadow, the cattle allowed themselves to be driven back to their home range. There were so many breaks in the fence Edie couldn't guess which one they had come through, so it didn't matter which one they went back through. On the other side they urged the cattle into a trot to chase them away from the fence, then turned and rode back the way they had come.

"Uh-oh," Alison murmured. "Looks like we're about to be caught trespassing."

Edie looked beyond her daughter to see two riders approaching them. Will Maddock was one of them. No one could fail to recognize that muscular frame mounted on a rangy, mouse-gray buckskin. The second rider was a girl, a wand-slim rider on a spirited sorrel with a blaze and four white stockings. Edie refused to hurry her bay gelding to reach their own land before Maddock intercepted them. They had a perfectly legitimate reason for trespassing on his property. A few yards short of the fence the four riders reined their horses in.

"Hello, Maddock," Edie greeted him coolly.

He acknowledged her with a slight nod, nothing more. There was nothing in his steady regard that ought to make her so aware of her unflattering old clothes, Edie thought uncomfortably. He was just so damned male that she was a little too conscious of how she looked, that was all.

Her gaze broke away from his to study the girl on the prancing, restless sorrel. She looked to be the same age as Alison, but considerably more self-possessed. Hatless, she had a thick mane of brunette hair, long and curling, and her eyes were an arrogant blue.

"This is my daughter, Felicia. Mrs. Gibbs and her daughter, Alison," Will Maddock said simply.

"Hello, Felicia." Edie acknowledged the introduction and Alison echoed it. Like her father, Felicia Maddock only nodded in response. Edie doubted if she was wrong to suspect that his daughter was a spoiled snob.

"Some of your cattle strayed onto our property. We herded them back," Edie explained.

"What can you expect? There isn't anything to stop them," Maddock replied in a dry dismissal of the effectiveness of the dividing fence.

"I'm aware of that," Edie countered stiffly.

"Good. Because it's your fence and your problem." He was stating facts that she couldn't argue with and pointing out where the responsibility rested.

But his calmness was somehow infuriating. "It'll be fixed." She was rigid.

"Let's go, Dad," his daughter urged with undisguised boredom. "You promised we would go swimming when we got back," she reminded him, and threw Alison a lofty look. "We have a heated pool."

Will Maddock's response was to tighten the grip on the reins. The big, blue gray buckskin he was riding showed how well-trained it was by backing up in double-quick time and stopping the second the pressure on the bit was eased.

"You're looking tired after only two days, Mrs. Gibbs," he observed. "You should get some rest." His gloved hand touched the brim of his hat in a farewell gesture before he glanced at his daughter and reined his mount away.

As cantering hooves drummed the ground to sound their departure, Edie dug a heel in the bay's side to ride it through the gap in the fence. She was so choked with anger she couldn't speak. Once on their land they both turned their horses toward the distant ranch yard as if it had been previously agreed.

"Will you promise to go swimming with me when we get back, mother dear?" Alison asked in a pseudo-cultured voice. "We have a heated pool." It was a deliberate and acid mockery of Felicia Maddock.

"Didn't you notice? I'm tired. I need my rest," Edie countered bitterly. She caught the glinting light in Alison's eye and laughed but unwillingly.

There was no sign of Jerry when they arrived at the ranch. They rubbed their horses down and grained all the stock. As they started toward the house, Jerry drove into the yard in his pickup.

"The next time someone has to go to town, it's going to be me," Alison stated. "It always turns into an all-day affair."

"Did you order the fencing?" Edie ignored her daughter's remark. They both knew that Jerry hadn't been loafing all day.

"I ordered it, all right." He fell into step beside them. The grimness of his expression was echoed in his voice.

"What happened?" Edie had a feeling there was more to that statement.

"I had to pay cash before they would even order it," he explained.

"What?" She stopped, stunned by his announcement.

"Same at the feed store, too, when I stopped to buy grain for the horses."

"Why? Didn't you open an account for us?" Edie demanded.

"I tried," he admitted, "but it seems we don't

have any credit established in this area, and the Visa card I had in my wallet was maxed out."

"Oh, hell. I should have known. We put the truck rental on it and all the gas."

"Whatever. It was embarrassing when they ran it at both places and it came up declined. So we either pay on the line or we don't get it. The lumber company did say that if we stayed here a year they would reconsider our application to open an account with them."

"*If* we stayed!" Edie repeated in anger.

"That's what they said." There was a wry twist to his mouth. "The word is out—no credit. It's going to be the same with every supplier."

"With what we have in the bank? Give me a break! But I can guess who put the word out," she muttered under her breath.

"Will Maddock," Alison supplied the name.

"He must have been laughing up his sleeve today." Edie jerked the front door open and stalked into the house.

"Today? Did you see him today?" Jerry held the door for Alison, then followed them both inside.

"Yes." Alison explained about finding the cattle and running into Maddock and his daughter when they herded them back to Diamond D land. "If his wife is anything like his daughter, she must be a real pain," she concluded.

"She's dead," Jerry informed them.

"How do you know that?" Edie glanced at him with some surprise.

"I heard somebody mention it—at the feed store, I think. Anyway, I had the impression he lost his wife some time ago." He shrugged.

Edie told herself she wasn't interested in Will Maddock's personal life. It had nothing to do with them. Their problems were more immediate.

"When will the fencing arrive?" she asked to change the subject.

"Part of it will be delivered tomorrow. The rest is being shipped in," Jerry replied.

The truck with the posts and wire came early the next morning. They elected to first replace the fence near the barns so they would have a place to turn the horses loose to graze. It was hard, monotonous labor—pulling out the old, rotten posts, putting in new ones and stringing the barbed wire. Jerry did the phases that called for brute strength, but all three of them were staggering with fatigue at the end of each day.

When the area near the barn was enclosed, they turned their efforts to the west property line where Diamond D cattle were wandering onto their land. Fortunately, the good weather held, turning springlike with pleasantly warm afternoons.

As the sun and work made her break a sweat, Edie removed her jacket and tossed it inside the cab of the pickup. Alison was farther up the fence row astride the buckskin gelding, roping the old fence posts, taking a dally around the saddle horn to pull them out of the ground and drag them back to the pickup to be returned to the house for firewood. She kept ahead of Jerry, who was setting new posts, and at the same time chased the curious cattle away from the fence line, herding any out that wandered in. It was Edie's task to string the barbed wire and nail it to the new posts. Dipping a gloved hand into a sack in the back end of the pickup, she scraped the bottom to come up with a handful of metal staples and slipped them into the pocket of the carpenter's apron around her waist.

"We're out of staples, Jerry!" she called in a tired voice.

Shirtless, Jerry's tough, sinewy back muscles glistened with sweat and dust that turned into rivulets of mud to streak his skin. He finished tamping a new post, paused to remove his hat and wipe his forehead with the back of his arm. With long, tired strides he started back toward the truck, stopping to take the shirt he had draped over the previous fence post. "I only have a half dozen posts left. I'll go back to the house for another load," he told Edie. "And staples for you. Have Alison help you."

"She's busy," Edie replied after a brief glance that saw her daughter spurring the buckskin toward some young steers racing with tails high through the downed fence line and toward a distant stand of branch-bare cottonwoods. "I'll manage."

With the slamming of the truck door, Edie picked up the trailing strand of the top wire. Even with the protection of leather gloves, she was careful to grip only the wire and avoid the pointed barbs spaced along the wire. Unwinding a long section from the reel, she strung it past one post and onto the second. There she tacked it to the far post and went back to stretch it tight to the first and hammer the staple to wood, holding it in place.

The pickup was bouncing over the uneven ground, disappearing in the direction of the ranch yard, when Edie remembered she had left the wire cutters in the pocket of her jacket. Shrugging, she decided she wouldn't need them before Jerry returned. With the top wire in place on the next pole, she strung the second and third strands, then went back to the top to repeat the procedure.

Her muscles hadn't quit aching for days. But Edie had learned to block out the discomfort and focus her concentration on the task. As she tacked the top wire to a second post, there was a prickling sensation of danger along the back of her neck. When she turned to walk to the middle post to stretch the wire taut, she saw Will Maddock sitting astride a big gray buckskin, relaxed in the saddle and watching her. Edie faltered for a second in midstride, her pulse leaping in alarm that she hadn't heard him approach. Aware that his presence had been noticed, Maddock still didn't offer a greeting. Pressing her lips together, Edie decided if he could be rude, so could she, and she continued to the second post.

"That isn't the way it's done," he criticized with drawling indifference. "That wire can pull loose from the far pole and whip right back at you."

"It's my fence and my problem, right?" Edie tugged at the top wire to pull it tight. "I can get along without any supervision from you."

There was a curl in the wire that resisted her efforts. Edie leaned against the loose section tacked to the far post to get some leverage. Irritated that she should have any difficulty when Maddock was watching, she carelessly put too much strain on the loosely secured section of wire.

"Look out!" The barked warning came too late.

Edie heard a pinging snap. Then there wasn't anything to lean against. She staggered for balance and heard the whine of recoiling wire. Sheer instinct raised her hands toward her face as the barbed wire circled her like a whip. A thousand needle-sharp points stabbed into her flesh, piercing her clothes to tear at her skin. She wasn't aware of crying out, but there was an echo of strangled screams in the air.

The wire had tangled at her feet, tripping her up and keeping her from regaining her balance. With each stumbling, staggering step, more flesh was ripped by constricting wire. Her attempts to unwind it only added to the agony. She couldn't even fall to the ground because the wire held her up. It seemed an eternity that she was trapped in the web of steel needles, writhing in pain, before a pair of hands held her motionless and gave her support. In actual fact it was only a matter of seconds.

"Are you just plain stupid?" A familiar voice spoke roughly near her ear. "Or just too damned stubborn to listen? You didn't want my supervision. Maybe you don't want my help, either. Where are your wire cutters? I told you this would happen, but damn fools like you know everything."

The barely controlled fury of his temper whipped at her, slicing into her pride the way the barbs cut her flesh. Yet all the while Maddock was talking, he was supporting her with one hand and loosening the strands of wire circling her body.

Each breath Edie took was a grunting cry. The straitjacket of wire didn't permit any movement without extracting a penalty of pain. Her eyes were tightly closed, trying to shut out the nightmare.

"Where are the damned wire cutters?" This time Maddock's voice demanded an answer.

"In . . . the pickup," Edie whispered, and cringed in expectation for the scolding that would follow.

"Of all the—" His large hands tightened on her arms. "Don't move," his voice rumbled the order with thunderous warning. "I have some in my saddlebags. Just stand still and don't try to get free. Do you understand? Don't move."

Hysterical laughter started to rise in her throat, because it was so ludicrous to think she could move. "I . . . can't." She gulped down the bubbling sound.

When he released her, Edie felt a surge of panic. What if he left her? She fought it down as she opened her tear-blurred eyes to watch him eat the distance between her and his horse with long, running strides and return at top speed with a pair of wire cutters in his hand.

"Have you had a tetanus shot lately?" With his powerful grip he began snipping through the wire strands as if they were pieces of string.

"No . . . I mean, yes. I have." Tremors of relief were quaking through her as strand after circling strand fell away.

When she was free he gripped her shoulders and lifted her out of the tangle of wire at her feet. Edie swayed unsteadily for a second, but his hands remained to solidly support her. His strength was a silent blessing. Edie tipped her head back to thank him.

"Maddock, I don't—" Before she could express the gratitude she was feeling, he shut her up with a look, angry sparks glittering in his flint gray eyes.

"I don't believe you could do something that dumb!" he raged again in a low growl. "Do you realize how lucky you were?"

"Because you were here? Yes." She nodded. Out of the corner of her eye she saw Alison driving the steers toward the fence.

"No, not because I was here!" Maddock almost shouted to be heard above the noise of the approaching pickup truck. "That barbed wire went around your body. It could just as easily have wrapped itself around your face! It's a miracle you aren't scarred for life. It wouldn't have mattered who the hell was here! Do you understand?"

The blood drained from her face at his explanation. Knowing how easily the barbs had ripped through her clothes and into her skin, Edie closed her eyes at the thought of what might have happened if it had whipped across her unprotected face. Her fingers curled into the sleeves of his black shirt, feeling the iron-hard flesh it covered and gaining strength from him. Distantly she was aware of the slamming of the truck door, but it made no impact on her until she heard Jerry's voice.

"Take your hands off her, Maddock!" he ordered, and grabbed at his arm.

As Maddock loosened his grip to send a fiery glare at her stepson, Alison came running toward her. "Mom, are you all right?" Her eyes widened at the sight of the torn blouse and the blood oozing from the many cuts. She turned on Maddock with a vengeance. "What did you do to her?"

"I didn't do anything to her!" he snapped. "Tenderfeet like you can do it all by yourselves!" With that he shook off Jerry's arm as if ridding himself of a pesky fly and strode to his ground-hitched horse.

It was left to Edie to explain, somewhat shakily, all that had happened. While Jerry stayed to put up the fence, Alison drove Edie back to the house to clean the cuts and put some antiseptic on them. Only a few were serious, but all of them were painful. Her back, shoulders and arms had suffered the most, but none kept her from working.

Enough land had been enclosed by the following week for them to focus on acquiring stock cows to build their herd. Jerry began attending the livestock auctions in the area. It slowed their progress in refencing since Edie and Alison had to work at something else on the days he went to the sale barns.

After three weeks of regular attendance, Jerry didn't have a single cow for his efforts. His story was one of frustration. Every time he made a bid on a pen of cattle, the price went sky-high. Jerry dropped out of the bidding whenever the price exceeded the cattle's market worth.

The day of the next sale it was decided unanimously that all three of them would take a break from their grueling work schedule to attend. The silent trio left their truck and trailer parked with the other ranch vehicles and walked to the sale barn. While Jerry registered and got his number,

Edie and Alison went to the snack bar for coffee before the auction started.

The area was a hive of activity. Boisterous male voices hailed one another above the ring of the cash register and orders being given to a harried waitress behind the counter. The smell of cattle and manure permeated the room, fighting with the aroma of freshly baked cinnamon rolls and apple pie. Edie was standing to one side while Alison debated whether she was hungry enough for two rolls instead of just one. For a brief moment Edie considered the fact that neither one of them had to watch their weight, not the way they had been working lately.

"Hey, Cully!" someone hailed the heavyset man at the cash register. Edie glanced around in idle curiosity. "You're in luck again today. That kid is here. I just saw him registering."

The man took his change and turned to face the stocky cowboy, pushing his way through the crowd of hats and boots and Levi's-clad men. "Slow to catch on, isn't he?" The man gestured to Jerry as Cully grinned and pushed his hat back. "Hasn't he figured out yet that Maddock ain't about to let him buy anything?"

Edie stiffened. To suspect this was what was happening was one thing, but to have it confirmed was quite another. She pretended to be interested in a sign over the counter, but her real attention was centered on the two men, anger making her senses twice as keen.

"Sometimes I wonder how high Maddock would drive the prices," the cowboy was saying. "I wish the kid wouldn't drop out so soon."

"Don't wonder too much," the rancher, Cully, warned. "Hank Farber wondered that last week and started bidding. He wound up owning a pen of expensive stock cattle. Maddock shuts off his bidding the minute the kid does."

"There's no question about it. Maddock wants that ranch."

"Hell! I don't blame him. It sits damned near square in the middle of his place," Cully declared. Alison started to say something to Edie, but she shushed her with a look and sent a glance toward the two men to indicate the reason. "It's got some of the best grassland and hay around here."

"After all Maddock did for Carver, I sure expected that old man to sell the place to him." The cowboy shook his head in bewilderment. "Carver never would have hung on to the ranch as long as he did if Maddock hadn't helped him out as much as he did. I know for a fact that Maddock made Carver a standing offer to pay a hundred dollars an acre over the market price. He could have squeezed the old man out of that place a long time ago, but he played fair."

"Maddock is fair, I'll give him that," Cully conceded, and grinned. "'Course he can afford to be. That old man, Carver, though, has a streak of cussedness a mile wide. His idea of a practical joke got a little twisted sometimes. Knowing how much Maddock wanted his ranch, he probably thought it was funny to sell to the widow instead."

"That bothers me. I mean, her being a widow and all." The cowboy frowned and shuffled his feet in discomfort. "I've heard she's quite a looker. She's sunk her money into that ranch, trying to make a home for her and her kids. They sure as hell are working hard trying to fix the place up. I saw them putting in new fence last week, all three of them. Maddock's kinda rough on her."

At least Edie had the satisfaction of knowing someone agreed that they were getting a raw deal. But the rancher Cully was laughing at the statement.

"Hell! Maddock isn't trying to cheat her in the first place," he declared. "He's just trying to, uh, persuade her to sell to him. As for her being a widow, that doesn't matter one way or another."

"Yeah, I guess you're right," the cowboy agreed reluctantly, and looked toward the door. "There's Tom Haven. I've been wanting to see him. See ya, Cully."

When the two men drifted away, Alison exchanged a look with Edie. "We'd better find Jerry."

He was in the auction area, halfway up the wooden bleachers that half circled the sale ring. Edie and Alison hurried up the steps to where he was seated and whispered to him what they had overheard, keeping their voices low so others around them couldn't hear.

"There's no point in staying around here, then, is there?" Jerry concluded when they had finished, the line of his mouth thinning out.

"We know the cards are stacked against us, but I think we should play out the hand we've been dealt before we ask for a new deck of cards and change dealers," Edie murmured.

"I didn't know you knew that much about games of chance."

"I've been watching *Celebrity Poker*."

"What do you have in mind?" Jerry eyed her with a glint of admiration and wary amusement.

"I think we should let Maddock go on believing that his dumb tenderfeet haven't caught on to his scheme. Then he won't be expecting us to do anything else," she replied. "We won't talk about it now, though."

"Okay." He glanced at Alison. "Where's my cup of coffee?"

"Oh, damn." A stricken look of regret widened her eyes. "I left it sitting on the counter. Somebody's probably taken it by now."

"Thanks a lot, sis." He shook his head in resignation and started to rise.

"No, stay here." Edie put a hand on his arm to detain him. "They're bringing the first group of cattle in. I'll get you a cup."

When the cattle were turned into the auction ring it was a signal for everyone loitering in the halls and snack bar to enter at once. Edie edged her way down the steps against the stream of ranchers and cowboys going the opposite way. She was nearly at the bottom when she happened to glance up from the wooden steps straight into a pair of slate gray eyes. The steps seemed to rock beneath her. The heel of her boot hooked the edge of the board, and she would have fallen headfirst down the last step if a familiar pair of hands hadn't caught her and lifted her to the ground. Edie was conscious of the warm, firm imprint of his hands making themselves felt through the material of her floral blouse. The sensation wasn't unpleasant.

"You'd better watch where you're going," Maddock said as he released her.

Her gaze flew to his tough, male features, the light of battle sparking in her hazel eyes. "That has a false ring to it, Maddock. Aren't you really hoping that we'll fall flat on our faces?" she challenged, and didn't wait for him to reply as she pivoted and fought her way against the current of crowd to the snack bar.

Chapter Five

The morning after the sale, Edie leaned against the board fence of the corral and gazed inside at a pair of frisky calves. Several months old, the Hereford calves were already showing the hefty build indicative of their breed. The pair was the only livestock they had succeeded in buying at yesterday's sale. Crossing the corral from haying the horses, Jerry vaulted the fence to stand beside Edie and watch the animals.

"It's up to you, Alison," he said to the tall girl perched atop the rail, "to bring home their mommas from Wyoming."

"I wish you were going instead of me," Alison sighed in apprehension.

"Maddock is convinced that Jerry will be buying our cattle. If he goes to Cheyenne, Maddock is going to guess that we're going out of state to purchase our stock cows. I don't know how long his influence will continue, but I don't want to find out," Edie replied. "He'll never suspect in a hundred years that we'd send you to buy cattle."

"Neither would I," Alison declared.

"How many horses have you bought at auctions?" Jerry challenged. "You know the procedures. Just make sure you get a health certificate and don't pay more than I told you."

"I don't think I like being an adult." Alison smiled suddenly. "Too much responsibility." She unfolded her long legs to climb down from the rail. "Why do you suppose Maddock let us buy these two calves?"

"Guilty conscience," Edie stated.

"He was probably afraid we might starve, so he let us have a couple of calves that we could butcher in the fall," Alison suggested, and laughed at the thought. "He doesn't know we have an income separate from the ranch."

"Yes—Joe's patents. Maddock probably thinks we are depending on this not-exactly-going concern for our sole support," Edie agreed, her dimples coming into play. "Wouldn't you love to see his face when he finds out differently?"

"I was just thinking," Jerry interrupted their laughter, "I'll bet these calves are a carrot Maddock is dangling in front of our noses to keep us attending the local sales."

"I wouldn't be surprised," Alison agreed.

Edie rested her chin in the cup of her hand to watch the calves nosing a half a bale of hay Jerry had tossed in the corral. She tried to smother a giggle and only partially succeeded.

"What's so funny?" Jerry eyed her curiously.

"I was just remembering all the grandiose plans we made last winter." She couldn't keep the amusement out of her voice. "We were going to become big cattle ranchers. And that's the sum total of our herd!" She waved toward the two calves. "It would take us longer to catch and saddle our horses than it would to round up and brand those calves!"

"I'm afraid you're right," Jerry chuckled.

"We did say we were going to start small," Alison reminded them.

Edie snorted. "This small?"

"Why not this small?" Alison decided to make a joke out of it. "We can start out with two the way Noah did. Next year we'll have four, then eight, then sixteen. Why, in twenty years we'll have a herd."

Both Edie and Jerry broke out in grins. "There's a problem with that theory, Alison." Edie tried to check her laughter long enough to explain and failed. "Maybe you didn't notice it but—"

Jerry interrupted. "Those are bull calves!"

Then all three were overcome with laughter. Holding her stomach, Edie leaned heavily against the fence, tears steaming down her cheeks. The laughter was a release for all of them—a release from days of hard work, frustration and tension. It turned something only mildly amusing into mutual hilarity. Alison fell against Jerry, laughing too hard to stand on her own. He circled an arm around her and reached out to draw Edie inside the curve of his other arm.

"Edie, you're the only person I know who can find something to laugh about when it looks like your dreams might be dissolving," he declared in a laugh-winded voice.

"Neither one of you would win a prize at being serious," she retorted.

"That's because of you!" Releasing Alison, Jerry circled his stepmother's waist with his hands and swung her in the air, lifting her above his head. "You're the greatest, Edie!"

"Put me down!" she shrieked in laughter.

Jerry set her on the ground and planted a kiss on her forehead. "I don't care who knows it," he declared. "Do you, Alison?"

"No." The two exchanged a look that transmitted a silent message.

In the next second Edie was covering her ears as the pair of them tipped their heads back and shouted to the sky at the top of their voices. "Edie Gibbs is the greatest mother in the world!"

"Help, you've stampeded our cattle," Edie laughed as the calves bolted to the far side of the corral.

The helpless laughter was on the verge of starting again until Alison sobered with unexpected swiftness, looking behind them. "Uh-oh," she murmured in a small voice. "We have company."

Edie turned, wiping happy tears from her cheeks. A blue-and-white pickup was parked in the yard, with the driver's door held open by the man standing near it. Maddock shut it when they all looked at him. Edie wondered how a man could be so powerfully built and not look like a muscle-bound freak. He started toward them, and the three of them moved forward together to meet him halfway.

A lazy smile was making attractive grooves in the sun-browned cheeks while his dark gray eyes were silvered with a glint of amusement and curiosity. Edie felt the magnetic pull of his male charm. Sexual and potent, it quivered along her nerve ends.

"I can't remember the last time I saw three people laughing so hard," he remarked. "What was so funny?"

Edie hesitated. "Oh, just a family joke."

"I don't think you would get it," Alison added.

"Is this a neighborly visit or business?" Edie hoped to change the subject. The indefinable warmth that had been present suddenly vanished.

"Business," he admitted.

"We haven't changed our minds about selling," she informed him.

"I didn't think for one minute that you would give up so quickly," Maddock murmured dryly, but his mocking look said they would eventually. "No, I wanted to discuss something else."

"Which is?" Edie prompted with an icy coolness.

"The below normal rainfall we've had this spring has hurt my grazing land. I don't want to risk overgrazing it, so I'd like to make you an offer to lease your land to run my cattle on," he explained.

"But if we leased our land to you, where would we run our cattle?" she challenged.

"You don't have any," he pointed out.

"Not yet," she admitted. "But we hope to acquire a small herd soon. We already have two calves." Let him think they were stupid and gullible, Edie told herself. Anger surged when she saw the glimmer of a smile he tried to conceal.

"I think there would be enough pasture for your *herd* and mine," Maddock replied with deliberate emphasis.

Playing dumb didn't suit her. "I don't think you want to lease our land because the lack of rainfall has affected yours, Maddock," she said. His eyebrows rose ever so slightly, she noted with satisfaction. "I think your land is overgrazed because it's overstocked. You've been buying a lot of cattle lately." There was a slight narrowing of his gaze. "We aren't interested in leasing you any of our land, but if you want to sell us some of your extra stock cows, we'd be glad to discuss that. Naturally we'd expect to pay fair market value for them, but you're a fair man, aren't you?"

He held her gaze for a long, hard moment. "I'm not interested in selling my cattle at the moment."

"It doesn't look like we can do business, then, does it?" she countered. "Because we aren't interested in leasing you any land."

"Okay." Maddock accepted her answer with a brisk nod. "Let me know if you change your mind."

"Yes," Edie agreed with a honeyed smile. "And you let us know if you change yours."

"Of course." His mouth formed a smile of grudging approval with a hint of admiration. Edie had a fleeting glimpse of it before he turned to walk back to his truck. Maddock had let her claim victory in this battle, but the war wasn't over. The war of the sexes was never over. A tingling shock ran down Edie's spine. Where had she gotten the idea that this was a man-woman struggle? That was ridiculous. It was the ranch they were fighting over. Maddock wanted it, and she was just as determined not to let him have it. It had nothing to do with sex.

Without wanting to, she recalled the firm grip of his hands when he'd caught her yesterday to save her from falling down the auction steps. And the previous time when he'd held her, supported her while he swiftly and expertly dispensed with the ribbon of barbed wire. That close, he'd emanated the warm, musky smell of leather, sweat and horse mixed with a trace of aftershave. The combination was unique to Maddock, a stamp of his male individuality.

Even now the virile scent of him lingered in her memory, honing her senses to a keen edge. Just for a second, Edie permitted herself to wonder what kind of lover he would be. Masterful, knowing . . . both of those without a doubt. But his hands, when they explored her body, would they . . .

Heat flamed in her face when Edie realized what she was visualizing. What was the matter with her? She had never indulged in such fantasies about Joe before she married him. Edie rationalized that away by reminding herself that she'd been innocent then, and she hadn't been tempted to use her imagination. Edie was shocked that Maddock had aroused her sexual curiosity when not a single other man had—not even Joe.

"Why the frown, Mom?" Alison's question was light, yet it pulled Edie sharply out of her reverie.

Maddock's truck had completed its circle and was bouncing over the rutted land away from the ranch yard. Edie was struck again by the abrupt way he kept entering and exiting her life.

"Just once I'd like to hear that man say hello and good-bye," she retorted.

"It would be a novelty," Jerry agreed. "Well?" He glanced at the two of them with a raised eyebrow. "Shall we get to work?"

"Yes." Edie didn't want to think about Maddock one second longer. "We're nowhere near finished, and I want Alison to leave first thing in the morning."

A violent spring thunderstorm arrived right after Alison's departure. The deluge confined Edie to the house, where there was plenty of work to be done. Jerry used the time to work on the tractor, which had been running roughly, and make certain the hay baler would be ready when they needed it.

Intermittent rain showers plagued the area for three days. The only ray of brightness came from Alison's call, telling them of a successfully accomplished mission and the arrival date for the shipment of stock cattle.

The rain made preparations for that great event impossible. Edie kept herself busy with the house, which had been neglected since they got there, but she would have preferred to be outside. All day long she consoled herself with the knowledge that the rain was a godsend. Proof of that was demonstrated by the way the parched ground soaked it up as quickly as it fell.

Yet at night when she was alone in the front bedroom with the rain drumming on the roof, Edie tossed restlessly in the double bed. She finally tossed the pillow next to hers onto the floor, but it hadn't helped to ease her tension. Most of her married life she had gone to bed alone while Joe had puttered in his workshop, so why did sleeping by herself bother her now?

She tried to convince herself that these yearnings tormenting her were natural. After all, hadn't she read that a woman's libido reached its peak in the midthirties? Grief had no doubt suppressed these longings. Now that it had begun to wane, it was natural they would surface.

And there was a logical reason why the image of Will Maddock's face kept flitting through her mind. With the cattle on the way, she was subconsciously trying to imagine his reaction to the news. That's why she kept seeing those smoke gray eyes looking at her with such unnerving steadiness, those hard-cast features etched with strong, suncreased lines and that mouth cut in a male shape. These recollections had nothing to do with the brief flight of fancy her senses had taken the last time she'd seen him.

Stifling a moan, Edie rolled onto her side and faced the empty width of the bed. Her hand reached out to the emptiness beside her. "I did love you, Joe," she whispered tightly. A little voice inside reminded her that there were many kinds of love, and the force of one did not negate the strength of another. Many kinds of love existed side by side, one not diminishing another. She hugged the blankets more tightly around her and closed her eyes, listening to the drumming message of the spring rain on the roof.

The sun came out the morning the semitrailer-trucks arrived with the cattle. With Alison back and teaming up with Jerry, it was easy for Edie to forget her restlessness and join in with their jubilant spirits. Herding the cattle to a section of the range where there was plenty of grass and water was a happy occasion.

It was after one o'clock when they reached the valley meadow. Within minutes the cattle were scattering out to graze in the knee-deep grass, lush and green after the rain. Everything was washed clean, the air crystal clear, the colors of the trees and hills more brilliant than before. Wildflowers were bobbing their heads in the tall grasses and peeking out of rocky crags.

"Let's eat our lunch on the saddle of that ridge." Alison motioned toward the hollowed crest between two hills, treeless and possessing an unobstructed view of the valley.

Her suggestion was seconded by Jerry, and the three of them rode their horses halfway up the slope and tied them in the shade of a stand of white-barked aspens. Rocky boulders offered hard seats for them to sit on while they ate their sandwiches and sipped at hot coffee from the thermos. Yet the plainness of the food didn't alter the picnic mood.

"I really feel as if we own a ranch now," Alison murmured.

Looking down at the valley floor where the mixed herd of Hereford and Angus grazed, Edie studied the shiny black hides that glistened in the sunlight and contrasted with the rust red coats of the white-faced Herefords. She, too, had the feeling that what had long been a dream had finally become reality.

"We've worked hard these last months," Jerry said in an equally quiet voice. "But looking down there at that sight is a reward in itself."

At the clatter of hooves on stone behind them, Edie turned to see a horse and rider top the crest and rein in. She rose to meet the silent challenge of Will Maddock's presence, a little pulse hammering in her throat.

"One of his spies must have told him about the cattle, and he had to see it for himself to believe it," Alison whispered.

Except for a cursory glance at the herd grazing in the valley, Maddock showed no further interest in the cattle. His attention seemed to be focused on Edie. To enforce the impression, he guided his horse over the exposed rock face to where she was standing. He rested his gloved hands on the saddle horn as he tipped his head down to look at her.

"The storm knocked down a tree on your fence line. I thought you should know," he said. "It's a good idea to check for damage after hard storms. Sometimes a small creek can turn into a raging torrent that wipes out a whole section of fence. Flash floods aren't uncommon here."

The sting of his criticism smarted. Edie was well aware that he was taking the opportunity to point out how inexperienced they were. A trio of tender-feet, he'd called them.

"It was thoughtful of you to come all this way to tell us." But there was a bite to her polite response.

"Oh, I don't know about that. But I had my reasons." On that cryptic note he turned his head to sweep an experienced eye over the herd of cattle below them. "That's a fine-looking bunch. They're carrying Wyoming brands, aren't they?"

"Yes," Edie admitted, and realized he could probably tell her the name and location of the ranch that the brands were registered to.

The buckskin stamped a foot at a buzzing fly, and the saddle leather creaked under its rider's weight. "You must have made a quick trip to Wyoming and back." Maddock addressed the remark to Jerry, who was leaning a hip against the boulder near Edie.

"I didn't go." Jerry calmly met the gray gaze leveled at him. "Alison bought the herd."

"Yes," she piped up a little smugly, and strolled over to stand near her brother. "It was amazing how much cheaper the cattle sold for there than the price they were bringing here at the local sale barns. Even with the shipping costs added in we saved money."

"So now you're in the cattle business." It was a flat statement that ventured no opinion.

"And we're going to be successful at it," Alison declared rashly. "You shouldn't underestimate the Gibbs family, Mr. Maddock."

There was a suggestion of a smile around his firm mouth. The glint in his eyes was unmistakable as his glance encompassed all three of them, lingering for a fraction of a second on Edie. "You can be sure I won't." Applying pressure on the bridle bit, he signaled the buckskin to back up, then pivoted the horse at a right angle to send it up the crest.

Chapter Six

"You're right, Mom," Alison muttered in an irritated breath. "It would be a novelty if he ever said good-bye."

Edie dragged her gaze from the crest of the saddleback ridge where Maddock had disappeared. She had just begun to enjoy a feeling of peace and contentment before he showed up. Now she felt disjointed, at odds with herself.

"It doesn't really matter what he didn't say," Jerry said, straightening from the boulder. "He did give us some sound advice. We should check to see what damage the storm did. We might as well split up and cover more ground."

"I suppose," Alison sighed, and Edie let her agreement be a silent one as they walked down the slope to the trees where they had tied their horses.

They mounted up without saying much more and fanned out in three different directions. Edie hadn't chosen the section of boundary fence she was to check; the choice had been made for her when Jerry and Alison picked the other two. At the time there hadn't been any reason to object until she saw the rider walking his horse and thought of an excellent reason—Will Maddock.

Her gloved hand tightened automatically on the reins of the bay gelding. It pulled up abruptly out of its trot into a prancing halt. She glanced anxiously around her, but both Alison and Jerry were already out of sight. What was more, Maddock had already seen her.

Edie was angry for not realizing that this would be the logical route Maddock would take back to his ranch. Or had she? Had her subconscious buried the knowledge? It was too late for such thoughts to be occurring to her.

She was supposed to check the fences in this region. She had a choice of either following Maddock at a distance or riding on at a normal pace as if it didn't matter. It didn't matter, she argued silently. She wasn't afraid of him.

Digging in her heels, she sent the bay horse forward at an easy lope. Maddock didn't exactly wait for her, but she caught up with him easily. The ground became rough beneath her horse. Edie had to let the bay choose its own pace or risk laming it, which meant she had to ride alongside Maddock.

"I see you decided to take my advice," he commented.

"About checking the storm damage, yes," she agreed stiffly, not turning her gaze from the front, but conscious of his gray eyes sliding over her. "About selling the ranch to you, no."

"I don't recall advising you to sell to me," Maddock replied dryly.

"That's true," Edie recalled with a touch of disdain that was alien to her nature. "I believe you said we would break under the pressure."

"You will eventually." He reached into his shirt pocket for a cigarette and, one-handed, cupped a lighted match to the tip.

"You're wrong, Maddock." Edie tried to keep her gaze from straying to his craggy profile and the way his eyes squinted against the smoke curling from the cigarette in his mouth. He was too rawly masculine. "I think we have proved we don't break under pressure . . . even your pressure."

"My pressure?" His mouth curved without smiling.

"Admit it, Maddock," Edie insisted a shade triumphantly. "You're upset because we outsmarted you and bought our cattle elsewhere after you tried to keep us from buying any cattle here. Can't sit well with you to be bested by a bunch of greenhorns."

"I don't care," he countered smoothly. "And I don't deny that I kept you from making any successful bids on cattle. You can call that pressure if you like."

"What else do you call it?" she retorted. When he didn't answer she demanded, "Did you really think it would work?"

"If you had been a bunch of fainthearted, dumb tenderfeet, yes, it would have worked, because you would have given up in another month and sold out. You showed you were stubborn and in-

telligent. But it doesn't change the eventual out-
come."

"That's where you're wrong, Maddock." Edie
was angry that he was so damned sure of himself.
"We aren't selling. And if the day ever comes when
we do, I'd sell it to the devil before I'd sell it to
you."

"And you're making a mistake." He blew out a
stream of smoke and gave her a long, hard look,
his hands resting on the saddle horn while his
body moved with the rocking motion of the walking horse.

"I'm not making any mistake," she denied, unable to withstand the force of that dark gray gaze.

"Yes, you are. You're taking this personally. I
have nothing against you or your family. If you
want to play cowboy, go somewhere else. I want the
ranch. It's that simple. You have it. I want it and
I'm going to do everything I can to persuade you
to sell—to me."

"Persuade? Force, you mean," Edie corrected
tightly. "Doesn't it matter to you that this ranch is
our home?"

"It isn't your home," he denied without hesitation or emotion. "Wherever it is you're from in
Illinois, that's your home."

"That *was* our home. *This* is our home now."
Strangely, that was true. This was where she felt she
belonged now. Their home and life in Illinois
seemed very distant.

"Don't sink your roots too deep," he warned.

The boundary fence was ahead of them.
Blocking their way was a tall pine tree, toppled by

the storm. Its trunk was charred where lightning had struck it. The top third of it was resting atop the fence. A post taking most of its weight had kept the newly strung barbed wire from snapping.

Ignoring Maddock, Edie reined her horse toward the tree and stopped near the fence. Since she expected him to ride on, she dismounted to untie the lariat hanging from her saddle. She glanced over the suede-covered seat of her saddle to see Maddock swinging off his horse.

"What are you doing?"

"I'm giving you a hand." He untied his coiled rope and walked toward the tree.

Hurrying, Edie reached it ahead of him and began tying the end of her rope around the tapered trunk. "I don't happen to need your help."

"I'm sure you can manage on your own." He expertly tied his knot while she was still fumbling with hers. "The same way you did with the barbed wire."

She flashed him an angry look and jerked the knot tight. Walking back to her horse, she stepped into the saddle and looped the other end of the rope around the saddle horn. Maddock was already astride his buckskin, the rope dallied around his horn and waiting for her.

Reining the bay at an angle away from the tree, she walked it forward until the rope was stretched taut across her thigh. Out of the corner of her eye, Edie was aware that Maddock had set his horse at a parallel line with hers.

The bay felt the weight at the end of the rope, the resistance, and fidgeted nervously. Patting its neck, she urged it forward and looked back. Pine branches were making rustling noises against the fence. Slowly the top half of the tree was beginning to move. There was the splintering crack of wood as the tree trunk began to split from the lightning-struck stump. Then it snapped, and the tree slithered off the fence and crashed to the ground, limbs cracking and breaking, the taut wire singing.

The rope went slack, and Edie immediately halted her horse, its dark head tossing nervously. She ignored the fact that Maddock was already on the ground walking to untie his rope from the tree when she dismounted. A white-hot tension was racing through her as she followed him.

Pulling the tree off the fence had tightened the knot. Edie had to work to get it loose. By the time she had it untied, Maddock already had his rope recoiled. His swiftness and adeptness made her feel clumsy and slow in comparison.

"I didn't ask you to help me, so don't expect any thanks." She jerked the rope free and began coiling it into a circle.

"I didn't expect any thanks. I didn't get any when I cut you out of that wire or when I saved you from falling down the steps. If neither of those warranted an expression of gratitude, this certainly doesn't." His indifferent glance was cool and gray. "Your manners leave something to be desired."

"My manners!" If Edie had felt a twinge of guilt, his last statement chased it away. "You don't even have the common courtesy to say anything as polite as hello or good-bye. But I imagine you've been pushing people around for quite a while. It's high time somebody started shoving back."

"You?" Mocking laughter glinted in his look, although there was no change in his expression.

There had been too much tension, too many seething emotions held in check for too long. The thread of control holding them had worn thin. At his taunt it snapped. Edie struck out at his face. The leather of her glove absorbed much of the stinging contact with his cheek, protecting her palm.

Her arm had barely finished its arc when it was seized in an inescapable grip. Maddock yanked her against his chest. His retaliation was too swift and caught Edie unprepared to resist. Her head was thrown back, and her wide hazel eyes were drawn to his face. The white mark on his cheek where she had hit him was turning red. There was a thunderous shade to his gray eyes, a violent Dakota storm about to break over her head.

An instinct for survival made her struggle. With her free hand Edie pushed at his chest and strained against the iron band that circled her waist. It didn't seem to matter how much she turned and twisted; she couldn't elude the contact with his powerfully muscled build.

"Let me go!" she demanded angrily, and tried to jerk her wrist free of his grip, but he used the downward movement to fold her arm behind her back and draw her more fully to his length.

"You did this deliberately, didn't you?" Maddock said softly.

"I'm not sorry I slapped you. I just wish I'd hit you harder."

He continued as if he hadn't even heard her, anger blazing in his eyes. "Don't provoke me. You won't like what happens next."

"I don't care what you do!" she gasped.

She stopped struggling, suddenly conscious that her writhing was provocation enough. She was no match for his strength. While he had easily checked her attempts to wrestle out of his hold, his hands had succeeded in fitting her intimately to his own body. Her hips were pressed firmly to the solid columns of his thighs and the thrusting angle of his hips. While trying to ease the pressure on the arm he still held behind her back, she had arched the roundness of her breasts fully against his chest.

"How long has it been?" Maddock demanded. "And don't tell me you don't know what I'm talking about."

A miserable cry of protest and denial came from her throat. His words only echoed the wayward thoughts that had been running through her mind these past days. That knowledge flamed through her body. She had to escape him before his nearness caused a purely physical response. In a last bid for her freedom, Edie kicked at his shin with the pointed toe of her boot and scored a direct hit. He cursed in pain under his breath and relaxed his grip just enough for Edie to twist free. She tried to run, but he grabbed at her arm.

"Oh, no, you don't!" His fingers closed on her sleeve, catching just enough material to half turn her around.

Her foot became tangled in the coiled rope she'd dropped. Edie lost her balance and tumbled backward. She was conscious of her legs becoming tangled with his as she fell, toppling him with her. The impact with the ground momentarily knocked the wind out of her. But not her fighting spirit.

Chapter Seven

"Got you!" Before Edie could recover her breath, Maddock rolled on top of her, captured the hands that would have pushed him away and pinned them to the ground above her head.

Edie couldn't move. She was aware that the fall had knocked her hat off, spilling the chestnut length of her hair over the ground. But she was more conscious of the pressing heat of his body and the way it heightened the earthy smell of him. She tried not to breathe and inhale his stimulating scent.

But there wasn't any way she could block out the feel of him, all that solidly muscled weight flattening her curves. Lying beneath him this way was strangely sensual. Edie was afraid to move in case Maddock discovered it, too. Her gaze became centered on the open collar of his shirt. She didn't dare look higher, aware of the tanned column of his throat and the hard, male features so close to her own. She could feel the warmth of his breath against her face, like a caress. One that she tried desperately to ignore.

There was a moment of stillness when neither moved. It stretched endlessly until some powerful, invisible force compelled Edie to lift her gaze. It traveled slowly up the corded muscles of his neck, dwelling for an instant on the pulse she saw hammering in his throat. In the space of another second her eyes became fascinated by the strong male outline of his mouth. Finally she met the magnetic darkness of his gaze.

"Maddock—" It was a plea, whether to be released or to be kissed, she never had a chance to find out for herself.

"Shut up, Edie." The husky order was issued as his mouth lowered onto hers.

The shape of her lips was explored with consummate ease, every curve and contour investigated with sexy thoroughness. Her mouth became soft and pliant under the influence of his kiss. Edie couldn't stop the quivering response that trembled through her. Her physical hunger for a man—this man—refused to be suppressed any longer.

When the sweet demand of his mouth seduced her lips apart, a languid warmth invaded her body until she seemed to melt into him. A fever was born, contagious and hot. Her arms were released and allowed to find their way around the breadth of his shoulders. His arms forced their way beneath her and held her with rough tenderness.

Turning her head, she eluded his mouth and gasped for a breath. "You're hurting me, Maddock," she murmured, because she doubted that he knew his own strength.

He levered himself above her, completely removing his weight. "Am I too heavy for you?" His husky voice was an evocative caress in itself.

Her lashes fluttered open as her gaze sought the face inches away from hers. She studied the sun-creased lines fanning out from the corners of his eyes and the slashing grooves that framed his mouth. She wanted to trace their paths as if they would provide the answer to the mystery of this man who could incite her to such anger . . . and such passion.

Edie could breathe again, but she didn't know if she wanted to. There was still his question to answer, and Maddock was waiting for it. "Yes . . . I mean, no." She saw the satisfaction glittering in his dark gray eyes as he watched confusion and desire warring in her expression. "Oh, Maddock, I don't know," she admitted finally, with a feeling that she had admitted a lot more than that.

"Never thought you'd be at a loss for a fast reply. This is an occasion," he murmured complacently and shifted his position to lie along her side with only a fraction of his weight resting on her.

His mouth moved to reclaim possession of her lips, consuming them with a lazy hunger that fed her desire. She felt the smoothness of a leather-gloved hand cup the side of her head, a thumb sliding down her neck to the base of her throat. Then the caressing hand was abruptly removed, and Edie was vaguely aware of some movement above her head. When the hand returned it was minus the glove. The sensitive skin of her neck delighted in the pleasing roughness of his callused touch, responding to it the way her lips responded to the masterful seduction of his kiss.

Once his hand and fingers had explored every inch of her neck, his mouth followed them up to claim the territory as his personal property. His tongue touched all the sensitive hollows while his hand continued its discovery trail, pushing the collar of her blouse aside to investigate her collarbone and the roundness of her shoulder. Quivers of sheer passion trembled through her. Somewhere in the back of her mind was the word no, but she was too conscious of the sensual stimulation his mouth was creating at a point below her collarbone. When he paused and lifted his head to let his fingers trace the area his lips had just claimed, she had to swallow a moan of protest.

"Is this mark from the barbed wire?" Maddock questioned in a low, taut voice that vibrated through her.

Edie moved her hand as if to touch the place, but the small scar was undoubtedly the result of that misadventure. "I . . . yes." What did it matter now?

Maddock pressed a kiss to the mark as if to speed the healing process and eliminate the blemish from her silken skin. "I'll never forget that day and the sight of you trussed up like a little brown hen in that wire," he murmured against her neck as he slowly worked his way up to her lips. "After I cut you free, my first reaction was to lecture you for getting yourself into such a predicament. But you wouldn't have listened. You were too damn mad—and scared, too. So my second reaction," he spoke against her lips, tantalizing their outline with the promise of a kiss while their breaths combined, "would have made the cockiest rooster proud. If your protectors hadn't arrived we would have been making love then instead of waiting until now."

A tiny animal sound of pleasure came from her throat under the driving possession of his kiss. His direct words had their desired effect on her mind. His hand found its way inside her blouse and his fingers slid inside the cup of her bra to feel her breast.

No other man had made love to her except Joe. Maddock would be the first since she'd been widowed, and the experience promised to be like nothing she'd ever known before. But wasn't it supposed to mean something? Did it? It was all happening too fast. Edie realized she wasn't ready for this, whatever it was.

With a muffled groan she twisted and rolled away from him, fighting the traitorous waves of regret. As she scrambled to her feet, common sense insisted that her decision was wise. What did she know about Maddock? What did she think of him? Was it loneliness that had made her respond, or something else?

"Edie?" His voice was low and puzzled.

She realized he was standing very close to her. The knowledge had a somersaulting effect on her heart, and Edie took a deep breath to calm her panicking nerves. The action drew her attention to the unbuttoned front of her blouse. She quickly tried to fasten the buttons, but it was a fumbling attempt. She damned the gloves that turned her fingers into thumbs.

A hand touched her shoulder, and she jerked away from the searing contact. "No." It was both a denial and a rejection. The next time he touched her, there was a disconcerting gentleness in the contact as Maddock turned her around to face him. Edie drew back as far as his hand would allow and refused to meet his probing gaze. "Let me go, Maddock," she requested stiffly. "I am not in the mood—" The rest of the sentence was lost in a gasp of pain when his fingers tightened to dig into her flesh. She was about to say she wasn't in the mood to argue, but Maddock interpreted the words as they stood.

"You sure about that?" He clamped a large hand on her hip and pulled her toward him, molding the lower half of her body to his length and impressing on her flesh how very potently he was in the mood.

She suppressed a shudder of longing. Her aching dissatisfaction wasn't helped by the knowledge of his need. She hadn't meant for things to go this far, even if that was the way it seemed. "Let me go."

For an instant Edie thought Maddock was going to ignore her brittle request. Then she was released and standing free, subject to the accusing rake of his gaze.

"I didn't do anything you didn't want me to do," Maddock stated.

Unable to meet his eyes, she reached down to pick up the half-coiled rope near her feet. She concentrated on coiling the rest of it while she answered him. "All right. I admit that I wanted to be kissed and even fool around a little, but I'm not so

desperate that I wanted to have sex with you."
Yeah, right, she thought. She'd responded to him
out of a need to be loved as only a man can love a
woman.

Her gaze ricocheted off his narrowed look.
Turning, she walked to her horse and tied the lariat to the saddle. Her nerves screamed at the way
his eyes followed her every move.

"How long were you married for?" Maddock
asked suddenly.

"Eighteen years." She stepped into the stirrup
and swung into the saddle. Feeling secure now
that she was mounted, Edie glanced at him.
"Why?"

He had gathered the reins to his horse and
mounted in one fluid movement. "I was just wondering. You never did tell me how long it's been."

"Since Joe died?"

Maddock shook his head. "Not quite what I
meant, no."

Edie felt her face flame with embarrassed anger.
"That's none of your damn business," she retorted.

He smiled ever so slightly. "No, it isn't. But I like
the way you stand up to me."

"Uh-huh. I don't think so. I'm certain that you
wish I were a helpless female incapable of fighting
back. You would've had my ranch by now, wouldn't
you, Maddock?" Edie challenged.

"Sooner or later we'll both get what we want."
He nudged his horse forward until his leg was uncomfortably close to hers. The line of his mouth
curved but it didn't smile.

"Go to hell!" She slapped the reins against her

horse's rump to send it lunging into a canter that swiftly carried her away from Maddock toward the ranch house.

Edie didn't slow her horse to a walk until she was out of sight. She choked on a sob and forced it down. Her pride and self-respect were soothed by the knowledge that although she had been vulnerable to his attraction for a little while, she had overcome it. No doubt Maddock enjoyed annoying her by pretending he was sexually interested in her. And she had almost been enough of a fool to fall for it. That brief interlude could be one more weapon for him to use against her. Well, she wasn't going to let it happen. It hadn't meant anything except that she was human and capable of being made to respond. She certainly wasn't going to hide from Maddock in the future because of it. After all, he was just a man.

Three days later Edie was with Jerry and Alison on the south boundary putting in the new fence. The other three sides to their ranch had been seen to. When this fence was in, they could begin on the inner pastures, which wouldn't be for a couple of days yet.

At the sound of a horse and rider approaching, Edie mentally braced herself to meet Maddock. But when she looked up, it was his daughter who was reining in her horse. And she was alone.

"Have you seen my father?" Even as she made the imperious demand of Edie, her gaze was straying with cool, feminine interest to Jerry, who was shirtless. His tanned muscles bulged as he drove a fence post into the ground.

"No," Edie replied, barely pausing in her work. "And I'm not expecting to."

"He said something about moving some cattle. I just thought he might have been by here." Felicia shrugged as if it didn't matter.

"I haven't seen him," Edie repeated, injecting supreme indifference into her voice.

"Who is he? Your hired hand?" The haughty question was spoken in a voice deliberately loud enough for Jerry to hear.

"No." With a sidelong glance at Jerry, Edie saw he had paused to look up, so she made the introduction. "This is my stepson, Jerry Gibbs. Jerry, meet Felicia Maddock."

The girl walked her flashy chestnut over to where Jerry was working. An overabundance of pride made her smile appear aloof, but there was no mistaking the avid interest in her blue eyes.

"Hello, Felicia." Jerry's wide smile was natural; his voice was a little winded from his physical exertion.

"It looks like you're working hard," the girl observed, and hooked a knee around the saddle horn, leaning a hand on the cantle. The provocative pose was reminiscent of the kind from the western calendars.

Jerry's gaze flicked over her with mild amusement and a little interest. "It's the only way the work gets done." He began tamping the post into the ground.

"Daddy's certainly going to appreciate all the improvements you've made on this place," Felicia remarked in an attempt at adult cynicism. "It will be just that much less he'll have to do when he buys it."

"Presuming, of course, that we sell it," Jerry reminded her, mocking her with his smile.

"You will," she replied with false confidence. "You can ask anybody. A Maddock always gets what he wants."

"Is that right?" Jerry continued with his work.

"You don't mind if I watch you, do you?" Felicia questioned.

"No, I don't mind." With that post in place, Jerry picked up his tools and moved on to set the next one. Felicia slid her boot back in the stirrup and reined her horse after him.

Alison pulled the barbed wire tight while Edie hammered a staple into the wood post to hold it. "I wonder if Jerry feels properly honored that Felicia is flirting with him," Alison murmured in dry sarcasm.

Edie glanced in Jerry's direction. The brunette was leaning on her saddle horn toward him, talking about something, but at this distance she couldn't hear what the girl was saying.

"She is pretty," Edie said, although she silently agreed that Felicia was out to make a conquest.

"The trouble is she knows it," Alison muttered.

Felicia Maddock stayed for about an hour, talking exclusively to Jerry. As far as she was concerned, Alison and Edie didn't exist. Felicia just wouldn't quit. Edie had to hand it to her stepson: Jerry did respond at the appropriate times, but he didn't slacken his pace.

As she turned her horse to ride away, she tossed

a light, "Don't work too hard, Jerry," over her shoulder.

"Don't work too hard, Jerry," Alison mimicked. "You'd better be careful, brother of mine. She wants to wrap you around her little finger."

"Oh, yeah?" He paused to wipe the sweat from his neck, and laughter twinkled in his eyes. "She's just a kid."

"She's eighteen if she's a day," Alison retorted. "And I wouldn't like to see her get her claws into you."

"I think Jerry can take care of himself," Edie said.

"Thanks, Edie." Jerry smiled. "To hear Alison talk, you'd think it was months since I'd seen a girl." Then with a wink he added, "Which it has been."

"You just watch that girl," Alison warned.

"I will," he promised with a roguish grin.

Jerry had plenty of opportunity in the three days it took them to finish the fencing, because Felicia Maddock "happened" to ride by every day. Each time she stayed about an hour, talking and flirting with Jerry, who neither encouraged her nor discouraged her.

Having the girl there automatically turned Edie's thoughts to Maddock. She studied Felicia, noting the similarities of their features and wondering if the differences came from Felicia's mother. This thought sparked her curiosity about Maddock's late wife and, ultimately, the question of why he hadn't remarried. With his virile good looks and standing in the ranching community, there wouldn't be a lack of candidates eager to fill the position. But Edie didn't ask a single question because she didn't want to admit an interest in him, not even a casual one—partly because the feelings he aroused in her were anything but casual.

Saturday was the day reserved for their weekly trip into town for supplies. The advent of June had also brought the annual influx of summer tourists to the area. The streets of Custer were crowded with vehicles and pedestrians, and it took almost twenty minutes to find a place to park. Then it was several blocks away from the main business district.

"From now on we'd better come to town in the middle of the week," Edie suggested.

"You won't get any argument from me." Jerry locked the door of the pickup before stepping up the curb to the sidewalk. "Do you want to meet me at the hardware store in an hour?"

"We should be through with our shopping and errands by then," Edie agreed after a questioning glance at her daughter.

"Most of them, anyway." Alison nodded.

With the crowd of tourists filling the sidewalks and the buildings of the colorful western storefronted town, it took longer than they anticipated. The hour had passed, yet Edie had acquired only half the items on her list.

"We'd better meet Jerry and catch the rest of the things later, Mom," Alison advised when they finally made it through the long line at a cash register. "At this rate it's going to take us all day instead of all morning."

Jostled by a customer who was attempting to exit the store at the same time Edie was going out the door, she wasn't able to immediately reply. "You're right," she sighed with a trace of disgust, "on both counts."

They crossed the street to the hardware store and went inside, but they couldn't find Jerry. None of the clerks recalled seeing him, but the store was crowded. It was possible he had been in and already gone. They went back outside.

"What do you think we should do?" The corners of Alison's mouth were pulled down by her fading patience. "Should we wait here in case he's late, too? Or walk all the way back to where the truck is parked to see if he's there?"

"With all these people, we could pass him on the street and never notice him." Edie frowned at the hopelessness of trying to recognize a person in this sea of faces streaming by.

"There he is!" Alison pointed across the street. An eyebrow arched coolly. "And will you look at who's with him? Miss High-and-Mighty herself," she declared at the same moment that Edie recognized Felicia Maddock. "I heard him mention to her yesterday that we'd be in town today."

"Alison, you make it sound as if she arranged to meet him," Edie chided.

"I wouldn't put it past her."

Edie noticed the way Felicia clung to Jerry's forearm. And she also noticed the smiling way Jerry observed the action, amused, indulgent and not exactly indifferent. For a brief moment she wondered if the Gibbs family was naturally susceptible to the Maddock brand of charm. With a beguiling smile, Felicia said something to Jerry. His reply must not have been what the brunette expected to hear, because she abruptly withdrew her hand from his arm, her expression freezing in an attempt to hide hurt anger.

"It looks like Miss Prissy Pants had her fur ruffled," Alison murmured with undisguised glee.

Edie flashed her daughter a reproving look, but Alison was watching her brother cross the street to the hardware store. When he reached the other side where they waited, he gave them a sheepish look.

"Sorry I'm late. I hope you haven't been waiting long," he said.

"Long enough to see you with Felicia," Alison murmured archly.

He glanced across the street in the direction that Felicia had taken. There was a wistful glint in his eyes that Edie noticed. "Yeah, I talked to her for a few minutes," he admitted without comment.

"What did you say that upset her?" Alison wanted to know.

"She asked me to buy her a cup of coffee, and I—" Jerry paused, a frown on his face.

"And what?" Alison prompted.

A wry smile twisted his mouth. "I told her that if I wanted to buy her a cup of coffee, I would do the asking."

"No wonder she looked like you'd slapped her," Alison murmured.

"But you wanted to ask her?" Edie suggested.

"Let's just say I might have if she wasn't—" He hesitated over the reason.

Edie supplied the obvious one. "Maddock's daughter."

"I could have overlooked that," Jerry corrected. "What I was going to say is if she wasn't such a spoiled brat." Adeptly he changed the subject. "I hope you haven't finished all your shopping."

"Hardly." Alison rolled her eyes expressively.

"If you don't need her, Edie, I could use Alison's help. I bought a couple of gates and a metal water trough. The lumberyard is so busy that they don't have anybody who can help me load them," Jerry explained.

"Sure, I'll help," Alison volunteered.

"I think I can manage without her," Edie agreed dryly.

"We'll meet you somewhere for lunch. That café by the corner?" he suggested.

"Okay. At one-thirty after the lunch hour rush is over," Edie suggested.

Chapter Eight

There was still time before Edie had to meet Alison and Jerry, so she wandered along the sidewalk beneath the shade of the overhang. A dress in a store window caught her eye, and she stopped to admire it. Made from a soft, melon-colored fabric, its design was simple, revealing a lot of skin and shoulder while avoiding the plunging look.

Its obvious femininity made what she wore look sad and sorry, Edie thought. In the plate-glass window, her slender, dark-haired reflection looked back. The real Edie ran a hand over her clothes, an uninspired combination of dusty jeans and a baggy T-shirt, a unisex, all-purpose outfit. Her gaze strayed back to the dress that needed the roundness of a woman's body to properly show off both.

"Hi, Mom." Alison's voice drew her attention away from the shop window. "We were just on our way to meet you. What are you doing?"

Turning, Edie noticed that Alison seemed particularly perky, all radiant and fresh with an extra

sparkle in her brown eyes. Jerry was with her, a typical hint of a smile in his expression.

"I was just admiring the dress in the window,"
Edie admitted. "Isn't it pretty?"

"It's gorgeous! It would look great on you,
Mom," Alison insisted the instant she saw it. "You
should get it."

"And where would I wear it?" Edie shook her
head, too practical to buy something that would
end up hanging in her closet. "What I need is a
new pair of jeans. I would get a lot more use out of
those than I would that dress, beautiful as it is."

"It's nice, though," Jerry said.

"And you could wear it to the dance tonight,"
Alison said brightly.

"What dance?" It was the first time Edie had
heard anything mentioned about a dance. Her
gaze darted curiously to her daughter.

"Jerry and I had some time to kill before meeting you, so we stopped at this bar," Alison began.

Jerry interrupted to assure Edie, "I had a beer
and Alison had a Coke."

"Yes, well," Alison hurried on with her explanation, "since it's Saturday night, they have a band
coming in to play at this bar. Rob says they're really
good. He's heard them play before."

"Who is Rob?" Edie frowned in amusement.

"He's this really cute cowboy who was in the bar
the same time we were there." That explained the
excited glow in her eyes.

"And this 'really cute' cowboy asked her if she
was going to come to the dance tonight and made
her promise to save a dance for him," Jerry teas-
ingly carried the explanation a step farther.

"I think I get the picture now." Edie laughed.

Alison looked self-conscious for only an instant before she shrugged it off. "He might change his mind and not even be there tonight. But I still think we should go to the dance. We've all worked hard lately. It's time we had a night on the town."

"I agree," Edie said. "But I don't need to buy a new dress to go to a dance."

"You haven't had a new dress in years, at least not one like that." Alison glanced again at the dress on the mannequin. "Let's go in and see if they have it in your size." She grabbed Edie's arm to pull her into the shop. "There wouldn't be any harm in trying it on. You might look terrible in it—who knows?"

When the clerk informed them they did have the dress in Edie's size, Alison took the packages from her mother's arms and thrust them into Jerry's. Edie wasn't given a chance to resist as she and the dress were hustled into a fitting room to change.

Everything was perfect—the length, the fit, the color, everything. She wasn't able to fasten the hook above the back zipper, but it didn't alter the appearance of the dress. She emerged from the dressing room barefoot since her cowboy boots had looked absurd, to view herself in the full-length mirror.

Alison was busy looking through a rack of dresses with Jerry standing patiently to one side. She didn't notice Edie when she came out of the fitting room, and Edie didn't immediately try to attract their attention, too anxious to see if the dress looked as good as it felt.

For an instant she was dazed by the image of a slim, fully curved woman with burnished brown hair. The dress enhanced a natural allure Edie hadn't realized she possessed. It was as if she was discovering all over again that she was a woman . . . and liking the sensation. With a three-quarter turn she looked over her shoulder into the mirror to get a back view of herself. Standing on tiptoes, she tried to get an idea of what the dress would look like with heels. Out of the corner of her eye she glimpsed the distinctive rolled brim of a cowboy hat. Automatically Edie assumed Jerry had noticed her and had walked over for a closer look. She reached behind her back with one hand to try to reach the unfastened hook.

"I wasn't able to fasten the hook but—" It didn't detract that much from the appearance. The material above the zipper simply didn't lie as smooth against her skin as it could. "What do you think?"

"I think it's a sin that a body like that spends so much time in men's clothes." The caressingly low pitch of Maddock's voice paralyzed Edie. Her heart leaped into her throat, robbing her of even the ability to speak. There was movement as the reflection of his tall, muscled lines joined hers in the mirror. "Let me get that hook for you."

The pleasant roughness of his fingers touched the bare skin of her backbone just above the zipper. The vibrations they produced shook Edie out of her trance.

"No. It isn't necessary." She would have stepped away from him, but he already had a hold on the material of her dress. Knowing his strength and the fragility of the fabric, she didn't try to pull away and risk tearing the material.

"A man learns early in his life the mysteries of all the hooks, snaps and zippers on women's clothes," he murmured.

"Were you a slow learner? You seem to be having difficulty with that hook." Edie was having difficulty keeping her breathlessness out of her voice.

"The skill comes in undoing them. There isn't any need to hurry when a man is refastening a hook," Maddock informed her smoothly, as if aware of the effect his touch was having on her.

It was a combination of his touch and the task. There was something about having a man fasten a dress that implied a delicious intimacy. Edie's senses were reacting to that feeling. When he had finished, Maddock turned her to face the mirror. Their gazes locked in the reflecting glass. His lazy gray eyes took note of the wariness in hers, while Edie tried not to stare at the way his jeans fit in all the right places. The tempo of her pulse went out of control when he made a leisurely inspection of her appearance.

"High heels are what you need. The perfect finishing touch," he observed dryly. The remark pulled her gaze from his tanned features, so masculine and tough, so disturbingly attractive, to the bareness of her own feet. "Don't you agree, Felicia?"

The mention of his daughter's name jerked Edie out of her foolish trance. She turned her head to the side where she encountered the brunette girl's cold regard. For a fleeting second Edie was surprised to see jealousy and resentment smoldering in Felicia's expression before it was disguised with a look of boredom.

"It would be an improvement," Felicia agreed with marked indifference.

"Mom! You look so hot!" Alison declared in a breathy exclamation when she noticed Edie standing in front of the mirror and moved away from the dress rack for a closer look. "Doesn't she, Jerry?"

"Yeah, you do, Edie. That's a beautiful dress." His agreement was restrained but no less sincere as his attention was drawn to Felicia Maddock.

"I thought you were in a big fat hurry to get back to the ranch," she said with an attempt at hauteur.

"I don't recall saying that." Jerry's denial was quiet but firm.

With a sidelong look through her lashes, Edie glanced at Maddock to see if he was observing this duel of wills between her stepson and his daughter. He was watching them, all right, but the instant she looked at him his gaze dropped to meet hers. She glimpsed the light of challenge in his gray depths, but didn't understand its cause.

"I had a skirt that was being altered. Daddy and I stopped by to pick it up," Felicia explained quickly, as if she didn't want Jerry to think she had followed him into the store.

"It fits you perfectly, Mom. You don't have to do a thing to it." Alison shook her head in amazement. "It's even the right length. Turn around so I can see the back."

Edie pivoted self-consciously, aware that her daughter wasn't the only one showing a lot of interest in the way the dress fit her. She was shaken by the sensation that she was modeling it for Maddock's benefit, seeking his approval. His gaze seemed to mock her with the knowledge when she unwillingly met it.

"You've got to buy it and wear it to the dance tonight," Alison insisted.

She felt the faint narrowing of interest in Maddock's look. Her throat became tight, nerves tensing. "No," Edie said, and raised a hand in a shielding gesture to lift the curtain of hair near her ear. "What I mean is . . . I don't think I'll go to the dance, so I don't need this dress. You and Jerry can go, but I'll stay home."

"You will not," Alison protested with an irritated frown, and turned to her half brother for help. "Jerry, talk to her."

"We've all been working hard, Edie. You need to go out tonight and have fun as much as we do," he insisted gently

"We'll talk about it later." Edie moved away from the mirror . . . and Maddock. She tried to sound light and uncaring as if it was all unimportant.

"Miss?" Jerry motioned to a sales associate to get her attention. "We'll buy this dress."

"Jerry—" Edie's voice was low and vibrating with impatience.

But he was too old to be silenced by the angry sparks in her eyes. The faint smile in his maturing face told her so.

"When was the last time you went dancing, Edie?" Jerry immediately provided an answer to his own question. "Had to be before you married Dad, because he had two left feet and nobody could drag him onto the dance floor. We all had to gang up on him just to persuade him to take us out to dinner."

Again she glanced at Maddock, who was listening without any qualms. Jerry's statement made Joe sound as if he hadn't been a very loving husband. She felt duty bound to defend him.

"I didn't mind," she reminded Jerry.

"I know you didn't mind. That was Dad. We all loved him for what he was, not what he did or didn't do. I'm only saying it's time you had fun," Jerry replied. "And don't say you don't know how to dance, because you are the one who taught me."

"I just don't feel like going." It was a weak excuse no matter how stiffly she issued it.

"Okay." Jerry shrugged an acceptance. "If you're going to stay home, Alison and I will, too."

"Jerry," Alison wailed in protest.

"You're both old enough to do what you want. You don't need me along." Edie felt she was being unfairly pressured.

"If you don't go, we don't go," Jerry repeated, and glanced at his half sister. "Agreed?"

A long, defeated sigh came from Alison as she nodded a reluctant, "Agreed."

"That is blackmail, Jerry Gibbs," Edie accused. "Emotional blackmail."

"I think that's what it is," he agreed with an impudent grin.

"Does that mean we're going?" Holding her breath, Alison glanced eagerly from one to the other.

"Yes." Edie grudgingly gave in to the pressure.

"Oh, good! I found this totally cute yellow outfit, Mom. Let me show it to you." Alison dashed back to the rack. "I thought I'd treat myself to something new, too."

The sales associate passed in front of Edie to hand a package to Felicia Maddock. "I'm sorry you had to wait so long, Miss Maddock," the clerk apologized. "The alterations to your skirt took a little longer than we expected."

"That's quite all right." There was a briskness of dismissal in the reply as Felicia glanced over her shoulder. "Are you ready, Daddy?"

"Whenever you are," he agreed blandly, but Edie thought she noticed a flicker of irritation in his expression.

His daughter paused to flash an aloof smile at Jerry. "Maybe we'll see you at the dance tonight. Daddy and I have been talking about going. He doesn't like me to go alone because sometimes it gets a little rough in places like that. You could ride in with us if you like. It wouldn't be out of our way to stop by your place," she offered.

Jerry was already shaking his head in refusal. Before he could voice it, Maddock was at his daughter's side, taking her arm. "I haven't decided that we're going tonight, Felicia," he stated.

Relief trembled through Edie. The prospect of Maddock attending the dance had filled her with all sorts of misgivings. Now it seemed likely he wouldn't be there, or he wouldn't have corrected his daughter. Edie wondered whether he was refusing because he didn't want his daughter chasing Jerry, or if it was because he wasn't interested in running into her.

Felicia seemed untroubled by his statement, although she surrendered to the pressure of his guiding hand. She smiled over her shoulder at Jerry. "We'll see you tonight," she said confidently.

As Maddock escorted her out of the shop, Jerry murmured, "He should make her stay home on general principal."

"I pity your kids, Jerry," Alison declared. "You're going to be too strict." She held up the yellow top and short, pleated denim skirt trimmed in matching yellow for Edie's inspection. "What do you think of it, Mom? Is rickrack too retro?"

"It looks great on the hanger. Why don't you try it on while I change out of this dress?" Edie suggested.

"Do you like it, mean daddy Jerry?" Alison teased him.

"Yes, I like it," he agreed absently while sending her a sharp look. "And I'm not going to be all that strict. I just know our kids aren't going to turn out totally spoiled like Felicia."

"*Our* kids?" Edie raised an eyebrow in curious surprise.

It had been years since she'd seen Jerry blush— not since his early teenage years. But a scarlet red was now spreading up from his neck to flame his face.

"I meant . . . when Alison has kids, and I have kids—our kids—we won't spoil them," he tried to bluff his way out of that slip.

But Edie knew that wasn't what he'd meant at all. When he had said "our" he had been referring to Felicia and himself. She was absolutely sure of it—and it was clear that he liked the girl a lot, even with the way she flounced around and acted like a princess. What was it about these Maddocks that could make you criticize them, find fault with them, dislike them even, and yet be so inexplicably drawn to them?

But all this escaped Alison's notice. "You're right, Jerry. If any kid of mine started acting like that brat, I'd make sure they didn't sit down for a week." She hugged the yellow outfit to her. "I'm going to go try this on."

Edie followed her to the dressing room to change back into her jeans and T-shirt and put her boots on. She pretended to accept Jerry's explanation for the time being. After all, who was she to give advice when she couldn't control her own wayward thoughts?

The only thing that needed to be done to Alison's outfit was to take the waist in a little—but that meant taking in the yoke of the short skirt too. The shop wasn't able to make the alteration in time for Alison to wear it to the dance that night, so Edie agreed to do it when they got home.

By the time they had lunch, did their grocery shopping and drove to the ranch, it was time to start the never-ending chores. Chaos set in as they tried to fix supper, eat it, pick out the skirt's seams and adjust the fit, take baths and get ready.

Edie was taking the last stitch in the waistband when Alison rushed into the room in her bathrobe. "Mom, help me! I washed my hair and now I have terminal frizzies!" She held the blow-dryer in one hand, a brush and curling wand in the other.

"How long is this going to take?" Jerry asked with a sigh. Already dressed in new jeans and a western shirt with pearl snaps and arrow-point pockets, he was sitting on the couch, twirling his hat in his hand in an attempt at patience.

"You can't expect me to go looking like this," Alison said heatedly.

"It wouldn't make a very good impression on that cute cowboy, Rob, would it?" He grinned. She wrinkled her nose at him, then laughed. "Edie still has to get dressed, and you still have to put your makeup on. I'm going to go to sleep waiting for you guys." He straightened. "If it's okay, I'm going into town now. You guys can drive the car. I'll take the truck."

"Go on ahead," Edie agreed, and knotted the thread. "It may take us a while."

"If you don't come with Alison, I'll drive back out here for you," Jerry warned.

"I'll be there," she promised.

"Save us a table," Alison called after him as he walked to the door.

"If you aren't there by midnight, I might be under the table."

"What are you talking about? You never have more than one beer."

He didn't reply. Then the door was slamming behind him.

It was nearly an hour later before they left the ranch. The summer sun was just dipping below the horizon when they reached the outskirts of Custer. There wasn't anyplace to park near the bar, but they finally found a spot more than a block away.

The bar was dimly lighted and crowded with people. Huge amps, positioned strategically throughout the room, blared with the country music being played by the band on the small stage. Jerry saw them before they even noticed him in the multitude of people. As Edie wound her way through the maze of tables and chairs ahead of Alison to the one near the dance floor, she realized there was another man with Jerry. Alison was quick to identify him as Rob Lydell, her cowboy.

"We were just about to send out a search party for you two," Jerry shouted above the din of music and voices, then managed an introduction to the young but sun-weathered cowboy who, Edie noticed, had an engaging smile.

The waitress stopped at their table. Jerry and Rob ordered two more beers, but Edie elected to have a Coke, as did Alison. At first it was difficult to hear the conversation, but she gradually learned to block out the general din and listen only to the people at her table. They laughed and talked; then Rob asked Alison to dance.

"He seems nice," Edie observed as she watched the pair circling the crowded dance floor.

"I like him—which is more than I could say for some of Alison's choices," Jerry agreed with a rueful smile. "Like lover boy Craig."

"I try not to remember him," Edie murmured.

When the band finished the ballad they went immediately into an up-tempo tune. The couple stayed on the floor to dance to it. After that song was over the band took a twenty-minute break. Edie tried not to notice that Rob's chair had slid closer to Alison's when they came back to sit at the table.

Some of Rob's friends stopped by to talk as a

prerecorded mix replaced the live music. Edie was glad that they had come to the dance. Jerry and Alison were meeting more people in this one night than they had since they'd moved here. They should have begun socializing sooner, except there had been so much work to do.

As the band returned to the small stage after their break, Edie leaned forward to mention her thought to Jerry. His attention was focused on the dance floor . . . and then he suddenly tensed. He took a deep breath, a swig from his bottle of beer, and seemed to force himself to relax. Curious, Edie followed the direction of his gaze and saw Felicia Maddock dancing with some cowboy. At that moment the brunette glanced toward their table and faked a look of surprise.

"Hi, Jerry!" She waved and smiled a greeting that was much too casual. "Told ya I'd see you tonight." Then she was being whirled into the center of the floor by her partner.

"What a snooty-pants. She can't even say hello to me," Alison grumbled in irritation.

"She's like that sometimes," Rob admitted, "but she isn't really a bad kid." As if he realized his opinion didn't exactly please Alison, he let the subject drop.

Jerry made no comment, although Edie noticed his gaze kept straying to the dance floor, keeping track of the young brunette. But he wasn't nearly as talkative as he had been before. For that matter, neither was she. If Felicia was here, so was Maddock. Almost unwillingly, Edie kept searching for him until she saw him standing at the counter bar.

There was an understated simplicity to his clothes—a white shirt unbuttoned at the throat and a buckskin vest hanging open. The western cut of his jeans fitted closely to his hips and legs, flaring slightly over his boots with their underslung rider's heels. He was engaged in conversation with a cowboy standing beside him. When his head turned in the direction of the dance floor, Edie looked immediately away, not wanting to be caught looking at him.

Aware of his presence, it was impossible to keep her gaze from straying to him. Yet Maddock didn't seem to notice her at all. Edie did a poor job of convincing herself that she was glad.

Alison was in high spirits as she returned to the table hand in hand with her cowboy. Her face was aglow. To Edie her daughter seemed to be floating on air. She felt a tad envious when Alison drifted to the chair beside her.

Rob didn't immediately sit down. "Want another beer, Jerry?"

Jerry seemed to have a hard time assimilating the question, not answering until he had torn his gaze from the couples leaving the dance floor. "Yeah, I'll have another," he agreed while drawing a deep breath.

"Would you like another Coke, Alison?" Rob inquired, and received an affirmative and smiling nod. His glance then sought out Edie. "How about you, Mrs. Gibbs?"

Mrs. The respectful term made her feel extraordinarily old. He'd be calling her *ma'am* next. "No, thank you."

The cowboy had barely left the table before Alison was leaning excitedly toward her. "Rob wants to take me home. Do you think it's all right, Mom?"

"I just met him, Alison," Edie protested. "I don't know anything about him. Neither do you."

"He's nice. You can see that." Alison was at her persuasive best. "What should I tell him?"

Maternal instinct insisted that Edie order Alison to come home with her, but it was overwhelmed by the memory of Rob's voice referring to her as Mrs. Gibbs. Her sigh was almost inaudible.

"I can't give you an answer just yet. Don't expect me to make a spur-of-the-moment decision like that, Alison. Let me think about it," she insisted with a vague smile of reassurance.

"But what if he asks me?" Her daughter frowned anxiously.

Edie shrugged. "Let him dangle a little. Tell him that he'll have to wait and see."

With a sigh, Alison straightened to glance at the returning cowboy and smile in welcome. Edie inspected Rob with a closer eye. Her conclusion matched Jerry's. Rob Lydell was a major improvement on some of Alison's past boyfriends.

She didn't notice Jerry rise to his feet until he touched her arm. "The band is playing a slow song, Edie. Want to dance?"

"I'd love to," she agreed without hesitation, and straightened from her chair. "It's been ages since I've danced, so if I step on your toes, don't complain," she added as Jerry guided her onto the dance floor.

"I'm not worried about you stepping on my toes." He grinned. "After all, you're the one that taught both me and Alison how to dance." He turned her into his arms.

Chapter Nine

Within seconds after they had joined the other couples on the dance floor, Jerry became silent and his expression grew serious. Edie glanced around to find the source of his distraction. She knew she had located it the instant her gaze found Felicia dancing with her father. Edie looked away, but not before her heart did a succession of flips at the sight of Will Maddock.

All her senses were on guard, alerted now to the rancher's presence and tracking him with super-sensitive, frustrated-female radar. When someone brushed a shoulder against hers, Edie didn't have to turn to know who it was.

Confirmation came with the stiffening of Jerry's arm around her waist and the low pitch of Will Maddock's familiar voice as he suggested, "Why don't we change partners?"

Edie couldn't think of a single reason to refuse, especially when Jerry was releasing her to welcome Felicia. Then Will's large hand was on her waist, and Edie found herself guided into his arms and matching her steps to the simple pattern of his. When she lifted her gaze to his rugged face, his gray eyes were smiling at her knowingly, as if aware of the effect he had on her. Yet Edie suspected it was all her imagination.

When his gaze drifted after the couple dancing away from them, she glanced at them, too. Jerry and Felicia were completely wrapped up in each other, oblivious to everything else around them.

"Young love." There was a dryness to Will's tone, and it glittered in his eyes when Edie glanced at them. "No one could pay me to go through those throes of agony again."

In spite of herself she smiled. "Neither would I." She was conscious of a very comfortable closeness, something warm and wonderful.

"My daughter is a true Maddock," he observed in the same tone as before. "Once she decides she wants something, she goes after it. I'm afraid she has decided she wants your stepson."

"Jerry is of the opinion that she has some growing up to do," Edie replied. "At the moment he finds her spoiled, self-centered and immature. If you don't mind my saying so," she added hastily, kicking herself for her unthinking rudeness.

But Will seemed to agree. She could hear it in his throaty chuckle. "I always believed that boy had a head on his shoulders, even if he is caught up in your dream of becoming a rancher." Before Edie could take offense at his remark, Will Maddock continued, "That's the trouble with being an only parent. It's hard to say no. I keep trying to make up for the fact that she doesn't have a mother. Normally I wouldn't approve of Felicia being with someone Jerry's age, but I'm hoping he will gently teach her that she can't always have her way."

His arm tightened around her waist as he avoided a collision with another couple. It broke the pattern, and Edie missed a step and brushed against him. The contact with the hard-muscled flesh of his body brought an instant recall of other times when she had been held this close. She had accepted the fact that she found him sexually attractive, but she was only just beginning to discover that he aroused her emotionally, too. His hand shaped itself to the small of her back, and she damn near melted.

Edie told herself silently to resist the sensual pressure of his hand. It was as dangerous as her growing emotional involvement. Directing her gaze away from the broad set of his shoulders and the tanned column of his throat, she sought the distraction of other couples on the dance floor. Alison was among them, her arms wrapped around the neck of her partner.

"Maddock, do you know anything about that cowboy dancing with Alison?" She drew his attention to the pair. "His name is Rob Lydell."

"Yes, I know him. What about him?" His glance was curious.

"He asked to give Alison a ride home tonight," she explained. "I've only just met him, and I wasn't sure whether I should let her go with him or not."

The corners of his mouth twitched in an attempt to suppress a smile. "I think it's safe to say

you can trust him." His tone and his amused attitude caused Edie to frown in confusion. "Rob
works for me," he revealed.

"I should have guessed," she murmured almost
under her breath. That Maddock magic again.
First Jerry was succumbing to his daughter's
charm, and Alison was all wrapped up with one of
his hired hands. And here she was, caught up in
some crazy longing for the rancher himself.

"If you'd like, I'll have a talk with Rob and make
certain you have no cause for concern about
Alison," he offered with parental understanding.

"It isn't that." She shook her head, impatient
and suddenly defensive. Some impulse made her
speak her mind, almost regretting her next words
as they tumbled out. "Why can't you leave us
alone?"

His glinting gray eyes ran over her face, following her thoughts. The line of his mouth became
mocking. "You know the old saying—if you can't
beat them, join them."

It wasn't meant to be taken seriously, she realized. He was only baiting her, trying to get a rise
from her. Well, she wasn't going to give him the
satisfaction. Her gaze was fixed on a point beyond
his shoulder. Maddock put a finger under her
chin, lifting it. She was forced to meet his steady
gray eyes.

"We Maddocks aren't such a bad lot, Edie.
You've got the wrong impression of us altogether,"
he murmured. "Our differences have been on a
purely business level. Your mistake was taking it
personally. I've told you that before, but you still
don't believe me. Your ranch happens to sit on

land I want. If you had bought any other place, I would have wished you the best of luck."

His fingers slowly stroked the underside of her jaw, tracing its firm set. Edie closed her eyes at the sensual ache his caress induced. Her fingers closed over his forearm to draw his hand away as the music stopped.

"Which doesn't change the fact that we still own the ranch, Maddock, and we aren't going to sell it to anyone," she replied tightly.

Turning out of his arm, she left the dance floor to return to her table. She was conscious that he followed her, escorting her back. At the table he pulled out her chair. As she sat down, both Jerry and Alison returned. She looked up to see the measured look Maddock gave the two before he nodded briefly to her and moved away toward the bar.

"You didn't mind changing partners, did you, Edie?" Jerry studied the stillness of her features with an anxious frown.

"Of course not." Her assuring smile was stiff, not fully natural.

But Jerry didn't seem to notice as his gaze traveled after the rancher, seeking him out among the others lined up at the bar. "What do you think Maddock would say if I asked to take Felicia home?"

"I'm sure you would have his permission," she replied, remembering Maddock's approving words about Jerry.

"Did he say anything about Felicia and me while you were dancing?" Jerry was quick to catch the note of certainty in her tone.

"Yes. Something to the effect that Felicia has made up her mind she wants you . . . and a Maddock always gets what he or she wants. So I don't think your request will come as any surprise to him." She smiled to take the little sting of bitterness out of her words.

But Jerry hadn't noticed it. "Excuse me." He rose from his chair to make his way through the crowd to Felicia.

"I don't know what he sees in her," Alison muttered. "She's a brat."

"But a very beautiful brat," Edie pointed out. "Where's Rob, by the way?"

"He stopped to talk to some friends. He'll be here shortly," Alison replied confidently.

"You didn't mention that he worked for Maddock." Edie observed the way her daughter nibbled at her lip. Obviously she'd known that.

"Just because he works for them doesn't make him like them," she reasoned. "Rob is nice."

"I'm not going to argue with that. If you want to ride home with him, I have no objection." After all, Maddock had vouched for him, and it was obviously what Alison wanted.

"Thanks, Mom." Her face brightened with a smile as she leaned over to give Edie an affectionate hug.

Rob returned to the table to sit beside Alison, and Edie was forgotten as the two spoke in low voices to each other. With Jerry gone as well, Edie felt superfluous. Everyone was paired up except her, and she didn't like the lonely feeling that gave her.

Rising, she laid a hand on her daughter's shoulder to gently intrude on their conversation. "I'm going home," she explained as the reason for the interruption.

"You can't leave now, Mom," Alison protested. "It's early yet."

"Maybe for you, but it's late for me." She glanced at the young man sitting so close to her daughter and smiled. "Good night, Rob."

"Good night, ma'am. I'll see that Alison gets home safely," he promised.

"I won't be late," Alison added.

"Tell Jerry I've left when you see him," Edie said as she moved away from the table toward the door.

Outside, the music and the noise of the bar was muffled. Edie paused and lifted her gaze to the night sky, brilliant with stars. A big, heavy moon lolled above the jagged horizon of the Black Hills. After the smoke-filled bar, the air smelled fresh and sweet.

As her thoughts wandered over the night's events, she strolled in the direction of the parked car. What was the best strategy in all battles? Divide and conquer. That was precisely what was happening. Jerry was with Felicia Maddock. Alison was with Rob Lydell, Maddock's hired man. And she was finding Maddock more irresistible with each meeting. It didn't bode well for the future.

She sighed and crossed in front of the dark opening to an alleyway. With her head down, Edie didn't notice the next building was a honky-tonk bar until the door slammed and three laughing cowboys staggered outside. They dawdled there, trying to decide where to go next. They were blocking the front part of the sidewalk, so Edie moved to walk behind them and continue to her car parked half a block away. At that moment they noticed her, and one of them let out a long wolf whistle. Not that she wanted that kind of attention from men who'd been drinking hard.

"Where are you going, honey?" One of the young cowboys moved in front of her to stop her.

"Can we come along?" a second spoke up.

The building was at her back as they crowded around her, yet there was nothing threatening in their manner. They'd had a few drinks and were ready for a good time. Edie wasn't.

"Sorry, fellas. I'm on my way home, so how about letting me by?" Her request was friendly but firm.

"The night's young," the third insisted. "It's too early to go home."

"Betcha she had a fight with her boyfriend," the first one guessed.

The second cowboy took up the thought before Edie could respond. "You aren't going to let him spoil your evening, are you? It would be a shame to let that pretty dress go to waste."

"We'll take you out," the first one offered. "You just tell us where you want to go and we'll take you." There was a chorus of agreement from the other two.

"Thanks for the invitation, but I want to go home—*alone*." She stressed the last word to leave them in no doubt. "Would you mind letting me pass?"

There was a slight shift, creating a gap between two of them. As Edie started to slip through it, the third cowboy made one last attempt to change her mind.

"Come on, honey. Take pity on three lonely cowboys," he coaxed.

A voice came from behind all of them. "You boys aren't listening. The lady said no."

Edie pivoted as she recognized Will Maddock's voice. The sight of his large frame standing by the shadows of the alleyway took everyone by surprise. The young cowboy closest to him recovered first and swaggered forward a couple of steps.

"Well, well, well. If it ain't the big bull himself," he drawled with exaggerated thickness. "I don't recall you bein' invited to this party."

"I invited myself. Now let the lady pass." There was a steel-hard quality to his voice, but his face was in the shadows and Edie couldn't make out his features.

The third cowboy continued to stand in front of Maddock in unsteady challenge. "Is that an order?"

"Yes."

Edie felt the tension build in the air. These boys were looking for trouble, and Maddock's attitude was all the provocation they needed. She could sense it rippling through the trio of cowhands out for a night on the town.

"What if we don't obey your order?" the freckle-faced one on Edie's left asked innocently.

"I guess I'll have to show you that it's the right thing to do." Maddock shrugged easily.

"Maddock—" She attempted to protest his handling of the situation, but he didn't give her a chance.

"Stay out of this, Edie," he ordered tersely.

"Edie?" The second cowboy looked at her, catching Maddock's familiar use of her name and drawing his own conclusion. "Is he the one who spoiled your evening and sent you home early?"

She intended to respond to that and attempt to defuse the scene, but it had already escalated beyond the point where any of the men would listen to her. She realized her chance was gone as the first cowboy took a step toward Maddock.

"I always wondered if you were as tough as everyone says," he murmured. "Guess I'll have to find out for myself."

"I guess you will," Maddock agreed.

The cowboy took the first swing, a blow that was warded off by Maddock's upraised arm. With every intention of stopping the fight before it went further, Edie took a step forward, but the shortest cowboy of the trio caught her by the waist to prevent her from reaching the scuffling pair.

"You'd better stay here, miss," he advised for her own protection. "We don't want you getting hurt."

Despite her struggles, she was held fast. When it became apparent that the first cowboy was getting the worst of it, the freckle-faced cowboy rushed in to help his buddy. The cowboy holding Edie blocked most of her view, limiting her knowledge of the fight to the grunting sounds of the protagonists, the thud of landing fists and thrashing bodies.

Finally there was semisilence, underlined with

heavy breathing and punctuated with soft moans. The arms holding Edie loosened as the last cowboy carefully let her go and moved out of her way. She saw Maddock standing there, breathing hard and swaying a little while his two opponents staggered to their feet.

"Had enough?" His rough voice made a winded challenge.

One of them nodded an affirmative answer and reached down to scoop up Maddock's hat and hand it to him. Edie stared in stunned disbelief as the cowboy's hand remained outstretched to shake Maddock's. The second cowboy did the same in a show of no hard feelings. Then all three were drifting across the street. Edie heard the good-natured ribbing start among them before they reached the other side.

"Are you all right?"

Maddock's question roused her from her stillness. *Men,* she thought, *why do they think everything has to be settled by a fight?*

"Who asked you to interfere?" she demanded, because as far as she was concerned, she hadn't been in any danger at all. The resulting brawl had been completely unnecessary.

"No one. The boys were looking for some adventure. It's better that I supplied it instead of you," he said, straightening a little and squaring his shoulders as if regathering his strength.

Her gaze narrowed in sharp suspicion as it occurred to her that Maddock had not simply "happened" to come this way. "Why were you following me?"

"I realized that I hadn't told you how pretty you

look in your new dress and those high heels." His compliment reminded her of that afternoon when he'd seen her trying on the dress barefoot. Some of her irritation faded with his remark. He lifted a hand to his cheek and wiped at it. She saw the glistening dark stain of blood on his fingers. "One of those damned cowboys cut me with a ring," he muttered under his breath.

"You'd better let me look at it." She walked over to him and took the handkerchief he produced from a rear pocket. Folding it, she dabbed at the blood oozing from the gash on his cheekbone. In the shadowed night she couldn't tell the extent of the injury. "I really can't see. Just not enough light here."

"There's a back entrance to this bar in the alley. The owner's a friend of mine. We can use his office in the rear." With the first step he took toward the dark alley, he swayed unexpectedly. Edie was instantly at his side to curve an arm around his middle, offering him slim support. Maddock paused, leaning some of his weight on her until his legs were steady under him. He draped an arm across her shoulders, his hand closing on the soft flesh of her arm, and started into the alley. "I haven't been in a fight for five years. If that third man had come at me, I don't think I would have been standing at the end."

"There wasn't any reason for that fight," Edie said with a surge of impatience. "They were letting me go when you showed up."

"It didn't look that way to me." The darkness of the alley enveloped them, and Maddock made his way to the rear door by instinct alone. "Either way, it's spilled milk now." He rapped on the wooden door.

"As usual, a woman has to clean up the mess," she murmured a little sharply.

"As usual, she does." His soft chuckle mocked her irritated response.

The door was opened by a portly, balding man in a tightly collared shirt with a string tie. His frowning glance widened to an open stare of shock as the interior light illuminated Maddock's face.

"It isn't as bad as it looks, Tubby," Maddock assured the man in a weary voice. But Edie felt the same start of shock at the smeared blood and purpling flesh around his cheekbone and jaw. Still she had taken care of too many of her children's cuts and bruises not to realize that Maddock's assessment was probably accurate.

"Come in, Will." The owner opened the door wider to admit them. "Sit here in my office and I'll get a wet cloth and the first-aid box."

The stout man disappeared, leaving the private office through an interior door where the sounds of loud voices and a jukebox filtered into the room. Edie helped Maddock into a straight-backed chair beside the desk littered with papers, rolls of register tape and delivery slips. Within seconds the owner returned with a clean, wet cloth and the first-aid kit. Edie took the cloth and knelt down to begin carefully wiping the blood smears from Maddock's face. The owner hovered beside her, gritting his teeth and making faces as if he was the patient.

"Do you think that cut will need stitches?" he asked. "Maybe I should call a doctor?"

The wound had already stopped bleeding. Edie studied it carefully. "It isn't as deep as it looks. I don't think it will need stitches," she concluded, but she was well aware that if it had been half an inch higher, it would have been his eye that was cut. Her concern was overridden by her feeling of annoyance at his testosterone-fueled showing off. The glancing blow from a ringed fist could have resulted in permanent injury. Her mouth tightened.

"Is there anything else I can do?" the owner offered. "Anything you need?"

"I think we can manage alone," Maddock replied. "Thanks, Tubby."

"I'll go out front and give Mike a hand at the bar. If you need me, just shout," the man insisted.

"We will." After the door latch had clicked shut, Maddock caught her eye with a glinting look. "The poor guy can't stand the sight of blood."

"It's a shame you don't suffer from the same problem. Maybe you wouldn't have ended up looking like this." Her glance moved over his face. There hadn't been as much damage as it had first appeared. Except for the gash on his cheekbone, there was a bruise along his jaw and a purpling area near the cut. It could easily have been much worse.

Setting the stained, wet cloth aside, Edie opened the first-aid kit and removed a bottle of antiseptic. She used the applicator attached to the lid and dabbed some into a corner of his wound.

Maddock breathed in with a sharp, hissing sound and recoiled.

"Hold still," she ordered without sympathy, and applied more.

"Ouch!"

"I'd like to know what it is about a little stinging that can turn grown men into little boys—the same grown men that take fists in their faces without a whimper," she said.

His gray eyes danced wickedly, not taking offense as they met her look. "Maybe I'm missing the soothing hand on my brow."

"You're getting just what you deserve." She added an extra squirt of antiseptic to what had already been applied.

"I was under the impression that women liked to have men fight over them."

"Not this woman," Edie retorted. "I don't think it ever occurred to you that someone could have been seriously hurt. You could have injured your eye, possibly lost the sight in it." She recapped the antiseptic bottle and straightened to return it to the first-aid kit.

Maddock caught her wrist and turned her around to face him as his strong features tilted up to view her expression. His steady gaze held her still.

"I was beginning to think you didn't care," he murmured.

"It was stupid of you to fight." She found it difficult to be patient with him. "You're too old for parking lot brawls."

"Too old?" He laughed heartily and pulled her

onto his lap. "I come to the aid of a damsel in distress and she accuses me of being too old!"

"I didn't mean it that way," she protested. How could she when she was so fully aware of the powerful strength of his arms encircling her and his potent maleness. The heat of his body was already stealing the force of her anger and kindling an entirely different response. "I meant you should have had more sense."

"Where you're concerned, Edie, I don't," he murmured, and narrowed the distance between their lips until she felt the warmth of his breath against her skin. "Hadn't you noticed?"

"No," she whispered.

As his mouth settled onto her lips in a deep, searching kiss, her eyes closed, and her arms found their way around his neck. In his arms she found the fulfillment her heart had been seeking. Emotion swelled within her in a flood tide of intense longing.

His hand roamed over her stomach and ribs and burned through the soft fabric covering her breast. Tremors of desire quivered through her, caused by his caress. The driving pressure of his kiss told of his need, assuring her that she was not alone in this irresistible spiral of feelings.

There was a rough possession in the kisses he burned into her face and neck, claiming every inch of her. "I'm not convinced anymore that any man can arouse you like this, Edie," he murmured thickly. "This isn't just about sex."

"But it's pretty damn sexy," she purred, rubbed her lips against his throat, savoring the taste of his skin. "I'm not sure what I'm thinking or feeling."

With each drumming beat of her heart, she was becoming more sure of her growing love for this man, but she kept silent, betraying her emotions not by word but by deed.

Maddock sighed and reluctantly lifted his head. His gray eyes smoldered with barely disguised impatience and desire, yet his actions were controlled. He removed his hand from her breast and forced it to wander restlessly to her shoulder.

"Tubby will be coming back to see how we're doing." He answered the question that was in her eyes. "I think we should leave."

"Yes," she agreed, and let him help her off his lap. "It's time I was going home." She was disappointed when Maddock failed to make an alternative suggestion.

"I'll walk you to your car," was his only offer.

Edie waited by the back door while Maddock let the owner know they were leaving and thanked him for the help. He took her hand to lead her out of the alley to the lighted street and walked with her the half block to her car. He opened the driver's door for her and waited until she was behind the wheel to shut it.

"My car is parked around the corner," he said. "I'll follow you to make sure you get home in one piece."

"Okay." She smiled an instant agreement, glad that she hadn't seen the last of him this night.

Shortly after Edie pulled onto the highway, she saw the headlights of Maddock's car reflected in her rearview mirror. It made her feel warm and wanted inside. All her adult life she had been the one who looked after others. It was a novel experience to have someone looking after her. She really liked the feeling.

The drive to the ranch didn't seem as long with his headlights winking in her mirror. There was a soft curve to her lips as she stopped the car in front of the house and climbed out. She waited for Maddock while he parked behind her car and stepped out.

"Would you like to come in for coffee?" she said as he approached. "It won't take long to fix some."

"I was hoping you'd ask," he replied, and took her arm as they climbed the porch steps to the front door.

Once inside, Edie paused to turn on a light. "Make yourself comfortable while I go to the kitchen and fix the coffee."

She had already started in that direction when Maddock called her name quietly yet insistently. "Edie?"

She stopped and half turned. "Yes?"

He walked up to her and stopped. "Coffee was just an excuse. We both know that."

Her pulse accelerated its tempo, and she suddenly had difficulty breathing. All conscious thought was swept aside by the dark intensity of his gray eyes, urgent and compelling. His hands molded to the soft curves of her shoulders, applying pressure to draw her toward him. The moment became prolonged as he slowly bent his head and nuzzled the sensitive curve of her neck. A sigh of aching pleasure whispered from her lips.

How wonderful, she thought, that someone so powerfully built could be so gentle. But Maddock seemed to be made of contradictions. He could punch the daylights out of the competition, yet he relied on sensual, tender kisses to obtain her surrender. He didn't take, but convinced her to give. He was a man hard enough to have a big heart.

"Edie, we've outgrown the stage of playing waiting games," he murmured, and lifted his head to frame her face with his strong hands. "Leave that to Felicia and Jerry. We don't have any reason to play hard to get and those other games. It wastes too much precious time that we could be enjoying in other ways."

"I'm not playing any games." Her emotions were much too serious to be toyed with. She hoped he knew that.

"I want to make love to you, Edie." The determination in his voice started a fluttering in her heart. "It's what you want, too. Don't try to deny it."

"I won't, Maddock." But she lowered her gaze to the leather stitching on his buckskin vest, feeling the tremors start.

"We've both been married. It isn't as if we don't know the score," he insisted, and lowered his hands to the sides of her neck, his thumbs caressing her throat. A stillness came over him as he felt the faint tremors quaking through her body. "You're trembling. What's wrong?"

"Nothing is wrong." Not really. It was more a case of nerves than anything else. It certainly wasn't a lack of wanting on her part. "It's just that I've never been to bed with any man other than my husband."

"I know that." He smiled into her uplifted gaze, but the puzzled light remained in his gray eyes.

"Don't you see?" The corners of her mouth

deepened in a tremulous smile. "It would be like the first time all over again."

A wondering look lit his eyes. "My God, Edie," he breathed, and gathered her into his arms, rubbing his cheek against the softness of her hair. A shudder vibrated through his muscled frame. "That's the most beautiful thing you could have said to me."

"It isn't that I don't want you to make love to me, Maddock. It's just that I—" A pickup rumbled into the ranch yard. Edie drew back. "It must be Jerry coming home."

After taking a deep breath and releasing it, Maddock gave a wry shake of his head and let her go. Outside, a pair of truck doors slammed shut. "And I thought it was only married couples who were interrupted by inquisitive children," he murmured suggestively.

A smile was tugging at the corners of Edie's mouth when Alison burst into the house. "Mom, there's a strange car parked . . . outside." The last word was tacked on belatedly after Alison noticed Maddock standing near Edie. "What are you doing here?" Surprise increased her natural bluntness.

"I was just making sure your mother arrived home safely," Maddock replied, and exchanged a glance with Edie.

"When I heard the truck," Edie spoke up to divert the subject, "I thought it was Jerry. I didn't expect to see you come through the door."

"Oh, Jerry's home, too." Alison glanced over her shoulder just as her half brother entered the house. His glance stopped on Maddock, too.

"You both came home together?" Edie looked

at the two of them with faint surprise. "But I thought—"

"It made more sense for me to ride with Rob as far as the Diamond D Ranch and come home from there with Jerry after he'd dropped Felicia off," Alison explained the arrangement, then cocked her head to one side to study Maddock. "What happened to your face? It looks as if you've been in a fight."

He touched the healing gash on his cheekbone as if he had forgotten it was there. "I fell down and cut myself," he lied blandly.

"Yeah? That was some fall," Jerry observed skeptically. "You cut one cheek and bruised the jaw on the other side."

Edie knew they weren't going to be fooled by Maddock's story. "There was an, um, minor incident tonight," she admitted.

"What happened, Mom?" Alison moved quickly to her side, and Jerry followed.

Maddock answered the question. "Some young men were mouthing off to your mother. I merely reminded them of their manners." His glance ran over the three of them, standing together, side by side. Wry amusement flickered across his features. "The Three Musketeers are united again," he murmured.

"One for all and all for one," Alison returned brightly.

"I'm having a few friends over for a barbecue tomorrow. I'd like you to come." He looked at Edie as he offered the invitation, but his gaze quickly encompassed the three of them. "All of you."

Edie was aware of the shocked silence emanating from her daughter and stepson, but she felt absolutely no hesitation about accepting his invitation. So much had changed in the space of one evening. She simply couldn't regard Maddock as an enemy any longer.

"Thank you, Maddock. It sounds fun." She smiled under the intimate look in those gray eyes.

"Come early—around eleven-thirty. I want to show you around my home." The softness of his voice carried its own message.

Typically, he left without a good-bye, but Edie discovered she was becoming used to that. With his departure Jerry and Alison finally had a chance to voice their curiosity. Jerry was first.

"What's going on, Edie?"

"Yeah," Alison echoed his question. "Why do we suddenly rate an invitation to Sunday dinner?"

Edie had a lot of guesses of her own, but she only voiced the safest one. "Maybe he's finally decided that we are here to stay."

Chapter Ten

The Diamond D ranch house was a white, two-story building with a pillared front. It faced the ranch buildings and had a spectacular view of the rough and broken Dakota terrain. This was Edie's first glimpse of the ranch headquarters, and she stared openly at its structures and network of corrals.

By the time Jerry had parked the car in front of the house, Maddock was outside to greet them. "Welcome to the Diamond D." He reserved a warm look for Edie. "I'm sorry Felicia isn't on hand to greet you, but she's still upstairs getting ready. Come inside."

His hand rested in light possession on the back of her waist as he personally escorted Edie to the front door with Jerry and Alison trailing behind them. The foyer just inside the front door to the house boasted a fine staircase to the second floor. To the right, decorated in soft rusts and golds, was the living room where Maddock began his tour of the house. A fireplace built of native stone gave the room a relaxed, comfortable air.

"There are three fireplaces in the house, two downstairs and one upstairs," Maddock explained as he led them into the dining room.

There was an informal quality about the room. It was easy for Edie to imagine Maddock sitting at the head of the table, holding forth to his guests about the ranch or politics or something as basic as Johnny's first tooth. Despite the richness of the solid walnut table, chairs and sideboard, there was something essentially casual about the room.

A cook was busy in the kitchen with preparations for the noon barbecue, so they didn't linger long there. But Edie did notice it was equipped with all the latest conveniences, with plenty of work space and a breakfast nook.

The last room he showed them on the ground floor was the den, paneled in knotty pine with leather-upholstered furniture. The bookshelves were lined with volumes on animal husbandry and agriculture interspersed with a selection of novels. Louis L'Amour and Larry McMurtry held pride of place, Edie noticed. Issues of ranching magazines were scattered around the room, giving it a lived-in look. A second fireplace was located in the den, constructed of burned brick.

As they returned to the foyer, Edie realized this was definitely a rancher's house where a man could feel free to walk in straight from the ranch yard without worrying greatly about what he tracked onto the floors. He could bring in a new-born calf, half-frozen by a winter's storm, and let the warmth of the kitchen help him nurse it back to life. Despite its imposing size, it was a home.

"We'll have the barbecue on the patio in the backyard by the pool." He paused beside the thermopaned glass doors that opened from the foyer onto the patio. "Last night I forgot to suggest that you bring your swimsuits along, but we keep a few on hand for guests in the changing room."

"Look!" Alison pointed to something or someone out of Edie's sight. "There's Rob."

"Yep," Maddock said. "He's helping set up the tables."

"Let's give him a hand, Jerry." Alison was eager to find a reason to see him again.

"Go ahead." Maddock nodded when Jerry hesitated to agree with his half sister's suggestion. "We'll be out shortly." As the two slid open the glass doors, the hand on Edie's back applied pressure to steer her away from the doors. Maddock wandered, apparently aimlessly, to the center of the foyer. "That concludes the tour of the house, with the exception of the upstairs," he corrected with a glance at the staircase. "There are five bedrooms in all, counting the master suite." He turned her around to face him, resting his hands on her hips. "What do you think of it?"

"Between the house and the ranch buildings, I'm convinced we'll never be able to do better," Edie admitted. "If your intention was to impress me, you've succeeded."

His mouth thinned with displeasure. Her reply wasn't the one he wanted to hear. "I'm not interested in impressing you. I want to know what you think of my home. Is it someplace you'd like to live? Do you like it?"

"I like it, yes." Edie hesitated to say more, certain she was reading more into his question than Maddock intended.

"That's why I wanted you to come today—so you could see where I live and get to know my friends. It probably seems like I'm rushing things . . . and I am," he admitted with a flash of wry amusement. "But I know what I want, Edie. I want to marry you. I want you to be my wife."

"Maddock." Amazement, a wondrous kind of disbelief and a little shock became all mixed up in the way she said his name. She hadn't expected a proposal! She knew the answer she wanted to give him, but the words wouldn't come out.

He gazed into her eyes, shining with happiness, and read her answer. A slow smile of satisfaction softened his firmly cut mouth. His head started to bend toward her and stopped when he heard car doors slam outside and voices signaling the approach of new arrivals.

Before the guests reached the front door, he claimed her lips in a hard, possessive kiss that revealed his desire and frustration. She clung to his kiss for an instant, then let him draw away.

"We'll talk about this later—after everyone has left," he told her as someone knocked on the door. But the light in his gray eyes promised there would be less talking and more action.

When he left her to welcome his guests at the door, Edie was lost in a bliss-filled daze. A faint noise came from the stairs, and Edie turned. Felicia Maddock stood poised on the steps halfway down. It was clear to Edie that the girl had been there for some time. She saw a look of hurt jealousy in the girl's blue eyes as they bored into her. Ignoring her father at the door with the arriving friends, Felicia came swinging down the steps directly toward Edie. Her expression was coldly haughty.

"I knew Daddy wanted your ranch," Felicia murmured. "But it never occurred to me he wanted it badly enough to marry *you* to get it."

With her poisoned barb delivered, Felicia swept past, not allowing Edie a chance to reply. With quiet concern she watched the girl walk to Maddock's side to welcome their guests. Was it possible that the motive behind Maddock's impromptu proposal was to obtain control of the ranch?

When Maddock called her forward to introduce her to his friends, Edie knew it wasn't true. Maddock fought for what he wanted and fought hard, but he was an old-fashioned man straight out of a classic Western movie. Riding the range. Protecting the womenfolk. Beating up cowpokes three at a time.

He was too blunt, too forthright. Sure, he had seen Edie as a thorn in his side at first. And his wheeling and dealing at the cattle auctions hadn't exactly been on the up-and-up, but again, he'd been protecting what he held dear—his land— with the typical stubbornness of a hard-knocks cowboy. South Dakota bred a toughness in its native sons and Will Maddock was one

No, Felicia had deliberately implanted that seed of doubt, hoping it would germinate and grow when nourished by Edie's fertile imagination. The ranch had been a wedge between Edie and Maddock, and Felicia wanted to keep it that way. But she'd made a mistake, because instinctively Edie knew Maddock well enough not to believe that about him.

Maddock kept Edie at his side as he led his party of guests outside to the patio. She managed to take an absent part in the conversation swirling around her and answer questions put to her by his friends, but her thoughts kept running back to Felicia.

Halfway through the meal of barbecued ribs and chicken, it occurred to Edie why Felicia had made such a vicious remark. It had been jealousy she'd seen in the girl's expression. For years she had been the only female in her father's life, spoiled and pampered and indulged by him. Felicia was the mistress of the house.

If Maddock married Edie, all that would change. Felicia felt threatened. Edie would not only upset her position as lady of the house, but she would also become the object of her father's affection and attention. And, childlike, Felicia didn't want to share him. Felicia resented Edie, just as she would resent any woman that she felt might come between her and her father.

The situation troubled Edie. Understanding the problem did not automatically provide a solution. There had to be a way to handle it if she just had time to think, but that was impossible with so many people around.

After the meal was finished, no one seemed inclined to move from the tables. When Edie noticed Felicia go to the buffet to replenish her iced tea, she saw an opportunity to speak to the girl.

"I'm going to get some more iced tea," she murmured her excuse to Maddock, and rose from the table. She crossed the patio to the end of the buffet where the insulated urn of iced tea was located. When Felicia saw her approach, she started to walk away. "Felicia," Edie called out quickly to stop the girl. "I'd like to speak to you for a moment."

"I can't think of a thing that we would possibly have to say to one another," she replied with obvious disdain.

"There is something we need to get straightened out," Edie insisted quietly but firmly. "I think you've misunderstood some things."

"No, you're the one who doesn't understand," Felicia retorted. Edie saw Jerry and Alison approaching the buffet table, but Felicia's back was to them and she was unaware there was anyone within hearing except Edie. "Daddy and I have tried to make it clear to you from the beginning. You aren't wanted here. You never have been. Regardless of what you might think now, that hasn't changed."

"Felicia," Edie tried to warn the girl that Alison and Jerry were listening. Anger had already turned Jerry's mouth grim and brought the fighting sparks to Alison's eyes.

"You wanted to talk," Felicia reminded her, "and you might as well listen to some advice. You've had your free meal, so why don't you leave?"

"I think that's an excellent idea, Mom," Alison spoke up, and Felicia pivoted in surprise. "I know when I'm not wanted."

"Jerry!" Felicia gasped in dismay.

"I always knew you were a spoiled, selfish brat," he said tightly. "You've grown way too big for your britches."

Before anyone could guess his intention, Jerry scooped Felicia off her feet and into his arms. She shrieked in alarm, but didn't struggle too hard to get free. Edie sunk her teeth into her lower lip as she realized that everyone at the barbecue was watching them, including Maddock, who had stood up.

"Jerry, put me down!" Felicia protested, but he continued to walk, carrying her in his arms. "What *are* you doing?"

Edie had already guessed when she noticed that he was walking toward the swimming pool. An instant later Felicia reached the same conclusion. She screamed something about him ruining her dress, but it was too late. He was at the edge of the pool and heaving her into the water. Jerry waited long enough to see her sputter to the surface, then turned to rejoin Edie and Alison.

"I think we'd better leave," he said to Edie above the confused laughter and the rush of people to the pool to help Felicia out of the water. Maddock was among them.

Under the circumstances, Edie felt leaving was the wisest choice. "Yes, I think we should." Explanations would have to be made to Maddock, but it could be done later. This was not the time.

"I wish I had a picture of that," Alison murmured as they entered the house through the sliding doors. "Only you could do that and get away with it, Jerry."

"She needed it," he muttered.

"I feel sorry for her. She's so confused and insecure," Edie sighed and glanced at the staircase rising from the foyer.

"Felicia?" Alison gave her a wide look. "Are you sure we're talking about the same girl?"

"Yes, I—" Edie wasn't able to finish her explanation as the sliding glass doors to the patio opened behind them. All three glanced back when they heard it.

Maddock came striding across the entry hall. "Where the hell do you think you're going?" The low demand was taut and angry, the hard steel of his gaze directed at Edie.

Alison and Jerry immediately closed ranks around her, providing a united front. "Under the circumstances, Maddock, we thought it was best to leave," Edie explained.

"I suggest that you change your mind," he ordered tersely. "You are staying here."

"We don't take orders," Alison retorted. "Certainly not from you."

"Edie had nothing to do with what happened by the pool," Jerry stated, moving forward to take the brunt of Maddock's anger. "I was the one who threw Felicia in the water. And I'm not going to apologize for it, either. She deserved worse than that for the things she said to Edie."

Maddock's stone-gray eyes flicked over Jerry

and Alison with impatience. "This is a private discussion between Edie and myself. You have no business interfering in it."

"Maddock—" Edie bristled at his censuring tone as the air crackled with tension.

"Be quiet, Edie," he snapped. "I'm going to get this straightened out once and for all. There will be plenty of times in the future when I'll be raising my voice at you over something. There isn't any way that every time we argue, I'm going to take on the whole Gibbs family. It's time they learned to keep out of any discussion between a man and his wife!"

"His wife?" Alison frowned and glanced at Edie. "What's he talking about, Mom?"

"This isn't the way I wanted you to find out," Edie said, and flashed an irritated glance at Maddock. Everything had mushroomed out of control. "He asked me to marry him." Just saying the words seemed to make it more real. In spite of her defensive anger, her voice softened as she made the announcement.

"Are you?" was Alison's instant and slightly incredulous reaction.

But Jerry had been watching Edie's expression and noticed the way her gaze had sought Maddock when she told them. He guessed what her answer had been and bent his head to kiss her cheek. "Dad would be happy for you, Edie," he said to ease her mind. "I'm glad you found somebody else, too." He smiled, then turned to Maddock and offered his hand. "Congratulations. You've got yourself quite a woman."

"Yes, I know." His roughly hewn features were gentled by the warmth of his look as Maddock held Edie's gaze. The possessive light burning in his gray eyes started a tingling in her nerve ends.

For Alison, none of it had truly sunk in. She glanced around in helpless confusion. "I don't understand," she murmured.

"I'll explain it to her," Jerry smiled at Edie and took his sister by the hand to lead her away so Edie could be alone with Maddock. "It's this way, Alison," he began as they walked away. "There is this emotion called love."

Edie didn't hear any more than that as his voice trailed away. Maddock had taken a step toward her, his large hands settling onto her shoulders while his gaze searched her face.

"Don't ever walk away like that again, Edie." This time it was a request. "Why did you do it? You know I asked you to stay until the others had left."

"Yes," she admitted, her voice growing soft. "But after that incident with Felicia—"

"What on earth did she say to you?" An amused look flickered in his gaze. "It was all I could do to keep from laughing when Jerry dumped her in the pool."

"It doesn't really matter what she said," Edie insisted.

"Yes, it does, if it was something against you," Maddock corrected firmly.

She realized it would all come out sooner or later. "She doesn't want you to marry me."

"I know." There was a wry twist to his mouth. "When I told her this morning, she threw a tantrum. That's why she was upstairs sulking when you arrived."

"Felicia tried to convince me that the only reason you wanted to marry me was to get the ranch," Edie admitted.

His hands tightened on her shoulders as his gaze became piercing. "You didn't believe that? Is that why you were leaving?"

"No." She smiled and shook her head. "You may want our ranch, but I don't think you would go to the extreme of marrying me just to get your hands on it. It wouldn't work, anyway."

"I never for a minute thought it would." His look gentled. "I'm sure that you plan to turn the ranch over to Jerry and Alison after we're married. But I still don't think any of you realize the mammoth job you're tackling. It'll be a long while before the ranch will show a profit."

"There's something you don't know about us." Her eyes danced with the one fact they had kept from him. "Joe left us an income independent of the ranch. We weren't gambling all of our money."

"I should have known," Maddock chuckled. "I think I stopped caring about getting the ranch when you outsmarted me and bought those cattle in Wyoming. That's just about the time I started falling in love with you, too."

She caught her breath, a sudden radiance shining in her expression. "Do you realize that is the first time you've told me that, Will Maddock?"

"Told you what? That I love you?" His gaze roamed over her face. "I thought I'd been telling you that every time I looked at you."

"You have," she said softly. "But it's nice to hear the actual words."

An encircling arm pulled her against his rugged frame while his large hand became tangled in her hair. She melted against him, her lips parting as his mouth moved over them in clear possession. Joy sang through her veins, pure and sweet, a pleasure so strong that she hadn't believed it could exist. The depth of her love for him left Edie breathless. Her hands were spread across his broad back, feeling the tautly rigid muscles.

Maddock finally called a halt to the kiss before it went out of control. His breathing was as heavy as her own as he lifted his head. Raw desire smoldered in the look that scanned her love-soft features.

"We're going to be married next week, Edie," he informed her. "If I could arrange it, it would be this afternoon."

"But what about Felicia?" She gently reminded him of his daughter's disapproval. "Maybe we should give her time to get used to the idea."

"Time isn't going to help her . . . and it would be hell for me," he declared with a wicked glint in his eyes. "I haven't done a very good job of raising my daughter. She needs you as much as I do—well, almost as much as I do," he qualified his statement.

"It isn't going to be easy for her," Edie warned, and caressed his hard cheek. "She's used to being the only woman in your life."

"I think Jerry can handle that problem." The corners of his mouth deepened with a smile. "I have the feeling that ranch is going to wind up in the Maddock family yet."

"You are incorrigible!" she laughed.

"No, I'm in love. And that can be contagious," he replied.

"It certainly can," she agreed and lifted her lips to his.

Here's a sizzling excerpt from
Janet Dailey's
BRING THE RING.
Available now from Zebra . . .

"I don't mean to shock you, Red"—he smiled without amusement—"but I don't wear pajamas in bed. Those were a gift from someone who didn't know that. Now, go and take your shower."

She colored furiously. "I don't want to take a shower. I don't want your clothes. And I don't intend to go to bed!"

Roarke stopped and turned back to her, his jaw set in an uncompromising line. "Let's get something straight. You're going to take a shower if I have to strip you and shove you in there myself. And unless you want to walk around in a skimpy bath towel, you're going to wear those pajamas. Lastly, you're going to go to bed. No more arguments."

With his decree ringing in the air, he walked over to a smaller chest and took out a pillow and some blankets.

"What are you doing?" she demanded.

"Since I'm going to be sleeping on the couch, I

thought I might like some covers," he answered shortly before a wicked glint appeared in his eyes. "Or were you going to offer to share the bed with me?"

"Absolutely not!" Tisha declared vehemently.

"Selfish," Roarke taunted. "I could make you sleep on the couch, you know."

"You're not going to make me do anything."

"Guess not." He waved her away. "Go and take your shower before you catch a cold."

"I hope you get pneumonia and die!" she called after him as his long strides carried him up the steps to the hallway door.

"Thanks. You sleep well, too. G'night." The door closed with a finality that left Tisha with the impression that Roarke was glad to get her out of his sight. For a moment she stood there, the silence of the room closing in around her, muffling the growls of thunder outside the window. A shuddering chill quivered over her as the dampness of her clothes began to seep into her bones. However reluctantly, she had to admit that the tingling spray of a hot shower would feel good.

With the pajamas still clutched in her hand, Tisha walked into the bathroom, locking the door behind her. For several minutes she stood motionless under the pounding spray as it beat out the emotions that had strained her nerves to the breaking point. When she finally stepped out of the shower stall and toweled herself dry, she was feeling a little more human.

And a little more vulnerable to a certain very sexy man.

Going through the motions of hanging up her

wet clothes, she told herself she was glad he had essentially rejected her. If anyone had tried to tell her that she could feel such lust for a man she didn't like, she would have called them a liar, but her own actions had proved her wrong. No matter how hard she tried, she couldn't wholly blame Roarke for the emotional storm that had broken open in the middle of the actual one.

She wrapped her long hair in a towel and piled it on top of her head as she reached for the pajama top. The silk felt cool and slippery against her skin, but the sleeves hung far below her fingertips. It took some time to roll them up to a point where her hands were free. With the buttons buttoned, the ends of the pajama shirt stopped a few inches above her knees. One glance at the pants and Tisha knew they were miles too long and too big around the waist, so she simply folded them back up and laid them on the counter.

Unlocking the door, she reentered the bedroom and walked to the bed, giving the lustrous Thai silk of the spread that covered it an absent-minded pat. Roarke did have incredibly good taste.

She felt a little guilty for liking his things, liking his house. She picked a spot near the edge of the bed and sat in a cross-legged position with her back to the door. Unwrapping the towel from her head, she began vigorously rubbing her long hair dry.

A knock on the door was followed immediately by Roarke calling out, "Are you decent?"

"What do you want?"

But the door opened without an answer, and

Roarke walked in. He still wore only a pair of jeans, but they were older than the pair he'd had on before. The light, faded color accented the deep tan on his chest. Tisha watched him from over her shoulder as he walked in.

"I brought you some cocoa to help you relax and get some sleep." His face wore an inscrutable expression as his dark eyes flicked over Tisha.

"Thoughtful of you," she said, turning away from him to continue rubbing her hair with the towel.

"There'll be a crew out in the morning to clear the road, and the phone line's already back up. I called Blanche to let her know I was putting you up for the night," he continued.

"I could have done that myself."

"I think the operative phrase is 'thank you.'"

"Thank you." Reluctant gratitude edged her voice.

"Do you want this cocoa or not?"

She could tell that he was still standing right where he'd stopped. It would have been quite simple to walk over and take the cup from him, but she didn't care to meet the indifference of his gaze.

"You can put it on the bedside table. I'll drink it later," she replied, keeping her head averted as she heard his footsteps moving down the stairs toward the couch. Through her long hair, she saw him walk by her without a glance. When he turned to retrace his steps, she asked, "Is there a comb I can use to get these tangles out of my hair?"

"There's probably one in the medicine cabinet."

"Thanks," she said shortly, uncurling a long leg from beneath her to slip off the bed.

She was halfway to the bathroom when his voice barked out at her. "Where's the bottoms of those pajamas?"

Tisha stopped and glanced back at him, surprised at the restrained fury on his face. "They were too big." She shrugged.

"Put them on," Roarke ordered.

"I told you they were too big!" she repeated, bristling at his bossy tone.

"And I told you to put them on. What are you trying to do—look like a sex kitten?" he jeered.

"Meow, meow," she said, adding a descriptive word for him that would've scorched his ears if she'd said it loud enough for him to hear. She glared at the tall figure standing at the steps. "The last thing I would try to do is entice you," she snapped. "I told you they were too big for me, but don't take my word for it."

Spinning around, she stalked into the bathroom and slammed the door, grabbing the bottom half of the pajamas from the counter. Fighting the long legs, she finally managed to draw the waist around her chest while her feet wiggled through the material to touch the furry carpet. She shuffled over to the door and swung it open.

"See what I mean?" she demanded, looking from Roarke to the baggy pajama pants crumpled around her feet.

"Roll up the cuffs," he growled.

"Fine." A sweetly mocking smile curved her mouth. "What do I do about the waistline? You're not exactly a size ten!"

"Improvise."

"How? And what's wrong with wearing only the top? It nearly comes to my knees. What's so indecent about that?"

Tisha took two angry strides in his direction. On the third the material tangled about her feet and catapulted her forward. Her arms reached out ahead of her to break the fall, but her hands encountered Roarke's arms and chest as he tried to catch her. Off-balance, they both tumbled to the floor, Roarke's body acting as a cushion as Tisha fell on top of him.

"Are you hurt?" he asked, gently rolling her off him onto the carpeted floor.

"No," she gasped, momentarily winded by the shock of the fall. "No thanks to you."

"Was I supposed to let you dive headfirst onto the floor?" he muttered.

"You shouldn't have made me put on these stupid pajama bottoms," she retorted, suddenly conscious of the heat of his body against hers. "I told you they were too big, but you wouldn't listen to me."

"Guilty, guilty, guilty," Roarke declared angrily, reaching over her to place his hand on the floor and lever himself upright.

His arm accidentally brushed her breast. Tisha drew in her breath at the intimate contact. That jellylike weakness spread through her bones as he turned his enigmatic gaze on her. He was propped inches above her, his bared chest with its curling dark hairs close enough to caress. The desire to touch him came dangerously near the surface, and Tisha turned her head away, a solitary tear trickling out of the corner of her eye.

"Tisha—"

"Oh, go away and leave me alone!" Her voice crackled slightly on the last word.

His fingers closed over her chin and forced her head around to where he could see the angry fire blazing in her eyes.

"I can't stand this," she said hoarsely.

"Tish, Tish—what are you talking about? I still don't understand what happened this afternoon."

"Neither do I."

His gaze was focused on her parted, trembling lips. She brought up her hands to ward him off. The instant her fingers touched the burning hardness of his naked chest, Tisha knew her body was going to betray her again. When his mouth closed over hers, she succumbed to the rapturous fire that swept through her veins. The hands that had moved to resist him twined themselves around his neck while his hands trailed down to her waist, deftly arching her toward him.

Her nerves were attuned to every rippling muscle of his body as they responded to his searching caress. It was a seduction of the senses, in which she knew nothing but the ecstasy of his touch. An almost silent sound of feminine bliss came from her throat as he pushed the pajama top away from her shoulder and treated her skin to erotic little nips. Then his mouth sought out the hollow of her throat.

"You're a witch," he murmured against her lips, then moved to nibble her earlobe. "A beautiful rainy-day witch."

And don't miss
TRY TO RESIST ME.
Available now from Zebra . . .

There was Sin, larger than life, filling the archway to the bedroom. Clad only in a pair of ripped denims, he walked into the kitchen. The hard, muscled chest looked deceptively lean—and she felt a flash of delight at seeing his bare skin, nice and brown, broken only by the V-shaped pattern of dark chest hairs.

His steel-and-silver hair was uncombed, its thickness in sexy disarray. A deep sleep had softened the rugged cut of his features, but his eyes were alert as he took in the look of shock on Mara's face.

"Good morning." His greeting sounded so natural that it made her wonder if she had her days mixed up. Was it Saturday? No, it definitely was Friday.

"What are you doing here?" she recovered enough to demand, then said, "I didn't see your car outside."

"You didn't look. My car is there, parked alongside of the cottage," Sin informed her, regarding her with lazy interest.

That explained it, Mara realized. Since she'd walked instead of driving, her angle of approach to the cottage hadn't given her a glimpse of the far side where his car was.

"Then you're the one who turned the thermostat up and made coffee," she concluded, relieved that it hadn't been an oversight on her part.

"I must be," he agreed, "unless there's a ghost haunting the cottage that you didn't tell me about." His mouth curved into a half grin. "Did you think you'd lost it?"

"I . . . I had a lot of things on my mind," Mara faltered in her own defense. "Adam's been sick with a cold all week. He's better now. So it was possible I might have overlooked a few things Monday."

"Not you," he said lightly. "You're Miss Perfect."

"Why are you here?" His comment annoyed her. "It isn't Saturday."

"I decided at the last minute to come up a day early. Is that all right?" Sin asked, knowing that he didn't have to ask her permission. "I don't recall reading any restriction in the lease that said I couldn't use the cottage seven days a week."

"Of course there wasn't," Mara retorted impatiently. "But you could have let me know you were changing your routine."

"I told you it was a last-minute decision. I didn't think you'd appreciate a phone call in the wee hours of the morning."

"Um, no." He had a point there, Mara thought.

"And it was well after midnight when I decided to drive up here a day early," Sin continued.

Mara doubted that he'd been alone at that hour of the night. That thought prompted another: maybe he hadn't made the journey alone either. She looked beyond Sin to the bedroom and glimpsed the sleep-rumpled brown satin sheets.

Sin followed the direction of her look and her thoughts. "There's no one with me, if that's what you're wondering." Amusement edged the hard corners of his mouth when her dark gaze flew back to him.

"You've been spending more and more of your weekends alone lately," Mara said. "Don't you get bored without anyone to entertain you?"

"Not yet but that's possible," he conceded dryly. "But if it gets too dull around here, I can always argue with you."

This conversation was going nowhere. Mara wondered why she hadn't just walked out the second she'd seen him bare to the waist, lounging in the doorway wearing only ripped jeans.

Scratch that thought. His physical charm was just about irresistible. But he took obvious delight in laughing at her, no matter what she said or did. She turned away and took out her annoyance on the items in the grocery bag, not caring if she crushed the bread or dented a can or two.

"I've had a long week, you know. Taking care of Adam isn't easy work. And I don't feel like arguing with you. Now or ever," she added tightly.

He studied her profile, noticing the strain etched in her features but unable to guess that he was the cause of most of it. Her eyes were large black smudges against the ivory cream of her complexion. The line of her finely drawn mouth was tense, her emotions rigidly contained.

Sin walked to where the coffeemaker was plugged in only a few feet from her. Opening the cupboard door above it, he took out two cups and set them on the counter.

"Why don't you take a break for a few minutes, Mara, and have a cup of coffee with me?" he suggested. "It's fresh and hot. The groceries can wait until later."

Oh, how sweet. Well, he didn't have to pretend a solicitous concern for her well-being, because she wasn't impressed. She flashed him an icy look as he filled the first cup.

"Forget it. I don't want coffee." The sharpness of her retort made his eyes widen.

He set the carafe back in the coffeemaker as a heavy silence filled the air, charging the atmosphere. His steady blue gaze stayed on her.

"No problem." His voice was low. "But I could use the caffeine. Gotta wake up, right?" He took a long sip from the cup he'd just filled.

Mara hesitated only an instant before answering coldly, "Go ahead." She continued unpacking the bag, her movements as brisk and rapid as she could make them without throwing things around. "But I don't need stimulating." The second the words were out of her mouth, she wished she hadn't said them.

"You sure about that?" Sin's voice changed subtly, a sensual quality entering it. "Makes a man want to prove you're a liar."

"Which says something about male arrogance, doesn't it?" Mara countered.

"Or female talent for provocative behavior," he said smoothly.

"I didn't mean it to sound so suggestive. I wasn't thinking—and, like I said, I'm tired." She clutched the loaf of bread in her hand, and she paused to pat it back to plumpness before realizing how silly she must look. She put the bread down and turned to confront him. "And I wasn't trying to be provocative."

"Whatever you say." Sin was closer to her than she had realized. She started to take a breath to make some reply when his hand touched her neck.

His fingers began tracing the base of her throat, exploring its hollow, and all her muscles constricted. Mara's heartbeat was erratic, speeding up, then slowing down as his fingertips lingered or moved over her sensitive skin. Her gaze was locked with his and she had the sensation of being drawn into the blue depths of his eyes.

"I'll bet ice cream doesn't melt in your mouth," Sin declared in a soft, but very masculine voice that felt like a caress.

The straight line of his mouth never varied. There wasn't a hint of a smile. He seemed oddly detached, as if conducting some simple exercise that didn't require his concentration. His fingers began outlining the neckline of her blouse. At the point, they brushed the top of her breasts before encountering a button. Then they started their upward slant to the base of her throat.

"What do you . . . No, it doesn't melt." Her voice

was soft, too, thanks to the state of sensual confusion she was in. "I eat it too fast."

No matter how she tried, the delicious daze wouldn't lift. Not as long as he was touching her, she realized. At first she had submitted to the caress of his fingers to prove it didn't affect her. Now that she knew better, she had to bring this sudden intimacy to a close.

Fighting the threatening sensation of weakness, Mara reached up and pushed his hand from her neck. Then she took a step away and turned her back to him, looking for a distraction. The loaf of bread was on the table where she'd left it. She grabbed it just for something to do.

"What's the matter?" Sin asked in a voice that said he knew.

"Nothing's the matter." Mara opened a cupboard door to put the bread away. She seemed to lack coordination. Her movements were jerky and out of synch. "Don't paw me like that, please. I'm not interested in sex for the sake of sex at this point in my life."

"Oh?" There was a lot of curiosity in the one-word question. "When do you think you will be?"

Instead of putting him on the spot, she'd tripped herself up. It was a question she couldn't answer and she knew she didn't dare try.

And here's a look at
CALDER STORM,
Janet Dailey's compelling new hardcover.
Available now from Kensington . . .

Trey hesitated, then headed in the opposite direction. Away from the dance area, people tended to gather in clusters or travel in twos and threes, making it easy for him to spot a solitary figure. There were few of those, and all male.

Then he spotted her coming his way, the neon light of a bar sign flashing over the sheen of her hair, and everything lifted inside him, his blood coursing hot and fast through his veins. His long striding walk lengthened even more, carrying him to her.

A smile broke across her lips. "You forgot to say which stage. There happens to be three of them."

The glistening curve of her lips and the sparkle of pleasure in her eyes acted like the pull of a magnet. When mixed with the pressures of waiting, wondering, and wanting, the combination pushed Trey into action.

His hands caught her by the waist and drew her

to him even as he bent his head and covered her lips with a long, hard kiss, staking his claim to her. There was an instant of startled surprise that held her stiff and unresponsive, but it didn't last. It was the taste of her giving warmth that lingered when Trey lifted his head.

Through eyes half-lidded to conceal the blatant desire he felt, he studied her upturned face and the heightened interest in her returning gaze. He allowed a wedge of space between them, but didn't let go of her waist, his thumb registering the rapid beat of the pulse in her stomach. Its swiftness signaled that she had been equally unnerved by the kiss.

"I was just about convinced that I'd have to turn the town upsidedown to find you," he told her in a voice that had gone husky.

"It wouldn't have been a difficult task," Sloan murmured. "After all, you know where I'm staying."

"I forgot," Trey admitted with a crooked smile. "Which shows how thoroughly you've gotten to me."

She laughed softly, paused, then reached up, fingertips lightly brushing along a corner of his mouth. "You're all smeared with gloss."

He pressed his lips together and felt the slick coating, but it had no taste to it. "You use the unflavored kind, too." Automatically he wiped it off on the back of his hand. "My sister claims that a man should taste her and not some fruit."

"You have a sister?" Sloan asked, absorbing this personal bit of information about him. "Younger or older?"

"Younger." By less than two minutes, but Trey didn't bother to divulge that and have the conversation diverted into a discussion of the twin thing. Instead, he took note of the change in her attire— the bulky, multipocketed vest and tan pants replaced by a femininely cut tweed jacket and navy slacks. "You ditched the camera and changed clothes."

"The others were a bit grimy from all the arena dust." Her matter-of-fact answer made Trey wish that he had taken the extra time to swing by the motel, shower and change his own clothes, but he'd been too anxious to get here. A quick smile curved her lips, rife with self-mockery. "This is my first street dance," she said. "So I had to ask the desk clerk what to wear. He assured me it would be very casual."

"Your first street dance, is it? In that case it's time I showed you what it's all about." Grinning, Trey shifted to the side and hooked an arm behind her waist, drawing her with him as he set out for the dance area.

"I should warn you," she said, slanting him a sideways glance, "I'm not much of a dancer."

His gaze skimmed her in frank appraisal. "I'm surprised. You have the grace of one." He guided her through a gap in the row of onlookers, then turned her into his arms, easily catching up her hand. The band was playing a slow song, which suited Trey just fine. "Don't worry about the steps," he told her with a lazy smile. "Dancing was invented solely to provide a man a good excuse to hold a woman in his arms."

A laugh came from low in her throat, all soft and rich with amusement. "Something tells me it was a woman who came up with the original idea. How else would she ever coax a man onto the dance floor?" she teased.

"And something tells me, you're probably right."